D0827567

WILD
ABANDON

What Reviewers Say About Ronica Black

"*In Too Deep* is more than a story of forbidden romance, dangerous liaisons, and perilous passions. It's…a high-speed thrill ride that keeps you guessing from one hairpin turn to another. As soon as you think you know where she's heading, Black gives you another subtle curve to remind you just who's doing the driving."—**Gabrielle Goldsby**, author of *Walls of Silence* and *The Caretaker's Daughter*

"Black juggles the assorted elements of her first book with assured pacing and estimable panache…[including]…the relative depth—for genre fiction—of the central characters: Erin, the married-but-separated detective who comes to her lesbian senses; loner Patricia, the policewoman-mentor who finds herself falling for Erin; and sultry club owner Elizabeth, the sexually predatory suspect who discards women like Kleenex…until she meets Erin."—**Richard Labonte**, Book Marks, Q Syndicate, 2005

"*In Too Deep* is…an exciting, page-turning read, full of mystery, sex, and suspense. Look for it at your favorite gay and lesbian bookstore, or order online at www.boldstrokesbooks.com."—**R. Lynne Watson**, *MegaScene*, Women's Issues

"Ronica Black's debut novel *In Too Deep* has everything from non-stop action and intriguing well-developed characters to steamy erotic love scenes. From the opening scenes where Black plunges the reader head first into the story to the explosive unexpected ending, *In Too Deep* has what it takes to rise to the top."—**Kathi Isserman**, *Independent Gay Writer*

"Ronica Black's debut novel, *In Too Deep*, is the outstanding first effort of a gifted writer who has a promising career ahead of her. Black shows extraordinary command in weaving a thoroughly engrossing tale around multi-faceted characters, intricate action and character-driven plots and subplots, sizzling sex that jumps off the page and stimulates libidos effortlessly, amidst brilliant storytelling. A clever mystery writer, Black has the reader guessing until the end."—**Cheri Rosenberg**, reviewer for *Just About Write* and *Midwest Book Review*

Visit us at www.boldstrokesbooks.com

WILD

ABANDON

by

Ronica Black

2006

WILD ABANDON

© 2006 By Ronica Black. All Rights Reserved.

ISBN 1-933110-35-X

This Trade Paperback Original Is Published By
Bold Strokes Books, Inc.,
New York, USA

First Printing: March 2006

This is a work of fiction. Names, characters, places, and incidents are the product of the author's imagination or are used fictitiously. Any resemblance to actual persons, living or dead, business establishments, events, or locales is entirely coincidental.

This book, or parts thereof, may not be reproduced in any form without permission.

CREDITS
Editors: Jennifer Knight and Stacia Seaman
Production Design: Stacia Seaman
Cover Design By Sheri (GRAPHICARTIST2020@HOTMAIL.COM)

By the Author

In Too Deep

Acknowledgments

Bold Strokes Books, Radclyffe and the entire team. Thank you. You have changed my life.

Jennifer Knight and Stacia Seaman, two women who worked tirelessly on this book to make it the best possible and, in turn, made me look good. It wasn't an easy job, and I will be forever grateful. Thank you.

Sheri, the cover, as usual, rocks. Thank you.

Gil, thanks, bro, you and your bike were my inspiration.

My family. Mom, Dad, Rob, and Beck. My everything. For embracing me and who I am. Thank you.

Caitie. No words will ever be enough, but I will spend forever trying. Thank you.

Dedication

For Cait
My love, my life

CHAPTER ONE

The woman beneath her writhed in sleek grace, undulating with pleasure so intense it caused the sweat to bead on her skin. Chandler ran her hands up the sharp curve of the moving woman's hips, sweeping them over the moist, flat planes of her clenching abdomen. Her fingers grazed the small swell of the warm breasts to the firm oval nipples. She pinched roughly and held them captive, along with the woman's cries of painful pleasure.

"Oh, please." The woman begged in her thick Spanish accent. *"Necesito...ahora...*Please."

Chan felt her own body tense and flood with need as the words penetrated her mind. *She needs, she craves, she begs for it.* Nothing in the world was more beautiful. Moved beyond comprehension, Chan eased down to kiss the woman softly on the delicate flesh just behind her knee. Then, extending her tongue, she worked her way up the woman's thigh to her full, soft outer lips. She lined them carefully and braced herself for the instantaneous reaction.

More Spanish flowed, begging and pleading; the more turned on the woman became, the more her native language took over. The fire from her words burned in Chan's ears where her own racing heart thudded with arousal. Her tongue, seeking and knowing, brought back the taste of the woman, sweet and ready, and she was no longer able to maintain the slow deliberation with which she'd been moving. Head spinning with want, Chan positioned herself carefully, ensuring that her weight would hold the woman down. She returned her hands to her lover's breasts, once again squeezing and tugging on the nipples.

Purposely, she breathed upon the moist flesh her tongue had exposed and at once felt the woman tense and buck. Inhaling, she closed her eyes, relishing the moment, wishing she could stop time. The woman was caught, balancing on the edge, begging for the ultimate push.

With that gratifying thought in mind, Chan worked her tongue farther inside the smooth, satin lips and carefully rimmed the engorged clitoris. Her lover jerked and strained, but Chan still didn't give in. Not just yet.

"*Ay, por favor.* I can take *no más.* I need to come." Olive-skinned fingers reached for Chan and dug into her hair, pulling her mouth closer.

Chan lowered her hands from the hard nipples, carefully running her fingernails down the damp, hot skin. Her tongue remained, extending its circular pattern along the edges of the thick patch of nerves. The woman arched her back as Chan exhaled upon the delicate skin once again, loving the reaction this drew. She moved her hands down and, with practiced ease, spread the soft, silken skin out and away from where her tongue played its torturous game. The flesh tightened, exposing the stiff, satin bulb of the clitoris. Its tip was red and full, like a firm little pillow.

Chan braced herself against her own arousal, clenching her legs together as she finally gave in and allowed her tongue to touch the sacred spot. Gently, she pressed back the hood so the underside of her tongue could work its magic on the exposed nerves of the head. The woman cried out again, words not known but their meaning clear.

Her insatiable lover was going to come. It would be the fifth time in thirty minutes. She was one of those women, the kind that could come nearly instantaneously over and over again in small bursts of orgasm. While Chan knew it had nothing to do with her, pleasing the woman relentlessly was satisfying for her ego as well as her libido. Most lovers wouldn't take the time to keep going, to make a woman come countless times before she finally begged to stop. Chan did, though, and loved every second of it, but unfortunately she didn't have time to do that today. Their normally two-hour tryst would have to end and soon.

Closing her eyes and inhaling her lover's alluring scent, Chan carefully pulled the firm flesh into her mouth. She sucked and stroked the length of it, relishing the way it felt against her tongue. The woman bucked wildly as her orgasm approached the point of explosion. It was going to be a good one, Chan having teased it out of her. Hands pulled and yanked on her head as the woman shoved against her, hips up in the air. Chan held fast, swirling her tongue over and over while powerfully sucking the flesh.

"*Ay,* oh my God. *Más, más,* so *bueno.*" Her head thrashed as her body tensed.

Chan felt the woman's legs tremble just before she finally shattered. Violently she came, clutching Chan to her while shoving her hips up to her mouth. The climax was powerful and strong, ripping through the woman's body quickly. It lasted longer than its predecessor, just as Chan predicted. Her lips burned with the pressure and her scalp screamed at the rough grip, but she ignored it all, too caught up in the beautiful sight before her. A sight that she had created, a pleasure she had gifted. When the woman finally calmed, her starving need to take all that she could from Chan sated, her body went limp and she fell back upon the bed. Chan pushed herself up and got to her feet, rubbing at her tingling lips. The woman's scent remained, reminding Chan of her feed. She studied the nude woman in silence while yanking on her jeans. Her head still swam with heavy arousal and she wanted desperately to climb back in the bed and stroke her to bliss. But she pushed on, knowing she couldn't, buttoning her jeans in frustration.

Sensing the movement, the woman opened her eyes in obvious surprise. They lifted to Chan, dark and liquid, pooled with pleasure. She stretched, languidly stroking her body against the sheets. "You leaving?"

"Yeah." Chan tugged on her shirt and balanced herself to slip into her boots.

"Why?"

"I've got other plans." Chan ran her hands hurriedly through her hair as she made her way into the master bathroom.

Her cell phone rang from inside her pocket as she splashed water across her face, scrubbing the scent of recent lovemaking from her skin with a bar of lavender soap. She dried her face and shoved her hand down in her pocket and grabbed her phone. Flipping it open, she noted the time and who was calling, then snapped it closed, making a quick decision not to answer.

"Another woman?" the woman questioned as Chan returned to the bedroom. Her tone was one of a pouting little girl.

"Yes." Chan propped one foot up onto the bed and hastily laced her boot tight.

"Oh?" The woman sounded annoyed and disappointed and Chan met her eyes, wondering why. They were in no way serious or exclusive. She didn't even know her name. Sophi? Sophia? Of course she'd heard it when they first met, but she couldn't remember. What they did required no names. All Chan had to do was answer her phone and say yes.

"My grandmother." Chan lowered her laced boot and raised the other. "Not that it should matter."

Maybe she should stop seeing the woman. It was becoming apparent that she was getting a little too personal, something Chan did not want. It was a shame, though, since they had only been together three or four times. But that's what always seemed to happen. Women wanted more, they needed more. More than Chan could give. She stood and retrieved her keys from the dresser.

"No good-bye kiss?" The woman beckoned from the bed.

Chan paused in the doorway and noted the sweet pink bliss that tinged her face and chest. Her eyes were deep and hopeful, her voice needy. Yes, it was definitely time to cut this one loose.

"No." Chan turned and walked from the bedroom, wending her way out of the woman's house.

She drove home in a daze. Her body still hummed with need, and she felt tight and full all over, as if she would burst from the tiniest of touches. The clock on the dash reminded her of the reason why she wasn't able to stay to have her own desires met.

It was Sunday and her grandmother was coming over to make dinner. Grandma Meg had raised her and her brother from early childhood after the sudden death of their parents in a car accident. She was like a mother to them, and for the most part the trio had remained close throughout the years, seeing each other often, supporting one another.

But lately, with Chan's busy schedule, they were seeing less and less of each other, and Chan had started to feel guilty. Granted, she wasn't the only one who was busy. Hank, her younger brother, had recently wed and bought a new home. Meg had her life too, gardening and playing golf. But like Chan, Meg chose to live her life alone and unattached. This played on Chan's mind. She worried about Meg's ability to cope with the inevitable loneliness as she grew older. Meg should have someone in her life. Someone to be there by her side. Especially since Chan had dropped the ball recently with the get-togethers.

Swallowing some bitter-tasting guilt, she slowed her truck and pulled into her drive. Meg's Buick flanked the sidewalk in front of the home.

Shit, she beat me here.

Meg had a strong preference for punctuality, which rivaled Chan's strong propensity for showing up late.

After parking her SUV in the driveway, Chan self-consciously smoothed down her jeans and muscle T-shirt, conscious that despite her adulthood, Meg still had a hold on her, silently demanding nothing but the best from her oldest grandchild. Her guilt gave way to nerves as she walked through the house. Noise from the kitchen greeted her, leading her right to where the older woman stood, two empty pots in hand.

Chan stopped next to the counter, shoving her hands down into her jeans pockets, all too aware of how she was dressed. The black sleeveless tee fit tightly, showing off the prominent muscles in her arms. The jeans were dark but worn, hugging her hips with a thick leather belt.

Her grandmother knew she was gay, but there were certain things Chan would never discuss with her—not out of fear or anything negative, but out of respect. Meg was more a parent to them than grandparent. She had raised Chan and her brother to speak with meaning and respect for others. And sex, Chan knew, was a topic Meg considered sacred, something only to be discussed at an appropriate time and place, neither of which ever seemed to happen. Chan had always found this curiously funny, given her own lifestyle and career choice.

Doing her best to shift into a more conservative mode, she glanced down and feared her butch-looking outfit and tardiness would give away her earlier whereabouts, as well as her earlier activity. She shifted, suddenly remembering how the Latin woman had sucked at her neck. As she quickly raised a hand to rub at the spot, Meg glanced over, obviously catching the movement out of the corner of her eye. She smiled, as if she knew exactly where her granddaughter had been.

Chan panicked a little and muttered, "Hi."

Meg lowered her gaze back to the pots. "I let myself in." Her tone was light and nonchalant but as always, she had a way of hitting her intended target dead-on with practiced poise and grace—the target being Chan's conscience.

"I'm glad you did," Chan said. "Sorry I'm late."

She was sorry, and she wished just once she could live up to the older woman's unspoken expectations. To show her she wasn't just half-assing her way through life, flying by the seat of her pants, going from woman to woman. No matter what the situation, when it came to her grandmother, Chan always seemed to find herself falling short.

She hasn't seen me in weeks and the day I invite her over, I'm late. Why? Because I was out doing what I wanted. Messing around. And I didn't even get my needs met.

Thank God Meg didn't know what had held her up. Or at least she was pretending she didn't know. It was no secret that she thought Chan was wild, free, promiscuous, burning the candle at both ends. That she needed to settle down, find a steady relationship, and quit her wild gallivanting and pulling dangerous stunts. Showing up late only added one more peg to the "tame Chandler" board.

Ignoring the usual pangs of guilt and the dull ache of her libido, Chan put on a happy face and stepped up to hug her grandmother, enveloping her smaller, thinner frame. Meg planted a firm kiss on Chandler's cheek, which caused another sudden alarm. Worried that the scent of her lover was lingering and noticeable, Chan stiffened and pulled away, her face red with heat. Her heart nearly jumped out of her chest as Meg spoke.

"You smell nice. What is that, lavender?" Meg began cutting some fresh vegetables, seemingly oblivious to Chan's fear and concern.

"Uh-huh." *Among other things.* Chan shoved her hands back in her pockets. She felt awkward and painfully exposed while Meg remained calm, radiating a quiet wisdom.

"It's good to see you." Meg looked up with a soft smile. "You look well."

"So do you." Chan shifted her feet and felt like she was eleven years old and secretly hiding her feelings for her girlfriends.

Meg, though, continued to slice and dice. "Dinner should be ready around four. Why don't you go relax and go about your day?" Her green eyes sparkled as she spoke. It was obvious that she was happy and in her element—cooking for others, giving the way she knew how. It was what she had always done.

Knowing the answer, Chan still asked out of habit, "You sure you don't need any help? Or company?"

"You know I don't like people in the kitchen when I'm cooking." She reached out for a large wooden salad bowl. "You go do whatever it is you need to."

Chan obeyed and headed down the hallway. As she passed, the framed photos along the wall reflected the sunlight, reminding her of times past. And of her first love: adrenaline. She paused midstride and smiled as her eyes focused. Picture after picture showed her on a motorcycle. Junior motocross, taking jumps, racing through the desert. All while straddling a high-powered dirt bike.

Her gaze stopped on the last photo, a uniformed rider performing one of the most dangerous stunt jumps. Her brother, Hank. He was still ranked among the best while she had hung up her motocross boots long ago. Nowadays she got her hit of speed from her Harley.

With thoughts of the past on her mind, she opened the door connecting to the garage and fumbled for the button on the wall. As light spilled in from the sun, her eyes adjusted and were drawn to the Harley that sat in the corner. She averted her gaze instantly, reminding herself that she couldn't go riding her cares away today. Meg was there, and Chan had too much work to do later that evening. Work she couldn't even begin to fathom concentrating on at the moment.

Needing to fill the void of sexual and mental frustration, she grabbed a bottle of Armor All and a rag and headed out to the driveway to wipe down the tires on her Dodge Durango. It was mindless and physical, just what she needed.

The warm March sun calmed her, and she was beginning to relax when the distant grumbling of a motorcycle caught her attention. Her body reacted unconsciously, kicking up her heart rate and tightening her throat. Her mind was suddenly stirred from its relaxed state, enabling thoughts of the wind. She could feel it invade, beating steadily against her face and body. She closed her eyes and imagined streaking down the black strip of road, pushing against the force that drummed in her ears. The daydream was as warm and comforting as the sun, threatening to lure her in deeper.

Her eyes flew open and, determined to push her craving aside, she fumbled with the stereo inside her truck. The Eagles strummed out of the speakers but did little to calm the need that beat within her. That heat grew as the motorcycle grumbled closer. Chan turned and faced the road. She needed to see the shining, powerful machine roaring between the legs of its rider. She needed to hear its strong growl, smell its heady exhaust, imagine the feeling of it, all raw and powerful, vibrating her center, her very core.

She squinted up the street and caught sight of the bike. Just as her body could wind no tighter with anticipation, her brother, Hank, slowed his new chopper up the paved road to her concrete drive. He eased the loud, shining beast up next to her and gave her his best shit-eating grin as he killed the engine. Hands resting on his long legs, he smiled at her in silence. Chan was nearly breathless as she glanced over the chopper. This was the first she had seen of his new ride, but she didn't allow her eyes to linger for long, knowing that doing so would be like staring at an eclipse. Dangerous, yet tempting. Instead, she glanced away and swallowed against the vise grip of her throat. Why did he have to bring it over today? She couldn't give in to it today.

"Hey, Chan," he greeted.

She could tell from his tone as well as his demeanor that he wanted something more than just Sunday supper. Doing her best to act calm and uninterested, she moved to the driver's door of her Durango and climbed inside.

"What brings you around?" she asked after turning down the radio.

Hank swung a leg over his bike to stand. She knew in her gut why he was there, what it was he sought. But she busied herself wiping down the dash, continuing to act aloof, hoping it would somehow shield her from the temptation he presented.

"Nothing. Can't I just come see you?" He sounded almost defensive and somewhat offended.

"Not usually." Chan leaned over to wipe down her door. She and Hank were very close and usually very bad for one another. They knew how to push each other's buttons, and when they were…together, they knew no limits. She had the scars and had suffered the numerous broken bones to prove it.

Hank removed his black bowl of a helmet, exposing his light brown messy spikes. The helmet was something new and Chan couldn't help but smile. "Where's Kelly?" she asked, referring to his new, young bride. The reason, no doubt, for his sudden safety concern.

"At some baby shower." He grinned, letting on that he knew it wouldn't take much to get her interested. It never did. Placing his helmet on the bike's seat, he approached and climbed in the passenger door.

Chan tossed him the rag and he started wiping down the dash. She contemplated him, her arms folded across her chest. He was bored. That explained his ride on his new machine and his last-minute arrival to dinner. Married life, she assumed, was doing little to calm the raging monster inside him. A monster she herself knew all too well.

Kelly was a great girl, and while a part of Chan was thankful for her levelheadedness and her love for Hank, she also knew that no matter what Kelly did, Hank would still hunger for what lay beyond that line—the line that most people never neared or even dared thinking of crossing. The line, according to Hank, that would've never been drawn if it weren't meant for crossing.

Hank finished rubbing down the interior of the truck, returned the rag to Chan, and stood. His green eyes squinted as he removed his shades to wipe some sweat from his cheek.

"So what are you doing the rest of the day?" He asked lightly, as if her answer wouldn't really make or break his day, but she knew differently. She knew it mattered. Her heart sped up as she thought of the intentions that were so poorly hidden under the nonchalance of his tone. Frustrated with her insides for reacting, she sighed and locked up the Durango with the remote.

It was Sunday, the day she usually spent going over files from her office, preparing for the week. It was work she had to do and she knew she should tell him so, just like she had with the woman. But as their eyes met, she knew she was in trouble.

"What did you have in mind?"

As the question floated from her mouth, her sensible side cringed. But damn it, he was her brother, and his mere presence sparked her adrenaline flow. Hank meant fun. Hank meant adventure. Hank meant throwing everything to the wind. And she loved that about him. Of course, she also hated that about him. Especially on days like today, when she should be inside, tinkering around the house, getting ready for Monday.

Hank eased his shades back on with cool poise. "I was thinking about taking the bike out for a ride." He grinned again, and his eyebrows rose just above his sunglasses. "Wanna come?"

Damn you, Hank.

She placed her hands on her hips and stared past him to his bike. At once she felt the fire ignite in her belly as she took in his new machine.

It was a wide-tire softail chopper, vivid black with electric blue and yellow ghost flames flowing across the tank almost as if they were alive. A matching tattoo of blue and orange flames shot up her brother's forearms from his wrists. She strolled over to the bike and ran her fingertips across the beautiful paint job, stroking it as if it were alive and purring. Her hungry gaze traveled to the similarly painted custom Jesse James fenders and beyond, where the remainder of the bike was beautifully chromed out and appeared to be made from Harley-Davidson parts.

Chan licked her lips, already imagining the vibration of the loud engine between her legs. She nearly shuddered as she rested her hands on the polished handlebars. "That's a nice bike you got there."

"Thanks. I thought you might like it." Hank took a step closer and motioned with his head toward her open garage. "What do ya say? Wanna crank up that bike of yours?" Her eyes drifted to the garage, and Hank lifted his sunglasses, gave her a wink, and walked inside. He caressed her bike, much like she had done to his only moments before. "Yep, she's just sitting here waiting."

The Harley-Davidson FXSTD Softail Deuce was customized by her very own hands. She had invested close to fifty thousand dollars in the bike, loving every last inch of it. Like Hank's, her ride was eye catching and tempting, the engine and pipes chromed out and shining, contrasting beautifully with the candy red paint of the tank and fenders.

Chan allowed herself a long look at the Vance and Hines pipes and the Screaming Eagle Mikini engine. She felt a surge of energy just thinking about the 105 horsepower.

"I'll get my boots," she mumbled, unable to tear her eyes away.

Hank smiled with victory. "Right on." He walked to his bike and swung a leg over, his hands tugging on his helmet.

She hurried inside the house and grabbed her Oakleys off the kitchen counter. Meg was busy smoothing out the top layer of a casserole, readying it for the oven.

"You going somewhere?" Her hands and eyes remained focused on her task.

Chan hesitated, nearly breathless with excitement. "Yeah, uh, Hank is here."

"Oh?" Meg glanced up. "Was that his motorcycle I heard? He told me he got a new one."

"Yes." Chan's nerves battled her heart rate, threatening to take over. Meg had never approved of the motorcycle riding, fearing for her grandchildren's safety, but she'd had no choice when it came to Hank. Chan, on the other hand, had no reason to keep riding, to keep pushing the limit.

She thought of that now as she struggled for words. "We're going to go take it out for a quick ride."

Her fingers tightened around her sunglasses as she waited for a response. She was thirty-two years old, and yet the worries remained.

Meg parted her lips but then closed them as she looked back down to her casserole. She slipped on a pair of thick mitts and slid the pan inside the heated oven. "I suppose it's useless to try and talk you out of it. I had always held out hope that maybe someday you would outgrow it." She lifted her eyes to hold Chan's. "Please be careful. And be back by four."

Chan nodded and pushed on her shades as she headed out the door, thankful that there hadn't been a major confrontation.

"Wear a helmet!" she heard Meg call after her.

But she ignored the request, feeling too alive to think about anything but speed. The absence of a helmet law allowed her to ride like she wanted. She was almost electric at the thought of the wind in her hair. She lived for speed and the feel of the open road. It was her addiction, her weakness; the only way she felt fulfilled.

The door to the house closed behind her and Hank asked, "She upset?"

"You know how she is." Chan straddled her bike and adjusted the mirrors, observing her reflection as she did so. She still had on her worn, dirty jeans, boots, and black cotton sleeveless shirt. Her brown hair was short but thick, tousled and careless, ready for the wind.

Hank seemed to think a moment before replying, "She never gives up, does she?"

"Nope."

Chan's entire body vibrated, including the small silver hoop earrings she wore, as she brought her pride and joy to life. The Harley roared and grumbled deeply, forcing Meg and everything else in Chan's life far from her mind.

Hank did the same, their bikes growling as if talking to one another.

Chan walked the heavy beast out of the garage and up next to her brother. He gave her a grin and took off. She followed quickly, flicking her wrist to awaken the engine, kicking up next to him.

As they rode loudly down the street, she felt the March sun once again, this time accompanied by the battling current that blew against her as she gained speed. She smiled at the sense of freedom and the thundering power between her legs.

Hank rode at her side, his helmet shining in the sun. She smiled, loving the exposure of riding without one, the tempting of fate. Meg's request disappeared into the wind, dissipating behind her.

They rode on, due east, leaving her neighborhood far behind, heading toward the mountains that edged Phoenix. She relaxed, as if she and the machine were welded into one. They turned onto the expressway, the one that would loop them around from the west valley to the east. They had no idea where they were headed, and they didn't care.

Merging onto the highway, the pair quickly sped up and eased their way over to the far left lane. The wind became a wall, blowing hard against her face and chest, testing Chan's strength. She clenched the bike harder and accelerated again, following Hank as he weaved in and out of traffic, leaving all the other vehicles behind. She rode like a demon, expertly leaning and accelerating, delicately stroking the road.

She pulled up next to Hank once again and grinned over at him, feeling so good she was nearly bursting with light from within. They were immortal, sleek, and strong, just like the wind. Nothing could touch them as they rode on the devil's wing.

He smiled back and sped up. She pressed on too and glanced down at the speedometer. They were pushing eighty-four.

Crazy. Careless. Confluent.

It had been like this since they were kids. She knew it was mostly because they had never properly grieved for their parents. The tremendous loss they felt was channeled into other, more daring outlets. They followed one another into the unknown, beyond their comfort zone, beyond any limit, imaginary or real. Climbing and jumping from trees had soon graduated to racing and jumping their bicycles, which then led to racing dirt bikes. And even though Chan had hung up her racing boots long ago, the love for speed still beat strong within her, like a starving animal that came out of its cave to feed every time it heard the engine of a bike.

Today, the animal had emerged once more.

CHAPTER TWO

The drone of the engine and the roar of wind were so loud, Chan almost didn't hear the shrill wail directly behind her, shrieking through the force field that was the wind.

She jerked as it penetrated not only her ears, but her consciousness as well. Even then she couldn't make sense of it. The siren was angry, screaming at them from behind.

Hank turned to look, his face as startled as her own.

They switched on their signals, slowed, and pulled off the pavement, turning up dust on the shoulder. Chan didn't notice how fast her heart was beating until she flicked off her engine, and then she was nearly overwhelmed.

She licked her dry lips, trying to decide if it was all adrenaline or maybe a little anxiety at what lay ahead. The absence of the wind left her ears feeling hollow, and the zooming traffic sounded strange and muffled. Her body still hummed with the vibration of the bike and road, her blood racing as if it too were an engine.

She glanced around her in awe. Everything was happening so quickly, for a moment she wondered if it was all real. Before she found her answer, a powerful voice came from behind.

"License, registration, and proof of insurance."

There was no "please," no friendliness in the tone. Hank shook his head, letting Chan know just how fucked they were.

She blindly found the back pocket of her jeans, where something soft kissed her fingers. Completely confused, she pulled out the rag she had used to wipe down the Durango. She had been in such a hurry, she had forgotten to leave it in the garage.

"Step off your bikes, gentlemen," the voice instructed.

Chan flinched, and eased slowly from the bike, shoving the rag down deep into her pocket and extracting her wallet. She was lucky she even had it. What had she been thinking, taking off that fast at the last minute? She looked to her brother and silently knew the answer.

Hank came to stand next to her. His serious eyes met her own as he removed his helmet and shades.

Turning fully to face the voice, Chan flipped through her wallet and pulled the documents to hand to the officer. Her face flushed with red heat, as the "gentlemen" comment replayed in her head. Now that she was facing front, maybe the jerk would see her very obvious size Cs.

To Chan's surprise, the officer was nearly on top of her, stepping up quickly to take the information. Chan's eyes focused first on the waist, where a thick black belt held a gun and pepper spray. And as the officer spoke again, Chan's gaze flew upward, lingered on the full breasts and strong shoulders, and then traveled up to the chiseled face, partially shadowed by the wide-brimmed hat. A lump in her throat formed and then burned as the officer raised her head to examine her.

"Sorry, Miss..." Her steel blue eyes looked down, focusing on Chan's driver's license. "Brogan."

Chan swallowed against the ball of fire as she took in the strong, perfect features of the cop.

Jesus.

She found herself sucking in more air as she stood straighter, unconsciously trying to look her best next to the woman's six-foot frame. She heard Hank clear his throat nervously beside her as he handed the officer his information. Chan watched the defined muscles in the woman's forearms ripple beneath her tanned skin. Her fingers were long and strong, her hands sleek but powerful. The burning continued in Chan's throat as the officer walked away, allowing an ample view of her long legs and tight, full ass.

The officer climbed inside the open door of her cruiser and Chan let out the breath of air she had been holding. "Holy shit," she breathed, wondering if her brother was as moved as she was.

"Yeah, no kidding. We are so fucked." He kicked the ground, apparently missing her real meaning.

"No, I mean her." She indicated the Department of Public Safety cruiser that sat several yards from where they stood, its lights still flashing.

"What?"

"Her...the cop," Chan said softly, almost to herself. "She's unbelievable." Excitement coursed through her veins. The woman was goddamned gorgeous. Chan had never seen anything like her. Every other woman she had ever laid eyes on vanished from her mind, including the one she had been with only hours before.

Hank folded his arms angrily over his chest. "You're serious?"

"Hell yes, I'm serious."

Couldn't he see it? Did he have no idea how a woman who looked like that could excite her? And in uniform, to boot? Granted, she usually liked her women a little wild, like herself. But there was something about this one, something about her confidence, stoicism, and control. She was tall, strong, and self-assured. Vastly different from the lovers Chan usually bedded.

She could use those handcuffs on me anytime. The thought made her shudder.

She glanced back toward the police cruiser. Was it possible that she was worse than a man when it came to noticing women? Maybe she was. Her occupation, her sexuality, and her libido all entered her mind. Yes, she definitely was.

"You're a man, Hank," she said, seeking some reassurance. Her reactions were understandable. Surely her brother shared them. "You're telling me you didn't notice?"

"Yeah, she's hot. So what?"

It seemed he couldn't get past the seriousness of their current situation, and Chan couldn't get past the tall, gorgeous cop. "So...I don't know what," she confessed. "I'm having a hard time just getting past her looks at the moment."

Her body continued to pump the sweet adrenaline. But this time what fed the raging fire wasn't speed. She was all worked up again, pulsing with desire. How a woman she had only laid eyes on seconds before could do that to her, she didn't know.

Hank snickered, seemingly reading her thoughts. "I swear, sometimes I think that's all you think about." His eyes were full of contempt. "Sex." He let that word linger a bit before he chided, "And don't forget Donna. You thought she was pretty hot too, remember?"

Chan turned on him quickly. Hank knew her better than anyone, and she knew he was right. Nevertheless, the sharpness of his words hit home. Thoughts of Donna flooded her, leaving a bad taste in her mouth. She couldn't believe he had brought her name up. It had been almost a year since their doomed attempt at something intimate, a strained relationship in which everything had to be Donna's way. They'd tried to make it work for almost a year—at least, Chan had. Donna had simply expected everything to go her way. When it didn't, she became harsh, curt, and judgmental.

The experience had been so negative, Chan had opted for casual sex ever since. If there were no strings attached, then she couldn't be pulled or controlled.

Hating the feelings that surfaced when she thought about Donna, she considered Hank's other words. Next to speed and the need for that adrenaline rush, sex did top her list. She studied the ground. Yes, sex was something she thought about an awful lot. Hell, she did more than think about it, she embraced it. There was nothing wrong with that, she decided, nothing to be ashamed of. After all, she had turned it to good use.

As she continued trying to convince herself that she was okay, there was movement from the cruiser and the cop walked up to them purposefully and confidently, her khaki uniform moving against her, clinging to her full chest and long legs. Chan could sense the hard muscles, almost feel them beneath her fingers, straining to tear out from under the well-fitted uniform. *God, yes.* She wanted to feel them, wanted to stroke their harnessed power. She wanted to run light fingers up one long, strong leg and then the other, making the woman shiver with desire. Then she would move up to her arms, caress the firm mound of the bicep all the way up to the shoulder.

The officer came to a halt in front of her and studied the thick metal clipboard in her hands.

Chan's pulse beat thick and heavy through her veins as she continued her covert visual assault of the woman, examining every last inch. She noticed the dark brown hair, pinned up and away from her face. Her ears were on the smaller side, with two pierced holes in each lobe, leading to her strong jaw. Her cheekbones were high and slightly bronzed, contrasting beautifully with her dark hair and light eyes. Her aquiline nose led to slightly pink lips, which were near perfect in size.

Chan thought about tugging on them with her own, caressing them until they were engorged with darkened blood.

"Ms. Brogan? Ms. Chandler L. Brogan?" the cop questioned in her strong, deep voice.

Chan stood very still, captivated in the way her mouth moved when she spoke. Captivated by everything about her. Regardless of the officer's demeanor, Chan's mind flew with possibilities. Serious blue eyes rose to look into hers. The stare was fierce and piercing. A light yellow ring surrounded each pupil, almost like a halo. Chan held her breath again, incredibly moved. She searched for a hint of interest or attraction, or at the very least a trace of recognition. But she saw nothing. Only the stoic look of a beautiful, professional cop.

Chan focused on the tiny brass plate on her chest. It read "S. Monroe." *Monroe.* Chan began wondering what the *S* stood for as the woman spoke.

"I'm not going to mince words here." Officer Monroe returned their licenses. "Both of you should be placed under arrest."

Chan's brain pounded, the reality of the words sinking in. *Arrest? Who?* "What?" she asked, hearing the panic in her voice.

The officer calmly and assertively explained, "You were speeding to an excess of twenty-five miles an hour over the speed limit." Her eyes held Chan's, unmoving and seemingly unfeeling. "That alone is grounds for arrest."

Chan couldn't fathom what was happening. How could she, this perfect creation of a woman, be saying such things, be thinking such things? It wasn't supposed to work like this. She was supposed to be swept away by Chan's presence.

Suddenly angry at herself for not seeing the situation for what it was, and for wallowing in illusions, Chan shook her head. What the hell was wrong with her? This wasn't the woman of her dreams…this was a cop. A cop who wanted to arrest her.

"No way. That's not possible." Chan was suddenly angry. She was a professional, a good citizen who had never been in trouble with the law. Why was this woman picking on her? Wasn't there a violent offender out there somewhere who needed her attention?

"What she means is—" Hank interjected, wrapping an arm around Chan's shoulders.

But Officer Monroe had words of her own. "You have two previous tickets, Ms. Brogan." Her voice was icy, causing Chan to shudder internally. "Both within the last fourteen months. Both on the bike."

Chan's face flushed. The woman was right, but she was wrong. One of the tickets was for changing lanes without signaling. The cop had been an ass, determined to meet some sort of twisted ticket quota. Of course, the other had been a little more severe. Chan had been speeding well beyond the limit. She had paid them both and shrugged them off.

Chan's blood began to boil. "One of those was for failing to signal. Hardly worth—"

"My sister's had a bad day." Hank interrupted again. "She—"

"As for you, Mr. Brogan," Officer Monroe cut in, "you have a previous ticket for reckless driving."

She studied them in silence, dropping the clipboard to rest against her thigh. "I observed you both weaving through traffic at excess speeds, with little regard to your lives or to those around you."

"You couldn't possibly know that," Chan spat defensively. This cop didn't know her, didn't know what regard she had for anything or anyone.

"I know that you were speeding up to ninety miles an hour, weaving through cars on a highway. Doing it all without a helmet or any other form of protective gear. That doesn't sound like someone who values their life to me."

"You don't know me," Chan grumbled. The officer had hit a very sensitive nerve, and Chan's body and mind reacted.

"I know what I see," came the reply.

"So do I." Chan held Officer Monroe's eyes.

She could size the cop up in a second. She knew her type, knew it all too well. Women who couldn't function without absolute control, which most of the time led them to try and control the lives of others around them. They couldn't stand disorder, spontaneity, or letting go. And she was just about to tell her so when Hank straightened beside her.

"Please excuse her, Officer." The fear in his voice did not escape Chan.

"No, I don't think I will." Officer Monroe's face hardened and Chan no longer felt a burning in her throat. All that remained was a large, round rock, making it nearly impossible to swallow.

She held her ground, her mouth dry, as the officer turned to walk briskly back to her car, where she deposited her clipboard.

"What the fuck are you doing!" Hank exclaimed, grabbing Chan by the shoulders. His eyes were wide with fear, his hands clenched tightly at her behavior. "She's going to arrest us!"

"I don't know!" Chan shot back. Her head hurt with all that was spinning around her. "What she said got to me, and I—"

But there was no time to explain.

"Place your hands behind your back, Ms. Brogan," Officer Monroe said as she stormed back up to them. A pair of cuffs jingled from her hand.

"No, this is a mistake, she didn't mean anything…" Hank said desperately.

"You have the right to remain silent." Officer Monroe yanked Chan's arm up and around her back painfully, causing Chan to turn. "Anything you say can be used against you in a court of law. You have the right to an attorney…"

Her hands were strong on Chan's wrists, wrapping the cuffs down tight against them. Chan nearly laughed as she realized that, only moments ago, she had been completely turned on at the thought of Officer Monroe handcuffing her.

A hard jerk turned Chan and led her away from her pleading brother, kicking up dirt as she was tugged along to the cruiser.

Holding the back door to the vehicle open, the officer pushed on Chan's shoulder. "Get in and be still."

Chan tensed for a moment and then relented, plopping down in the backseat. She remained silent as Officer Monroe closed the door, locking her inside the police car. Her breathing came quick and shallow. She felt like a caged animal. A dangerous caged animal. Tears nipped at her throat but she fought them back, too proud to cry. Her big mouth had gotten her into trouble, real trouble.

She watched as Officer Monroe returned to Hank, and then she let her eyes fall to the floor as the police radio reported on various situations. She knew she didn't belong here, but she didn't know how to get herself free. Her mind fought for a way out. She would have to apologize for her behavior. And if that didn't work, she guessed she would have to spend a few hours in jail. Christ, what would her colleagues say if they ever found out about this? What would her clients say? Hank was right, she was fucked.

She glanced up as Officer Monroe returned and slid in behind the wheel. Her shoulder moved as she scribbled on the clipboard.

Chan shifted a little, ignoring the pain in her arms, working up the nerve to speak.

"Excuse me?" she said in a weak voice. She hated the way it sounded, hated herself for this situation.

Officer Monroe continued writing. "Yeah?"

"I just wanted to apologize. For my behavior." It certainly wasn't the first time she'd had to bury her pride in order to get out of trouble.

Officer Monroe was silent for a moment. She stopped writing and looked at her captive in the rearview mirror. "Do you really mean that, or are you just trying to get out of an arrest?"

Again Chan felt anger burn through her, but she bit it back. Why was this woman getting to her so?

"I mean it," she whispered, sounding defeated. And a part of her *was* defeated, having to say such things to this stranger.

"You know, you're lucky you got me," Officer Monroe said. "Anybody else would've hauled you two off right away. But I tried to be nice about it."

Chan sighed, her shoulders slumping.

"I know," she admitted, seeing things from the cop's perspective for the first time. Something she had trouble doing lately. Even with her paying clients.

"You really should lose your motorcycle license for a while before you get yourself killed."

Chan shook her head, hating the sound of the words, not to mention the idea. And again she felt the sting of the woman's judgment and the resentment at being told what to do. Chan had a real problem with authority, but she shut her mouth and breathed deep, waiting for the right words to come.

"It's just that…I need to push the edge, just like…" Chan paused, searching. "Just like you need control." Immediately, she regretted the words.

Officer Monroe stiffened and looked away, staring out the windshield.

Chan continued, desperate to explain. "You probably go crazy if you don't have everything in your life under control." She wasn't trying to be a jerk; she was being sincere, trying to relate to her in a way that she knew how. Chan knew people. It was her job to know people.

But Officer Monroe remained still, looking straight ahead. When she did move, it was to crawl out and open Chan's door. Her strong hand wrapped around Chan's bicep and lifted her up out of the car.

Chan cringed as her fingers dug in.

Officer Monroe then turned Chan around quickly and released the handcuffs. At once Chan brought her hands around to the front to massage her wrists.

Officer Monroe closed the door and rested her hand on the open driver's door, her face turned away from Chan's. "You're free to go," she said coldly.

Chan froze, studying the side of her beautiful face. "I am?"

"Thank your brother." As she said the words, she pivoted and looked at Chan with her cool blue eyes.

Chan inwardly gasped as she witnessed the pain in their depths. Had she done that with her words? Was she the cause?

"Look, I really am sorry—" she began.

"No need, Ms. Brogan," the officer interrupted, sliding into her car. She closed the door and switched off her lights. The cruiser moved away and sped up as it merged back onto the highway, leaving Chan in silence, squinting through the dust.

In a daze, she walked up to Hank, who was sitting on his bike, looking like he had just weathered an awful storm.

"What happened?" she asked.

"She let us go."

"I know, but why?"

Hank shrugged and pulled on his helmet. "I told her I raced bikes and that I was egging you on."

"You said it was your fault?"

"Yeah, but she didn't believe me."

Chan's eyes returned to the road, where the car had disappeared from sight. "So why did she let us go?"

"Beats me." He started his engine and waved the tickets at her. "Maybe she thought you were hot too and decided just to give us the tickets." He was being an ass, and she knew he would never let her live this down.

She rolled her eyes at him and straddled her bike. As she cranked the engine back to life, she continued to wonder.

Who are you, Officer Monroe, and why did you let me go?

CHAPTER THREE

Several hours later Chan sat alone in her quiet house, staring right through the file in her hand. Frustrated and unable to focus on the words, she tossed it on top of the numerous others that were scattered along the coffee table. She sat back against the sofa and allowed her gaze to drift beyond the beckoning files.

Darkness settled in around her; the sun, as well as Hank and Meg, were long gone. The clock on the mantel chimed, letting her know it was nearing eight o'clock. She knew she should read over the files, but she just didn't feel like it. Besides, she knew enough and she was confident that she could handle and appropriately analyze anyone or anything. Just like she had done with the tall, stoic cop. Chan smiled, feeling a bit cocky at her no doubt very accurate assessment of the woman who had very nearly arrested her.

Interrupting her thoughts, her wayward gray cat, Mitote, meowed at the back door, wiping the grin from her face. He was ready and driven to go out prowling for the night.

"It was nice seeing you too," she commented dryly as she rose to open the door for him. Surprisingly, she found the door to be unlocked. "Huh," she said aloud, fairly certain that Meg and Hank wouldn't have had reason to unlock it. "Guess I need to be more careful."

She shrugged and then shook her head as Mitote trotted outside, tail high in the air. She knew he wouldn't be back for days, a typical tomcat that only came home to eat.

She chuckled to herself as she recalled finding the small feline sitting at her front door staring up at her after a particularly emotionally trying week. She had just ended things with Donna, and the experience had left her feeling insecure and unsure of herself—of her feelings, her ways, her desires. She had opened her front door to find the kitten just sitting there, small and gray, with deep green knowing eyes. His presence forced her to take a mental step back and realize that life wasn't about all that currently ailed her.

He had been just what she needed, an affectionate companion who silently encouraged her to see through the fog. And she had named him accordingly. Mitote meant "fog" in ancient Toltec.

Running a hand through her damp, clean hair, she wished Mitote an adventurous night and headed to the refrigerator. She was freshly scrubbed and comfortable, all ready to settle down and get to work. But she just couldn't seem to concentrate.

She tugged the fridge door open and thought of the cop again. The blue eyes, full of pain and something else…loneliness.

Chan cracked open a bottle of Killian's. She knew that look all too well. It was the same look she saw every time she stared into the mirror. She just couldn't seem to connect with anyone. No one seemed to hold her attention or respect. And Donna served as a constant reminder as to why.

Yeah, she was just fine the way things were. So why was this cop invading her thoughts?

The beer was cold and crisp, and her mind stirred and heated. Despite her best efforts, she knew herself well enough to know that she wasn't going to be able to sit still and concentrate. She needed to do something to get the cop off her mind.

She took another sip as she thought. At once the idea of speed entered her mind. Hopping on her bike and flying down the darkened road would surely do the trick. But now, with her most recent ticket, it was out of the question. She couldn't risk getting in trouble again, especially so soon after her run-in with Officer Monroe.

She fumbled with the bottle cap as her brain downshifted to her second favorite way to spend time. Sex. Yes, a woman was just what she needed. She laughed suddenly as she realized she wasn't that different from her prowling cat after all.

Suddenly buzzing with purpose and sure of her remedy, she headed into the bedroom, where she pulled on her favorite pair of jeans. She ran her hands down her thighs, loving the way the denim clung to them. Her heart beat faster as the thought of her escapade excited her. Next, she pulled on a tight-fitting Banana Republic T-shirt that kissed her breasts and abdomen just right. The army green of the T-shirt matched her eyes and showed off some of the lightness in her brown hair.

Seeing that it needed work, she moved into the bathroom, ran some gel through the tousled locks, and brushed her teeth. After that, she yanked on her thick brown belt and stepped into her matching boots. With a quick spray of cologne and one last look of approval, she was out the door and starting the engine to the Durango.

She drove in silence, hoping that the pickings would be good. It was Sunday night, after all, not exactly the best time to find a one-night stand. But there she was, determined and convinced.

The outside of the bar was dark, with a few cars scattered around the parking lot. She parked the SUV and dug in the console for her cigarettes. She only smoked when she drank, and she had a feeling that she would be putting away more than a few that evening.

Her vision adjusted quickly as she pushed in the door and scanned the lesbian bar, which was illuminated by a few neon beer signs and a couple of blacklights. The two women sitting alone at the bar turned to look her way, and then dropped their heads to once again study their drinks.

Chan approached the heavyset bartender with the well-kept mullet.

"How are ya?" the bartender asked, placing her hands on the worn counter.

"Not bad," she lied, digging in her pocket for cash. "Captain Coke," she requested, laying out a ten. "Easy on the Coke."

The bartender nodded and turned to busy herself making the drink.

From behind, Chan heard the sorrowful cries of Melissa Etheridge sing out from the jukebox. She was feeling the pangs of love, and Chan wondered who else was as she looked around, focusing on no one in particular. There was only a handful of women in the bar. Two where she stood, two sitting dangerously close at a table, and one all alone in the back corner.

"Three fifty," the bartender declared, sliding the rum and Coke her way.

Chan grabbed a book of matches and turned to walk away. "Keep them coming," she instructed, carrying her drink and cigarettes.

She made herself comfortable near the far corner booth, liking the privacy and darkness that surrounded it. Behind her the lone woman sat in silence, hidden by the darkness. Chan thought about voicing a polite greeting but changed her mind, not yet ready to have a mindless conversation with sex as the main motive. She sipped her rum, resisted the urge to twitch at its strength, and lit a cigarette.

As she blew out the comforting smoke, the bartender walked over and stopped at the table behind her, asking the occupant, "Can I get you anything else?"

Half listening, Chan sucked on the cigarette, her eyes trained on the door, looking for prey, just like a cat ready to pounce.

"No. I'm ready to leave." The voice behind her was deep and smooth, and dangerously familiar.

Chan nearly choked as she hurriedly exhaled and tensed in her seat. *No. It can't be.*

Suddenly nervous, she lowered the cigarette and debated turning to look. The bartender moved past her to return to her station.

Chan's heart thumped in her chest. More movement came from behind her as the mysterious woman with the familiar voice took several steps to leave, passing by Chan's table. Without thinking, Chan reached out and touched her arm, needing to know, dying to know.

The woman straightened at the touch, but didn't turn around. Chan allowed her eyes to glide quickly over her long, strong body before coming to rest on the back of her head, where dark chestnut hair fell just below her shoulders. Her fingers burned from the warm softness of the woman's flesh.

"Officer Monroe?" she rasped. The stranger turned then, fastening her intense blue eyes on Chan's.

"Ms. Brogan," she responded coolly. Her arms were strong and toned, her breasts high and full in the tight-fitting black tank top she wore.

Chan inhaled at the sight of her. "I…uh…"

The officer's gaze fell to her arm, where Chan's hand remained. Feeling awkward and shook up, Chan withdrew her hand at once. "Please, sit."

Officer Monroe stared at her for a moment, as if deliberating. "I should get home."

"No, please!" She half stood, desperate for her to stay. "Let me buy you a drink." Chan waved the bartender over and eased herself back down. "Please. It's the very least I can do." Chan watched her, searching for that crack in her wall, needing to know she had reached her. Seeing nothing of the kind, she continued, "You were kind to Hank and me today."

The bartender approached and stood looking from Chan to Officer Monroe.

"Bring her another one," Chan ordered.

"No, thanks," Officer Monroe responded politely, excusing the confused bartender, who retreated back to the bar, shaking her head.

Chan was just about to protest when the cop sat, making herself comfortable across the table. She studied Chan coolly for a few moments before she finally spoke.

"I don't like smoke." She stared pointedly at the thin trail of white smoke snaking up from Chan's cigarette.

Immediately Chan stubbed it out and pushed the pack away. "I'll stop. I mean, I only smoke when I drink." The words were offered quickly and Chan waited, nerves on edge, for a response.

The officer's face gave away nothing, nor did her eyes, making Chan all the more nervous.

"I don't do that much either," Chan continued. "Drink, I mean." She looked away then, ashamed at her behavior. What the hell was she doing? Why did she care? Why was she so eagerly accommodating her, this virtual stranger?

Finally, Officer Monroe spoke. "I'll stay, but only if you tell me you didn't ride your bike here tonight."

Chan laughed aloud at the joke and then fell silent as she realized that the officer was serious. Again, she felt the need to please her. She would do or say anything to keep her there.

"No, uh, no. I drove my Durango," she quickly explained.

Just like that, the night had changed on her. Not only had she found a woman of interest, she had found *the* very woman she was trying to forget in the first place. What did this mean? What should she do? More importantly, what should she say?

"Come here often?" *Brilliant, asshole. That's sure to knock her off her feet.* Chan resisted the urge to whack herself in the forehead at her less than suave choice of words.

Officer Monroe grinned slightly. "No."

Chan nearly sighed with relief and returned the smile. "Me neither."

To Chan's pleasant surprise, the woman continued to speak, saving Chan from voicing more ridiculous come-ons.

"So where's your brother?" A flicker of mischief made itself known as her lips tilted to one side.

Chan's blood flushed with heat, making her skin tingle. The gorgeous cop was incredible. And Chan was drowning in her presence.

"He's at home." The words came out, but Chan didn't seem to have voiced them. Her mind whirled, her sole focus on the woman seated across from her. Officer Monroe was here, and that meant she was gay. And suddenly all of Chan's crazy thoughts and fantasies from earlier in the day were screaming to a halt in front of her. The recognition she had searched for in her eyes was now smack-dab in front of her.

Houston, we are go for launch.

"With his wife," Chan continued, smiling and glancing down at her drink. Her nervousness and desperation suddenly receded, leaving a calm, cool demeanor that came from knowing what the woman was and what she wanted.

"So what about you, do you have a wife?" Chan raised her eyes to watch her once again.

"No, I don't," she replied softly, her eyes glinting with lightning.

Chan rimmed her glass with a finger as the sweet adrenaline she always craved flooded her insides. "Aren't you going to ask me if I have a wife?"

"No."

Chan clenched her legs as the heat from the officer's stare traveled to her center. "Why not?"

"Because I don't need to."

"You don't?" Suddenly Chan's heart flip-flopped. Maybe she was reading her wrong. Maybe she wasn't interested.

"No. I already know you're not attached." The grin returned. "Your brother happened to mention it while he was trying to explain your behavior."

Chan's face burned with embarrassment. She dropped her head in her hand and reached for her drink, which she gulped at.

"He did, did he?" She tried to sound unaffected, but the officer's gaze was intense and stirring her insides.

"Yes."

Silence fell, making it difficult for Chan to breathe. What else did this woman know? Chan squirmed a little in her seat, not used to being on the other side of the coin. She was the one who knew things about people, private things. Not the other way around.

"Can I ask you something?" she asked, curious, turned on, and more than a little dizzy.

The officer nodded.

"Why did you let me go today?"

"Honestly?"

"Please," Chan asked softly, watching the woman's dark brown bangs caress her forehead.

"Because there was…" She glanced at Chan briefly and then lowered her eyes.

"Because there was what?"

"Because there was something about you."

Chan's entire body beat to the drum of her heart. She sipped more of the drink, almost disbelieving that she had heard correctly.

When Officer Monroe raised her head to look at Chan again, the attraction in her eyes was undeniable. Chan couldn't speak. She couldn't swallow. She just sat. And stared. Never before had a woman moved her so. Chan wanted her, wanted the woman to have her as well, wanted it all. The officer seemed to sense what Chan was feeling. Her blue eyes burned brightly with desire right back at her. Chan reached for the drink again and wet her mouth so she could speak.

"You want to get out of here?" Her voice was tight and strained. *Please, God, say yes.*

Officer Monroe swallowed and then licked her lips as Chan nearly died with desire across from her. When she nodded, Chan felt like melting, her body turning to mush.

They rose from the table, and Chan's insides growled with starvation, her mouth watering at the sight of the woman's bare skin peeking through the fabric of her torn jeans.

The bartender voiced a good night somewhere in the foggy, dim distance as they pushed out the door into the cool desert night.

CHAPTER FOUR

Once again Chan was alone and driving in silence, only this time the frustration and the determination to forget were absent. What resonated inside of her instead was a craving, a desire so strong it left her weak.

Her palms were sweaty as she made the turn onto her street. Officer Monroe's headlights shone on her from behind, tickling her with promise. Chan pulled in the drive and eased the Durango into the garage. She stepped out and waited for the woman she so badly wanted.

Officer Monroe climbed from her black Chevy truck and slinked her way into the garage. Chan smiled with nervous anticipation as she pushed the button to lower the door.

"Come on in—" she started to say, but the cop stifled her words, shoving her against the door to the house. Chan gasped in surprise as the woman pinned her with her weight. Her mouth was a fraction from Chan's, her alluring scent teasing her nose.

"Shh," she instructed, lightly touching Chan's lips with her finger.

The garage door closed, leaving them alone with the dull glow of the overhead light. Glacier eyes stared into Chan's, fanning her fire, letting Chan know she had something to say.

"I'm going to make you come," Officer Monroe whispered, her lips teasing Chan's as she spoke. She raised Chan's arms up above her head. "I'm going to make you come over and over again until you beg me to stop."

Chan moaned slightly and started to speak but the officer stopped her, conquering Chan's mouth with hers. Chan closed her eyes and felt her knees weaken as the officer devoured her, sucking on her tongue and then probing her with her own. Officer Monroe's body pressed up against her, her thigh grinding between Chan's legs. The cop groaned with pleasure.

"Do you want it?" she asked as she tore her mouth from Chan and bit at her ear. "Do you want me to make you come?"

Chan trembled beneath her as hot blood gushed to the fleshy spot between her legs. She couldn't comprehend what was happening, unable to make sense of the woman at her neck, the cop who had tried to arrest her. But it was her, it was Officer Monroe. Only now she was off duty and on Chan with the same confident, strong control she oozed while in the uniform.

"Yes." Chan's voice quaked in response to the officer's hot hungry tongue licking at her ear.

The officer grunted her pleasure and grinned at Chan as her right hand drifted down to Chan's crotch.

"Good," she purred. Her fingers flew, unbuttoning Chan's fly.

The light to the garage door switched off, leaving them in the darkness. Chan felt the cop's breath against her skin as she flattened her hand and slid it down the front of Chan's underwear. Chan gasped and bit her lower lip as the sexy officer's fingertips found her wet and aching.

"Yes," she groaned against Chan's neck. "I wanted to make you come the second I saw you." She stroked Chan's swollen clit as she spoke, driving her like a Ferrari, fast and fluid.

Noises crept from Chan, short, throaty, and raw. She clenched her eyes, feeling the white-hot heat branch out into her, consuming her quickly. Her hips began to buck against the strong hand as the hunger demanded to be fed.

Officer Monroe's left arm pressed into Chan's hands above her head, while her right arm stroked Chan like a talented bow. Chan's head slammed back with the pleasure, her mouth opening to take air from above. She heard the woman laugh in the darkness and felt the heat from her breath once again in her ear. The talented hand stopped its sensual play, causing Chan to twitch with need.

"Wait," Officer Monroe demanded softly. "I want to see you. I want to watch your face as you come." She released Chan's arms but the hand at Chan's crotch remained as she slowly turned Chan to face the door. "Now," she instructed. "Take me inside."

With a weak hand, Chan felt for the doorknob and gently pushed. Dim light from her living-room lamp filtered out, softly showing the way. Chan stepped slowly and as she did so, Officer Monroe's fingers squeezed her flesh, causing Chan to rise up onto her toes.

The cop stepped into Chan from behind and whispered in her ear. "Keep going."

Chan took another step and felt her breath hitch in her throat as the cop squeezed again. Chan wanted to yank her hand out, to turn and kiss her, to take back control. But as her knees shook, she knew she couldn't. She was weak with pleasure, pounding with need.

She reached back to brace her hands on the cop's strong thighs as they took several more steps together.

The cop's left arm found Chan's waist as she was just about to crumple with orgasm. "Not yet," she said devilishly.

"I can't," Chan breathed, shaking, almost unable to stand. What was happening? Her brain swirled with hot foggy desire. Who was this woman and what was she doing to her? More importantly, why was she letting her?

"Yes, you can." Her tongue teased Chan's ear, awakening her arms and legs with goose bumps, pushing her qualms away. "Which way is the bedroom?"

Chan shuddered and leaned her head back against the officer, trying desperately to anchor her body, her will, and pointed to her left.

"I promise, if you keep going, it'll be worth your while." The cop stroked her again, sliding her fingers up and down the sides of Chan's clit. Her teeth found Chan's neck while her other hand rose up to pinch Chan's nipple through her shirt.

Chan cried out, arching her back with pleasure, wishing to God she would just take her now. Attuned to Chan's excitement, the cop slowly stopped her stroking and lowered her hand from Chan's breast to her hip.

Chan nearly collapsed again, needing so badly to come. She clenched her eyes tight and felt the salty stings of sweat. The near stranger had total and complete control of her. She knew it but realized she no longer cared. Even if she had, she was too wound up, too weak to fight back. Her aroused and racing mind slammed a realization home.

"What are you doing to me?" The words were strained and weak. Chan didn't realize she had spoken them aloud until the officer chuckled softly and knowingly, and then once again spoke in her ear.

"Take me to the bedroom."

Breathing deep and getting her bearings, Chan turned and walked carefully with her down the hallway. The cop's fingers played with her, rubbing and teasing while her breath spoke of pleasures to come.

Somehow, Chan managed to keep walking, until eventually she stood writhing against the powerful woman in the doorway to her room. Sweat dampened her shirt, and her legs shook involuntarily. She felt like a puppet, wet, wanting, and nearly limp, willing to do anything for her master.

"Turn on the light," was the next soft, yet seductive command.

Chan reached out and fumbled for the switch. The bedside lamp came on, the light piercing her eyes as it spread, kissing the king-sized bed.

The knowing hand eased up from her pants and Chan clenched her legs in response. Her body screamed at the separation, throbbing and aching with need. Her head swam, leaving her feeling dizzy with desire. From behind, Officer Monroe's hands steadied her shoulders, turning Chan around to face her. Chan did so carefully, as if she were intoxicated.

Blue eyes burned her skin, running over her face and neck. "I want you to watch now," the cop said. "Watch me undress you."

Chan licked her lips as the long fingers rose to her shirt. Slowly, the cop inched the T-shirt up, her fingertips lightly grazing Chan's skin as she did so. Chan raised her arms, her eyes locked with the incredible woman's as the shirt was pulled from her.

They stood still then, chests rising and falling with arousal. The cop dropped the shirt and then pulled on Chan's waistband, tugging her closer. Her tongue lined Chan's lips before trailing to her neck as she forced down the jeans.

Chan gasped as she felt the hot tongue trace the cool skin of her chest and then her abdomen as the graceful hands freed her of her pants. The cop's fingers came back up slowly, caressing Chan's thighs as she rose back up before her.

The fever of the woman's wants and desires was evident in the brush of color on her cheeks. Her eyes were focused, and darkening and alive. She moved into Chan, her hand claiming the back of her head, pulling Chan to her mouth. She took her hard, aggressively plunging her tongue into Chan, then hungrily tugging on her lips.

Chan groaned into her, her hands clinging to the powerful back, knotting in her shirt. Chan felt the sweat on the woman's bare skin and instantly craved more. She flattened her hands and tried to ease up her tank top.

As she did so, she heard a growl and then felt the cop pull away. Strong hands wrapped around Chan's forearms and pushed them from her. Chan stood staring, confused, but too turned on to care.

The cop grinned at her again, like a hunting, slinking panther, and she backed her up to the bed.

When the back of Chan's legs bumped against the mattress, the cop released her and lifted her hands to Chan's bra, leaning into her, allowing Chan to inhale her scent once again. She flicked her wrist and released the clasp. She stepped back and gently brought the straps of the bra off Chan's arms so that it fell to the floor. Her eyes swept up and down Chan's body, lightly touching her in all the right places.

Chan shuddered beneath her stare. The air, too, caressed her, tickling her breasts and puckering her nipples, causing the pulse to return to her center.

"Take off your panties," the cop said with heavy intensity.

Hesitating only for a moment, Chan brought her hands up to her hips and slid her fingers under the double bands of her satin thong.

"Slowly," the woman added, causing Chan to move with deliberation, gliding her panties down over the flare of her hips, below her pulsing center and down her sensitive thighs.

Chan stepped out of them carefully and stood before her conqueror completely nude, her body aching and alive with need. She didn't know what it was about the cop that kept her going, kept her moving, kept her obeying. Never before had she felt so alive, so hungry for another. She was willing to do anything for her. Anything.

Her brain, her thoughts, any sense of pride or reason she had were gone, eaten alive by the fierce appetite of desire that burned into her with this woman's every touch. Instinctively, she reached out for the cop's shirt, wanting to undress her, but a strong hand and a soft command stopped her.

"Lie down." The officer eased Chan onto the mattress, and crawled atop her with assured grace, immediately claiming Chan's neck with her teeth and tongue.

Chan groaned up into her as the woman's skilled hands came to life, squeezing first her breasts and then her nipples. A firm thigh shoved into her engorged flesh as the cop devoured her skin, making her way down to Chan's navel.

She stopped at her hips and looked up at Chan from all fours. "I'm going to make you come now," she said, wrapping her hands under Chan's legs and up around her hips, lifting her off the bed.

Chan didn't have time to respond before she was raised up to the cop's mouth and the woman fed like she was dying, her tongue assaulting Chan's flesh with weighted pressure, swirling in deliberate circles. Chan clamped her hands down on the bedcovers as her shoulders took all the weight. She thrashed her head from side to side, the pleasure too much, too intense. She felt the skillful tongue glide lower where it plunged into her, swirling again, this time against her tight walls. As she neared climax, possessive hands squeezed her buttocks, holding her tighter.

At just the right moment, the woman's mouth maneuvered again, sucking in all of Chan's flesh and then attacking it with her tongue. Chan cried out, tensing and tightening, writhing with the pleasure the cop was creating. And she nearly screamed out as the orgasm came and she shoved herself up into the cop over and over again.

Officer Monroe moaned as she took her, continuing to suck her core vigorously, holding on until the last of the orgasm shook through Chan. Apparently satisfied that the climax had been milked thoroughly, she finally lowered Chan back onto the bed.

Chan lay breathing heavily, her body weighted and tingling. A surge of intensity shot through her suddenly and she raised her head to find the cop licking up her warm arousal from her inner thighs. Chan grabbed her dark hair and knotted it in her hand. The aftershocks were too much to handle with the seeking tongue. Her breath came sporadically, as did her voice.

"Stop...I..." she started and then swallowed. She couldn't take what the cop was currently doing. "That was..."

"Shh," the cop instructed, rising up. "I'm not done." She crawled forward and wiped her chin with a grin. "Turn over."

Confused and nearly spent, Chan merely stared at her. "Huh?"

"Turn over," she said again, this time helping her.

Chan rolled onto to her stomach and began to wonder when it would be her turn to take charge. Her thoughts were quickly stifled as she felt the cop's fingers between her legs. She slid carefully inside Chan, gliding against her slick walls. A bolt of heated pleasure shot up through her, lifting her hips up off the bed.

"Do you like that?" the cop asked.

"Ye...yes," Chan grunted.

"Good," she cooed, continuing to fuck her. "Now, relax."

She stopped her strokes as Chan settled her hips back onto the bed. Chan felt the fingers shift slightly and then in an instant a new pressure was up in her, in her ass. Tensing with the pleasure that she knew was soon to come, Chan moaned her delight as the cop began pumping her again, one finger in her ass and the others in her slick hole, pressing against her G-spot.

"Jesus Christ," Chan mumbled, lifting herself up to all fours, clutching the bedcovers.

The powerful cop drove into her from behind, killing her with pleasure. The bed began to squeak as she fucked her, harder and faster. Chan closed her eyes tightly and then opened them wide as she felt the cop's mouth and tongue on her, biting her cheeks and then rimming her ass, licking where her finger disappeared up inside. The sensation sent her over and she came again, incredibly hard, bucking back against the cop's hand, loving what she was doing.

She pushed and rocked until her arms shook with exhaustion and her head spun with lack of blood flow. She collapsed down onto the bed and felt the cop move, kissing her way up her back.

Chan breathed with difficulty, her arms smashed beneath her body, her face in the bedcovers. Her ears buzzed and rang, making the officer's voice sound fuzzy and distant.

"Turn over."

Chan lay unmoving, unable to comprehend anything but her pounding blood. She felt the officer's hot mouth find the back of her neck, where she bit just hard enough to get her attention.

Chan moved slightly and met the seeking eyes. "Wha?" Her mouth remained pressed against the bed. She couldn't lift her head, it was way too heavy.

Officer Monroe twisted her hand around inside Chan, rousing her from her stupor.

Slick with sticky sweat, Chan jerked and turned slowly over. She breathed deep, letting the ceiling fan cool her hot body with its caress.

The seductive stranger looked down on her with her hypnotic eyes and full, pink lips. Chan gulped, recognizing the hunger that still beat in the vein on her neck. The cop grinned again, and Chan's racing heart almost stopped at her unbelievable beauty. She was by far the sexiest creature Chan had ever laid eyes on.

"You're..." Chan could barely whisper but she wanted to tell her. "So beautiful."

Officer Monroe moved a quick finger up to her lips where she lightly traced, shushing her. She bent down and kissed Chan where her finger had just touched. Her mouth was warm and soft and heavy. Chan moaned softly and felt her pull away. Her blue eyes danced as she whispered, "One more time."

The words floated to her but had no meaning. Chan was flying high, high above her body and the bed. Fingers raked lightly down Chan's stomach to her glistening flesh and carefully circled, encouraging Chan to spread her legs.

She did so quickly, her body taken over by desire once more. The amazing hand found its way back inside of her, back into both holes.

The cop began to pump her again, painfully slowly as she spoke. "One more time."

Chan shook her head, the meaning finally sinking in. No. She couldn't. It was too much. Impossible.

"One more time," the seductress said yet again, softly demanding it of her. She took Chan's hand and brought it to her mouth, where she slowly began to suck on her index finger.

Chan took in a quick breath at the sensation and relaxed against her. The cop fucked her slowly, carefully, moving Chan's finger from her mouth to lead it up her shirt, where her breast lay exposed, bound by no bra. Chan relished its warmth and groaned, pinching the woman's nipple. The alluring officer licked her darkened lips and clenched her perfect jaw. She was aroused, hungry like a wolf, eyes flashing with want and need.

Chan had seldom seen a woman look like that before. So turned on, so moved by what she was doing. Chan wanted her then, wanted to touch her, to take her where she had been taken. She rose up and pinched the nipple again, tugging her forward for a powerful kiss.

The cop responded with a heavy groan and kissed her back furiously. Chan's hand found her hair possessively and grasped it, holding her to her. Then, with another groan, the stronger woman pushed herself upon Chan, slamming her back down against the bed. Her free hand tore Chan's from her dark hair, pinning it above her.

"Stay here," she insisted, breathing rapidly, her eyes flashing with lightning once again. She released her and moved down the bed. With one last look of starvation, she lowered herself, resting her mouth on Chan's meaty center.

Chan sucked in a hot breath of air as the hand continued to probe deep within. She arched her back with pleasure as the need to come took hold of her again. Reaching down, she tugged possessively on the cop's head, holding her as she fucked her with her mouth and with her fingers. The orgasm that was building was bigger than before, looming larger and larger.

"Yes!" Chan cried out, her voice deep and throaty. "God, yes!"

The beautiful woman pushed up into her vigorously, moaning into her flesh as her hand and tongue worked their magic. Chan closed her eyes and saw her face, her eyes, her grin. She saw the look of hunger, the flash of desire. She was beautiful. She was intense, she was raw, she was unbelievable. And so was the insane amount of pleasure she was pouring upon Chan. Filled up completely, Chan raised herself up off the bed, offering her entirety, almost like a sacrifice to the goddess the woman was. Tensing, shaking, she held the cop's face in her mind's eye and then broke all at once. She shouted, she grunted, she died. Her body fought the powerful cop, forcing itself upon her and then trying desperately to back away. The woman fought back, grabbing onto Chan's hip, holding her to her, silently demanding that she take it all, every last bit.

They battled for what seemed like an eternity until Chan had no more strength left in her and relented, dropping down onto the bed as if she had no bones in her body. She lay still, like a rag doll, panting, her mind swimming. She was vaguely aware of a tongue licking the sweat off her abdomen. Her body twitched, her nerves frayed and dangerously exposed.

"Can you speak?" the cop asked, very delicately removing her fingers from inside her.

Chan cried out softly at the absence within and shook her head as she tried to focus on her blurry face.

"I...I..." she croaked, her eyes unbelievably heavy and drifting closed. The world around her seemed heavy and thick, too hazy to focus on. Everything became one. A soft, deep hum, lulling her to sleep.

The woman kissed her then, or maybe Chan dreamt it. She felt soft lips touch her own oh so gently and then pull away, quickly disappearing into the haze along with the woman's scent.

CHAPTER FIVE

Patrol Officer Sarah Monroe slipped her thin T-shirt on over her sports bra. She stood from the bench in the women's locker room and pulled the string on her mesh athletic shorts, tightening the fit. As she held her arms above her head for a brief stretch, the bright blue spine of her latest purchase caught her eye. She reached inside, unable to be patient any longer.

The book was by one of her favorite romance authors and it had just arrived that afternoon. She licked her lips with anticipation and turned it over to skim the back cover as she had a dozen times in the last hour. More than anything she longed to get lost in the pages, to escape into the hearts of the imaginary characters. The love and passion she found in books and film felt incredibly real to her. The stories touched her like nothing else could. And most importantly, the characters couldn't hurt her, betray her, or even die. No, they were perfect. Safe. Just like the ideal love they shared.

As she fanned through the book, she heard someone approach and open a locker near hers. Startled back from her world of make-believe, she tucked the book away and grabbed a pair of socks.

"Hey, Monroe."

"Hey." Sarah mentally sifted through names as the young fair haired officer busied herself at her locker, quickly tugging off her shirt and shoving down her pants. Leslie Carver.

She caught herself looking her colleague over, eyeing her fit body appreciatively. As she studied her, the vision of another woman invaded her mind. Chandler Brogan. The woman she had been with the previous night. The woman who had been on her mind constantly ever since.

Frustrated, she did her best to shake the thought away.

"Working out?" Carver questioned, reaching back to unlatch her bra. Her small perky breasts gathered to taut points as the cool air hit them.

"Yeah." Sarah sat poised on the bench, one leg crossed over the other, sock in hand. Leslie Carver was beautiful, but she didn't compare to Chandler. Sarah felt her cheeks heat, but she didn't know if it was from frustration or desire in remembering how Chandler looked in the nude.

Why am I sitting here thinking about a one-night stand? She forced her focus away from Chandler and onto the temptation standing next to her. The woman was attractive, more than most. And Sarah knew she was gay.

"Me too." Carver moved about with an air of self-assuredness, seemingly oblivious to Sarah's wandering gaze. But a part of her had to know Sarah was watching. She was obviously eating it up while pretending not to let on.

"Listen," she said, unabashedly squeezing into a sports bra, "a couple of us are going out later after our shift." She stuck her hand in the bra, adjusting her breasts. "Wanna go?" Her dark eyes met Sarah's as her mouth spread with a knowing grin.

Sarah contemplated the invitation, once again averting her gaze. She knew she could have the woman and thought about what it would be like to conquer her. But her answer came out before she even realized.

"No thanks. I can't." She tugged on her shoes and laced them up hurriedly. *What am I doing? Why did I say no?*

Her colleague took it well, almost as if she expected Sarah to turn her down. "Some other time then?" She straightened, pulled her tank top down over her bra, and rested a warm hand on Sarah's shoulder.

Inwardly cursing herself, Sarah replied, "Sure."

Leslie Carver gave her a smile and breezed out of the locker room, leaving Sarah alone with her thoughts. She closed her locker and sat with her head in her hands. Truth was, she knew exactly why she'd said no. She didn't date. Nor did she socialize. Especially with people from work. It was just the way she was. She didn't let anyone in.

She stood and stroked her dark mane back into a ponytail as she moved to the door, then made her way down the hallway to the weight room.

As she scanned the room, which hung heavy with sweat, her mind flashed over her current life. She had a lot going on, a lot to think about. Most of it things she wished she could bury down deep, never to think of again. But her present life was demanding that the past be dug up, however awful and life shattering it might be. Which was all the more reason why she needed to concentrate right now. She had to focus; her future depended on it. Any day now she would hear back from the FBI. She had just finished phase two of testing the week before. The Bureau was all she had ever wanted, and she couldn't afford to screw it up over her current issues. It was too important to her.

Her eyes caught the bulky body of her longtime friend, fellow cop Dave Houston. At once her insides flooded with guilt. Dave was her closest friend, her only friend. But she hadn't yet told him about the FBI. She could lie to herself and say it was because she wasn't yet in. But she knew better. She was a shoo-in.

Dave greeted her by handing over a water bottle, taking a quick squirt from the one he still held. "You ready?"

"Yeah." She was more than ready. It was time to focus and forget all the rest.

She had worked hard to build a nice life for herself. A tidy, comfortable apartment, a great job, an attainable goal with the FBI. *And no one to share it with.* The thought stabbed her and seemingly from out of nowhere, Chandler's face forced all else from her mind. Coming for her, over and over. *Damn it. No.*

She pushed it away only to have her mother's voice enter her head, reporting the bad news. Forcing up memories, ghosts, demons she had long ago buried. Fresh, potent anger and resentment followed close behind, leaving her feeling tightly wound, ready to rage, causing her to question her own sanity. *No.*

She clenched her water bottle and walked with purpose next to Dave.

Bodies around them pumped and pushed, grunted and strained as they tried their muscles. But she ignored them, too worked up over her inner turmoil. Leslie Carver waved as she walked by, almost touching her. It forced up another issue. Her own secret little problem. The real reason why she kept women at bay.

Worked up before she had even started, Sarah laid down on the bench press and lifted the bar of weights before Dave had a chance to spot her.

He scurried behind her, cursing as she pushed out rep after rep, determined to clear her mind. She couldn't stop or the thoughts would catch up. Her workouts were all she had. Nothing else could chase her troubles away. So she pushed on, enjoying the strain, welcoming the pain.

"Jesus, Monroe. Easy," Dave warned.

Sarah clenched her jaw and bent her knees, lifting her feet to place them flat on the bench. She needed more of an isolation on her chest, and the new position would do it. She gripped the bar again and squeezed, positioning just right for the next lift.

"You've had enough," Dave said sternly.

"No, I haven't, " she replied. "One more set."

"It's too much, you've had enough."

She squinted up at him and refused to submit. "Fine, I'll do it without you." With that she tensed her body and hoisted the bar up over her chest. She had to keep going, had to keep focused.

"Why are you so worked up today?" he questioned as she pumped out the first rep of her fifth set.

"No reason."

Sarah groaned as the thoughts of Chandler invaded, regardless of her internal fight against them. As she pushed the bar up time and time again, she imagined pushing the thoughts away. But they still came. The way Chandler moved, the way she smelled, the way her hardheadedness had melted into an unbelievable burning passion. The bar weighed down on her, pushing her to fail, causing her arms to shake. She grunted in frustration rather than pain.

"Bullshit!" Dave grabbed the bar, lifting its weight from her trembling arms and bringing it to a clanking rest above her. "You've gone way overboard today. Don't tell me it's nothing."

She sat up, the memory of the way Chandler's skin tasted all too real and heating her damp skin.

"So?" Dave continued with irritation, tossing a towel at her. "You gonna tell me what's going on or not?"

Sarah wiped her face with a weak hand and fought off the dizziness she was feeling from her hard workout as well as from her thoughts about Chandler. She tossed the towel back to Dave, hell bent on remaining strong. "I gained half a pound last week."

Dave scoffed and adjusted the elastic waistband of his sweat shorts with obvious frustration. "You're unbelievable."

Sarah could tell he was upset at her refusal to give him a meaningful response, but to her relief, he didn't pursue the matter and left her alone the rest of their workout, enabling them both to lift in peace.

By the time they'd finished, Sarah's upper body trembled with the stress of going five sets on each and every lift. She stretched her taut muscles and resisted the urge to flinch in distress in front of Dave. He would only bite into her again about overdoing it. They headed slowly over to the treadmills, where they always finished their workouts. Sarah climbed on and set the pace at a brisk walk, which quickly led into a jog as Dave walked casually beside her.

"You know," he began, his voice heavy with concern. "You can talk to me."

"'Bout what?" She was a little surprised he was starting in again. But she remained focused on her running. She was getting in her groove now, all of it becoming one, her steps, her heart rate, her breathing. It felt good, somehow seeming to soothe the tightness in her muscles.

"Anything." He wiped his face with his towel. "When I think of all the things you've helped me through..." His voice trailed off.

Sarah's legs continued to melt into the treadmill as she listened to him. It was true, she had helped him through a lot. Problems with his wife, problems with his folks. She had always been there for him and she always would. And she suspected he would do the same for her if given the chance.

He seemed to study her for a moment, squirting a stream of water in his mouth. Swallowing it, he said. "So what's going on? You only work out this hard when something's eating you."

"I told you. It's nothing." Sarah refused to let his questioning trip her up. Like a soldier marching perfectly in line, she pressed on. She wasn't in the mood to talk about anything, not even to Dave.

She kept running, feeling the seed of guilt growing in her stomach. While she usually kept most things inside, she did talk to Dave quite a bit. Rarely about anything serious, but they joked around and spoke of life in general. When she was quiet and driven, Dave worried, because he knew her better than most people and she trusted him more than she trusted anyone else. But how could she tell him about this? About her own private demons from her past? About the man who called himself her father who now lay dying? About the job she had always wanted but secretly feared she wouldn't get? She couldn't, there was no way. Dave would try to understand, but in no way could he help her battle the demons that were hers to fight alone. And he would be hurt that she hadn't told him about the job. So she was stuck dealing on her own.

She pressed on with her run as Dave pressed on with his quest to get in her head.

"I'm not stupid, Sarah. I know something's under your skin," he announced, wiping his chin with his thick forearm. "Look, you've helped me out. You give good advice when I need it. And Nicky acts like we wouldn't have a marriage if it wasn't for you. She's always asking me to invite you to dinner. I wish you'd come more often."

Sarah reached up to check her pulse, loving the high from her steady jog, but hating the guilt she was feeling in regard to Dave.

"How about it?" Dave asked from his squeaking treadmill, now trying a different angle to reach her. "Dinner tomorrow night?"

"Can't." It was bullshit but she didn't want to give in. She was afraid that if she did, her wall would come crumbling down and she would fall apart in front of him.

She pushed the down arrow key on the treadmill and slowed her pace to a fast walk. Her hand returned to her neck, and she forced herself to concentrate on her pulse.

Dave kept on. "You got other plans?"

Satisfied with her heart rate, she glanced over at him as her brain settled. His body was thick, solid with the bulk of muscle. He was far from cut, but beefy in his build with little visible fat. Sweat shimmered on his head where he kept his reddish hair shaved close to the scalp.

She took a squirt of warm water from her plastic bottle and returned it to the holder. In a gentler tone, she said, "I just can't, okay?"

"If you're seeing someone, you can tell me—"

She jerked her head and cut him off. "I'm not." Dave knew she didn't date. And when she had, with Danielle, she had kept it quiet. Danielle Turner had been a huge mistake and the negative feelings still stung, even though it had been a few months since their breakup.

The couple of times Dave had asked questions regarding her love life had won him the silent treatment. So why would he think she was seeing someone now? Was her attraction to Chandler that obvious? Frustrated to think she could be that transparent, she tensed her body.

"Okay, okay." He sounded resigned. "But if you ever do get involved, I hope you'll tell me. Even if it's, you know…"

She listened to his sentence trail off and cocked her head, her curiosity awakened. "Even if it's what?"

Dave appeared uncomfortable and almost embarrassed as he turned his head to face forward. His eyes focused on his water bottle as he said, "Another woman."

Sarah almost laughed. Dave had never had the nerve, and she'd never given him the reason, to question her sexuality before. *So why now, big guy?* She observed him in silence, taking note of the fear draining the color from his face. He must really be worried about her to bring up something so intensely personal and quite possibly upsetting to her.

"Thank you," she managed, not sure what else to say. She knew Dave would never tell anyone about her private life, but she just wasn't ready to get into it. She felt too emotional right now, her walls too weak. She had to remain strong, for her own survival.

They walked on in silence and as Sarah slowed her breathing and tried to relax, she wondered if she was being too guarded. Over the years it had become second nature. At first she'd retreated into herself knowing that her parents were always too drunk to care, and eventually it became a habit. She took care of herself. She never needed anyone else. Now she wasn't sure how to be any other way.

But Dave's hint at a female lover brought back more images.

Chandler writhing on the bed, calling out for her, begging for release.

Sarah's breath caught in her throat as the memory stirred her. Chandler was such a passionate lover, comfortable in her body as well as in the bedroom. Sarah had wanted the gorgeous tomboy the second she had turned around on the bike, all wild and free, strong willed and hardheaded. And the sex with her...

Sarah breathed out long and steady. The sex with her had been unbelievably hot, something she knew would be difficult to forget. But forget was what she had to do. She couldn't risk seeing Chandler again; there were things about herself she couldn't afford to expose, so there could be no repeat of their steamy encounter. Right now, she didn't need the stress of having to maintain the persona women seemed to expect of her. And she'd discovered the hard way that if she revealed herself as anything less, there were ugly consequences.

Instantly anxiety and anger flooded her as she thought of Danielle.

"You aren't who you make yourself out to be. You're a fake, Sarah."

She let the words echo in her mind. The breakup with Danielle had been nasty and heated, leaving her feeling more ashamed than ever. And broken.

Danielle was convinced that she knew it all. Her criticism and harsh words, however, had made Sarah think. Not just about her problem in regard to sex, but to all of it. The anxiety and anger she felt when she thought about the past. The distance she felt with other people around her. Her inability to express her feelings. She had an idea as to where they all stemmed from, but she could only deal with one thing at a time. And she was finally ready to start, scared by her own mind and the memories that lurked there. The appointment was set, waiting for her to take that first step with someone who could hopefully help.

Dave coughed next to her, alerting her that she should probably say something more to help ease the quiet thickness between them. But what could she say? She knew she should be able to voice her worries and concerns to him. But she had never been able to open up to him—or anyone else, for that matter—about deep personal issues. He knew it and most of the time he respected her privacy, but today he was homing in on her trepidations like a hound sniffing for blood. She held her ground, though, unable to trust. Even though Danielle had gotten close enough to know she had a problem, she didn't know why. No one did.

"I'll come to dinner another night," she finally offered, hoping it would get him off her back.

"Yeah?"

She gave him a look letting him know she was serious and not to push it.

Dave smiled, pleased at himself. "I'll let Nicky know. How about Friday?"

"Sure." She kept walking, staring straight ahead. "Just make sure that damn bulldog of yours doesn't try to hump my leg."

Dave laughed, his relief evident in the way his eyes danced. She was joking around with him again, and she knew it made him relax. It was what she always did, hid her true problems with light humor or meaningless conversation. She suspected Dave appreciated it too most times. It was a way for him to unwind as well.

"Killer likes you," he said, joking back.

"Yeah, well, Killer better knock it off if he knows what's good for him."

She inwardly cringed as she thought of the slobbering, bulky dog with the smashed face latching on to her leg, sliming her pants. Killer was one of the main reasons she didn't have pets. They were messy and unpredictable, and she couldn't imagine having to clean up after one in her apartment. She couldn't even venture getting a fish.

Her home was her haven. Immaculately clean and organized, it was where she felt completely safe and in control. Instantly, Chandler's words about control and how it probably played a big part in her life rang in her ears. Sarah shook her head. Chandler didn't know just how right she had been.

Eventually, they headed off toward the locker rooms, their bodies glistening with warm sweat, their heart rates slowing down to a normal pace. They had finished their preshift workout and Sarah was looking forward to taking a hot shower and stepping into her clean, crisp uniform. She only hoped that work would help to ease the turmoil that still churned in her mind despite her heavy workout.

Unconsciously, she rubbed her tight, twitching bicep as several other DPS officers passed them by, heading into the gym.

"Houston, Monroe," seasoned cop Bill Fletcher greeted with a nod.

A young rookie walked at his side, a cocky grin on his boyish face. He squeezed his fists, pumping his cut arms as he openly admired Sarah, seemingly convinced that she would show equal interest.

She caught his attempt at eye contact, but walked on unimpressed. Her lack of attention caused the young muscled man to turn slightly and call out.

"Hey, Monroe!" When she and Dave stopped walking, he continued. "Is that any relation to Marilyn?"

Sarah stiffened at once and felt Dave flinch beside her. She turned to face the rookie, who stood grinning, his light eyes glinting with mischief. His mentor stood at his side, looking more than a little nervous as Sarah approached. She respected Fletcher and as she walked up, she gave the rookie the benefit of the doubt. He didn't know her, but he had no manners, something she needed to take care of. Her fellow officers knew that she would not tolerate any kind of sexual misconduct or harassment. Some had learned the hard way, but most had wised up the easy way.

"Did you say something to me?" she asked, stepping up into the rookie's face, testing to see if he would continue with his rude behavior.

He merely smiled, his eyes traveling over her face and body with blatant approval. "I think you're hotter than Marilyn," he said, ignoring her warning tone. "Tough, sexy—"

Sarah knocked the wind from him, smashing him up against the wall, her forearm pressing against his throat. Around her, Dave and Fletcher spoke up, trying to get her to calm down and release him, but she couldn't hear them. All she heard were the little bastard's words, ringing in her ears. She couldn't handle disrespect, not from anyone.

The rookie choked against her, flailing his arms wildly, trying to smack her away. She pressed him harder, her nose against his, her eyes boring hatred into him.

"Say you're sorry," she seethed. She felt Dave's hands on her shoulders but she continued, her body rigid against the younger man's.

The rookie looked at her with wide eyes. He tried to speak but he couldn't. He could barely breathe with the pressure of her forearm. She eased up a little to allow him to voice his apology. Around them, a small crowd began to gather.

"Say it!" she demanded, slightly lunging at him once again, threatening the return of her restricting forearm.

"I...I'm sorry," he stammered, his hand flying up to his neck, rubbing reassuringly.

"Don't ever let me catch you talking to a female like that again," she added, holding his eyes, stepping away from him.

The rookie slumped against the wall, his face red from the encounter and from obvious embarrassment. He looked around frantically and stalked off, shoving his way through the gathering men.

Sarah breathed her anger in and out, thick and heavy, as Fletcher bumped her shoulder to chase after his rookie.

"Get control of her, Houston," he voiced, giving Dave a wary glance before he disappeared into the crowd.

Dave's hand clenched down on her shoulder, making her muscles jump as she came treacherously close to reacting with violence once more. His small hazel eyes were round and serious, worry shining from them.

"Come on!" He tugged her along after him, yanked open the janitor's closet, and shoved her inside. They stood alone in the darkness as he shut the door and pulled on the string of a bare bulb.

Stabbing a finger at her chest, he demanded, "What in God's name was that?"

Sarah squinted against the harsh light. "Come on Dave, the guy was a—"

"No!" he yelled. Dave had never raised his voice at her, and it startled Sarah to silence. "Damn it, Monroe, this tough guy act of yours is going to get you fired!"

She felt her face heat with emotion as he spoke. She wasn't upset at him, she was upset at the world. Everyone knew she didn't take shit. Everyone but the rookie. Now he knew it too. So what was the problem?

"I'm telling you as your friend. You have got to get yourself under control." A crooked vein throbbed in his neck. The freckles above his lips danced as he spoke. "This is serious shit, Sarah. People are starting to notice." His hand gently squeezed her shoulder. "You have got to lighten up."

Sarah bit back her anger and held his intense stare. She could see the reason in his eyes and she knew he would not be treating her this way unless something was not quite right. Yet she couldn't see the problem. She wasn't a loose cannon. There was always a good reason for any action she took. She never did anything she shouldn't. Did she?

"I'm always under control," she replied with calm, cool conviction.

"You call that control?" Dave spat. "You nearly took his head off!"

Upset that he was questioning her choices and behavior, she reacted defensively. "I knew exactly what I was doing."

Dave shook his head and took a step away from her, lowering his hand from her shoulder. "Then that frightens me even more."

As he spoke, a tiny part of her deep down began to burn with what she recognized as anxiety. Was she out of control? She shoved the possibility from her mind and stared down her longtime friend. She had known exactly what she was doing; she always did. And what always came first and foremost was her own protection. The rookie's words and his attitude had threatened that, crossing an invisible barrier they both knew was there. He had gotten what he deserved. If anything, they should be patting her on the back; she had done them all a favor putting the meathead newbie in his place.

Dave stared at her like he was waiting for something. This wasn't like Dave, she'd never had a confrontation with him before. It made her uneasy and the closet seemed to close in on her inch by inch. It was obvious Dave was upset with her and her heart sped up at the realization. All over some smart assed rookie. Keeping her anxiety in check, she said, "I think you're overreacting."

"Are you serious? "

"The guy was out of line. You were there. You saw him."

"I saw a kid showing off in front of an attractive woman. Dumb, yes. But not worth risking disciplinary action over."

Sarah resisted the urge to roll her eyes. Something Dave would never understand was that being a woman on the job meant having boundaries and ruthlessly enforcing them. Her male colleagues had no idea what she would have to put up with if she showed the slightest weakness.

"If we're done here, I've got work to do," she said coolly.

"We're done." Dave gave her one last look of disappointment and shouldered into the door, leaving her alone in the cramped closet.

CHAPTER SIX

Sarah sat in her cruiser underneath the overpass staring in a daze at the rush of steady traffic. The headlights streaked past her, hypnotizing her.

Dave hadn't said a word to her since their conversation in the closet. While other cops had glanced curiously her way at their nightly briefing, having heard or seen what happened, Dave had avoided her eyes and sat across the room. That was the first time he had ever sat anywhere but next to her and the first time he'd ever questioned her behavior. Her mind raced to find the reason why and latched onto Danielle.

The weeks since their breakup had been stressful for her as shadows from her past stepped into the light once again, forcing her to relive and remember. She had fought as best she could, refusing to let the shadows win. But the painful memories hovered, leaving her guarded and edgy just like she used to be when she was fourteen, poised for fight or flight at the drop of a dime.

She closed her eyes softly as she realized just how many times lately she had chosen to fight in response. Just a few weeks earlier, she and Dave had been called in as backup on a routine traffic stop. The officer who'd pulled the guy over ran his license and was alerted that he had a warrant outstanding for rape and battery. It took three of them to wrestle the man to the ground and get cuffs on him.

Sarah had seen scum like him all too often and she was relatively calm as she escorted him to the cruiser. Their suspect was in obvious pain, his face coated with the sheen of sweat. She could smell the beer on his breath and she kept her face slightly averted, avoiding the images that seeped from her memory. As she brought him up next to the cruiser, she placed a firm, black-gloved hand on his shoulder, thankful to be getting rid of him.

The guy took this opportunity to share what was on his mind. "I usually don't like 'em so big," he grunted. "But you'll do just fine."

Rage surged through her as the words sank through her skin and stabbed her insides. She slammed him up against the car and held a hand around his neck. "What did you say?"

He snickered, flying high with wild eyes, unafraid. "I said I usually like 'em smaller, like around thirteen, their cherries just ripe for poppin'."

Sarah felt a darkness invade her body like a cold steel demon. Voices, memories, smells from the past all came screaming back at her. She tightened her grip on his throat and lowered her left hand to his crotch, where she squeezed his testicles with all her might. The man whimpered, his face contorting in pain.

"How does it feel, huh?" she demanded, squeezing and yanking on his sac, determined to make him suffer. Just like his young victim had.

His eyes rolled back in his head as the lack of oxygen began to affect him, but Sarah eased her grip on his neck only enough to ensure that he would feel the pain from his crotch. As he struggled to breathe, the stagnant odor of nicotine radiated out from his damp skin and the alcoholic wave that rose up from his throat nearly made her nauseous. Her mind took over, sucking her into a wormhole that led to the past.

She heard laughter so loud and out of control it was threatening. She eased her way up to the kitchen wall where she stood, tall, gangly, and silent.

At the table six adults sat, laughing, carrying on, cussing. A thick haze of cigarette smoke hung around them like their own private cloud cover, harboring them, encouraging them, encaging them. When they got like this they couldn't see beyond that haze. They couldn't see the real world. They couldn't see her.

Her father sucked on his near-empty beer bottle, draining the fiery fuel that she had long ago come to hate. "Shit! You're killing me, Scottie, killing me." He laid down his cards with force and rose from the table, shoving back his chair with a screech so loud it made her jump. "*I need another beer.*"

He made his way to the fridge and she knew from his sloppy movements that he was already drunk. The door to their old Frigidaire banged open as his head disappeared inside.

"*Get me another one!*" her mother called from the table.

"*Get it yourself!*" he shouted, slamming the door closed. "*We're out.*"

Sarah took a timid step back, afraid of the look on his once-handsome face.

"*Go get some more,*" her mother responded, a Pall Mall cigarette hanging loosely from her bright red lips. Her eyes were heavily painted and firmly fixed on her hand of cards.

"*Why don't you get off your fat ass and go?*" Roy Monroe sauntered over to his chair, where he plopped down and nearly fell. He gripped the table for support and cursed to himself.

Sarah's mother calmly plucked two cards, never offended by her husband's drunken verbal assaults, and laid them facedown on the table. Raising her eyes, she said to their longtime friend Scottie, "*Hit me.*"

Scottie, all grease and no good, grinned. His fingers riffled two more cards and then pulled back to smooth through his wet-looking hair. He leaned back in his chair and retrieved the pack of cigarettes he wore tucked away in the front pocket of his T-shirt. With practiced grace, he lit one and sucked on it so hard his shiny cheeks caved. As he blew the smoke out of the side of his mouth, he eyed his feuding friends. "*Why don't you send Sarah?*"

"*No, Roy can go,*" she heard her mother say.

"*Fuck you, Harriet. I'm the one who works his ass off for you. I'm the one who pays for the goddamned beer, and for all your shit!*" He was getting louder and Sarah took another step back, this time hiding behind the wall and losing her visual. Quickly, she retreated down the hall to her bedroom, their voices loud enough to follow her.

"*Fine, send Sarah,*" Harriet Monroe shouted. "*Jesus, Roy. Calm the hell down.*"

"*No, I won't calm down, damn it! I'm sick and tired of—*"

"*Sarah!*" her mother called, and Sarah froze in front of her door, eyes closed, as the bickering continued.

She wished she could disappear. Disintegrate and float away, every last molecule to another place. A safe place. A home like her *friends had, one where parents didn't drink and didn't fight.*

She jerked at the sound of her name being called again, this time high on a scream. Wiping away a tear, she walked slowly back toward the thick haze of smoke in the kitchen.

"There she is." Scottie's beady eyes assaulted her twelve-year-old body with blatant approval. "Hiya, Sarah."

His grin made her feel sick. He had been looking at her like that for a few weeks now, and it made her extremely uncomfortable.

"Sarah, say hello. Don't be rude," her mother chided, still concentrating on her card game.

Sarah raised her arms to hug herself against Scottie's lingering gaze and meekly said, "Hi."

Her father dug in his pockets for the wad of cash he always seemed to have. "Go down to the store and get us a case of beer." He caught hold of her arm and yanked her close, plopping some money into her palm. "Get yourself some gum or something, but hurry back. Don't fuck around."

His mood instantly changed at the prospect of getting more beer and he stood up and danced his way over to the kitchen counter. He switched on the transistor radio and turned up the volume. "Don't fuck around, 'cuz I wanna dance!" He sauntered toward his wife, smiling, humming, and snapping his fingers. Tugging her up, he held her close to his body. "Come on, baby, dance with me."

"Roy!" She resisted, but then laughed as he squeezed her ass. They glided across the kitchen, holding each other tight as her father sang along with the radio.

Scottie and the others clapped and cheered and then rose to join in, each man taking hold of his woman—with the exception of Scottie. He had no girlfriend, and he moved toward Sarah like an evil demon searching for a soul. She shoved the money down in her pocket and turned to go, but a strong hand on her arm stopped her.

"Oh, no, you don't." He pulled her into him with ease and she stiffened at the contact. A rough hand brushed her cheek and she could smell the nicotine on his fingers. His free hand quickly brushed her backside and he grinned as he hugged her closer. "Dance with me, darling."

Her heart thudded its resistance and she raised her arms to push him away. "No, I have to go."

"Not so fast," he whispered in her ear.

Her eyes flew to her parents for help but they were in their own world, laughing and dancing, oblivious to her as always.

Scottie squeezed her closer, tighter. She could hardly breathe, and she felt something hard jabbing against her hip. "You're such a pretty girl, Sarah. I bet the boys is just all over themselves over you."

Around her, laughter filled the room. He pulled his face back and spoke again, but she was panicked and she couldn't hear him. The alcohol on his breath assaulted her nose, burning it. She fought back a gag as he rubbed against her, grinning, groaning. Scared and confused, she shoved him away as hard as she could.

"No!" she cried out.

He staggered back and dropped his hands as his eyebrows rose. "I was only teaching her to dance," he said with startled innocence.

Her parents looked her way as she stood breathing heavily with fear.

"Sarah! Don't be rude to Scottie," her mother insisted.

As the words stabbed her heart, she turned and ran. The screen door banged behind her and she hurried down the steps as the tears ran down her cheeks in warm rivers.

"Sarah! You get back here!" Her father's voice, loud and angry. "Don't forget my beer!"

Sarah reached down and sipped her now-cold coffee as she refocused on the present. After she'd almost choked the prisoner to death during that callout, Dave had told her to take the rest of the night off. No report had been filed against her. Lucky. Or maybe it was more than luck. Obviously Dave had done his best to sweep the incident under the rug. For that, she was grateful.

She could still remember how she'd felt pinning that pervert to the cruiser, staring at him as he choked. Everything around her had seemed like a fog, including time itself. When Dave tore her off the guy, she was shaken and startled to realize where she was, shocked that she wasn't alone and in the dark place of her past.

Dumping the rest of her coffee out the window, she placed the cup back in its holder and readied the radar for use. Maybe she had been a little hotheaded lately, she thought as she switched on the speed detector. While she could excuse each encounter and convince herself that she was in control, she knew it must look bad to others, especially Dave, who cared for her so much. And she knew she couldn't afford to have that kind of behavior reported to the FBI. Her chances would be blown to hell.

She eased down her window and positioned the black, bulky radar toward the oncoming traffic. She would make it up to Dave. She owed him. Maybe it was a good thing, her making that appointment. Exhaling, she tried to relax. Yes, she thought to herself, things would be just fine.

CHAPTER SEVEN

I really do," Chan's client Bob Rogers said with conviction. "I really think she married me for my penis."

Chan followed his pointed stare to his wife of two years, a heavily made-up brunette in her late thirties who sat on the opposite end of the couch. Sherri Rogers seemed amazingly unmoved by the accusation, or perhaps she was concealing hurt and anger beneath her air of quiet reserve. Chan couldn't tell, an unusual situation for her; normally she could read her clients well. But she was in an exceptionally cranky mood for a Tuesday, and she knew it had everything to do with her unforgettable night with Officer Monroe. Listening to one discontented couple after another didn't help. Mainly because, despite their issues, they had something she didn't. Each other.

Chan fought back the sting of loneliness and focused on her clients. "Bob, come on now. Sherri didn't marry you for your penis." Chan glanced Sherri's way and met eyes filled with a surprising nonchalance. "Right, Sherri?" *Come on, help me out here.*

"Right," her client said, all smiles.

Bob was obviously unconvinced. "But that's all she wants all the time." His eyes grew wide as he spoke. "To fuck."

Chan thought for a moment. So many of her clients came in with the opposite problem. The men wanting sex, their wives uninterested. "Do you enjoy having sex with her?"

Bob squirmed a little and started to speak, but then closed his mouth and folded his arms across his chest, the gesture revealing his defensiveness. "I...Well, yes, at the time."

Chan gave him a few seconds to cool down, then, in a softer tone, said, "But that's not your point, is it? You see her wanting it all the time as a negative. Like it's no longer about intimacy and lovemaking." Maybe Bob was just as sensitive as her female clients. Maybe there came a time in everyone's life, male and female, when sex just wasn't enough.

Her thoughts strayed to the mysterious Officer Monroe. Chan was surprised at how empty she'd felt when she had awakened the next morning all alone. Had that time finally come for her? Was she now destined to overanalyze every sexual encounter, hoping, searching, needing something more? Something that had seemed to elude her for years and quite possibly always would? The discouraging thought hung heavy in her mind.

Bob's voice quivered as he continued to try to put words to his feelings. "I'm saying that I feel a little used here."

A hot spark ignited in Chan's belly. It burned quickly and spread up to her throat. Used. The word played out, fanning the fire. Was that how she felt about her one-sided night with the beautiful cop?

Officer Monroe hadn't allowed Chan to reciprocate. She had pleased Chan, then disappeared into the night, leaving Chan only half satiated. The pleasure had been so great, the seduction and domination soul altering. Chan had wanted, more than anything, to touch her conqueror, to feel her tremble, to hear her cries of pleasure. But it had been a one-night stand. One night, one chance, and it had ended as many did. Regrettably. Only this time the regret was simply that Chan had fallen asleep. This encounter left her bothered as few others ever had. She wondered why. Was it because she was the one who usually did the pleasing, the disappearing?

Oblivious to her lapse in concentration, Bob continued to speak, the hurt evident in his voice. "I mean, it's all the time. And it's not like we're having normal sex."

Chan raised her eyebrows, curious as to what he meant.

He rubbed the back of his neck. "She insists that I take Viagra."

Chan glanced Sherri's way. Bob didn't have erectile dysfunction. "Why is that, Sherri?" Chan was sure she knew the reason but she wanted to hear it from her.

Sherri hesitated a little before she spoke. "Because he goes longer."

Clever girl. It was nice to hear from a woman with a healthy sex drive who wasn't ashamed to take what she wanted. Even so, she studied the couple for a moment. She had to reverse the roles and view them as she did every other couple. Just because Bob was a man and Sherri was the one who took what she wanted, it didn't make Bob's feelings any less valuable. Their relationship was taking an unhealthy turn, and a selfish, uncaring partner was just that regardless of their gender.

Chan's desk alarm beeped, graciously allowing her a little more time to think on this one. "That's it for today, guys."

"But what about me?" Bob whined.

Chan sighed and tried to think of a temporary solution. What would she tell her female clients?

"Don't have sex with her. Tell her no." But as she studied him, she knew he wouldn't take her advice. Bob was a healthy man, after all, and Sherri a healthy, attractive woman. She cleared her throat and did her best to explain. "Bob, I think you could work on taking back some of the control you allow Sherri to have. It's important for you to respect your own feelings and voice them. Don't ever do anything you're not comfortable in doing. And, Sherri, as Bob's lover, you need to respect his feelings."

Control. Again she thought of the night with Officer Monroe, and suddenly she understood Bob better. As in most relationships, one person gives more than the other, dysfunctional or not. She made her livelihood on this certainty, and when couples couldn't seem to communicate or work through their problems, she stepped in to guide them. But she now knew firsthand just how easy it was to give in to a demanding partner. She had done exactly that with the cop, willingly, caught up in the moment. She'd also spent the next day feeling lonely and frustrated. It was the first time she had ever felt so completely empty after lovemaking.

"We'll talk about it some more next week, okay?" Chan gave Bob a pat on the back while escorting them to the door.

They exited in silence, leaving Chan to return to her chair, where she sat gratefully and began to massage her temples. She was confused by her feelings, and concerned. The sex with Officer Monroe had been incredible, unlike anything she had experienced before. So why was she so down? She stewed in her chair, wishing the woman had at least left her number. And her first name. Chan wanted to see her again.

The realization startled her. Maybe that was why she was so shook up. It was obviously just a one-night stand, but Chan wanted another. She shivered as she relived the unforgettable evening. It wasn't just the unbelievable things the mysterious cop had done to pleasure her, it was how she had done it. With fiery passion and complete control and confidence, coolly demanding what she wanted. This was what moved Chan most, and yet left her feeling strangely yearning. With a long sigh, she rose to get some coffee. She was going to need it to get through the rest of the day.

Entering the main office area, she ran her hand through her hair and allowed the steady buzz from the overhead lights and the strong scent of freshly brewed coffee to soothe her. To her left, several of the reception staff busied themselves filing charts and answering phones. She stopped at the counter and poured herself a steaming cup of the dark morning fuel.

As she sipped, she tried to ready herself for the rest of her day. She had five more people to see, and if her current mood prevailed, it would be a miracle if she made it through.

"Good morning."

Chan turned with mug in hand, expecting to see one of her colleagues. But the surprise of seeing Hazel Jackson caused her to nearly choke. Hazel was a plump older woman who saw one of Chan's colleagues. She had been coming to the practice for years and always showed up early for her appointments, talking relentlessly to the staff.

Chan nodded a greeting and tried her damndest not to stare. No matter how many times she saw Hazel, she was still shocked by the woman's choice of headgear. Planted across her forehead was a large, thick, super-absorbent maxi pad. During the warm season, which was a good seven months in Arizona, Hazel insisted on wearing this version of a sweatband, asserting that it was the only thing that could keep the sweat out of her eyes, especially since she had to wait out in the desert heat for the city bus.

She had the soft side resting against her skin and a purple shoelace running horizontally across the sticky side of the pad, tying it secure around her head. Chan knew she should be used to seeing it by now, but she still had to force her eyes away.

Seemingly oblivious to her discomfort, Hazel dug in her large book bag and retrieved a long-stemmed purple sunflower wrapped excessively in aluminum foil that nearly covered the entire stem.

With an eager smile, she held it out to Chan and said, "I brought one for everybody."

Chan took the flower tentatively. Last week it was a strange concoction of cookies that were so hard and flat they could have doubled as clay pigeons. Every time Chan looked at them she had the urge to yell "pull!" and toss them into the air.

Suddenly feeling like laughing, she bit her lower lip and tried her best to look the woman in the eye. "Thank you, Hazel. You're very kind." With laughter threatening her, she again looked away. But Hazel, as always, didn't seem to notice.

"If you keep the flower until it dies, the seeds turn into crystals, and if you plant them, you'll grow magic flowers." Her voice was alive and excited and she seemed completely serious about what she was saying.

Chan wasn't surprised, having heard far crazier things from her before. She didn't know what Hazel's problems were beyond the general comments passed during team meetings at the practice, but she knew enough to know that the maxi pad sweatband was the least of them. That, coupled with the insistent gift giving, led her to believe that Hazel was quite comfortable with the attention her behavior got her. Trying to modify it had to be a frustrating process. Chan relaxed a little, relieved she wasn't the one responsible for her care. Today, her patients and their sexual problems were more than enough for her to handle.

"I wrapped it with a wet paper towel so it would live longer," Hazel confided. "The foil should help keep the paper towel wet."

Chan glanced at the wrapped flower and then, unable to resist, at Hazel. "I suspect it will," she said, eyeing her forehead, the area she had been resisting looking at.

Hazel stared at her intensely, still smiling, completely and totally happy in her gift-giving. "You have a good day now."

"You too, Hazel. I'm sure I'll see you next week."

Chan walked back into her office just in time to hear her cell phone ring. She plucked it quickly from her briefcase and answered.

"Chan?" It was Meg. It seemed a little strange that she would be calling this early on a Tuesday morning.

"Meg, hi."

"Good morning, dear. I hope I'm not interrupting?"

Chan eased down into her leather listening chair. "No, no. I have a few minutes. What's up?"

"I wanted to tell you that I ran into an old friend of yours this morning."

"Oh?"

"I was out for my daily walk and he pulled up next to me, said he recognized me as your grandmother."

Chan suddenly felt wary as she continued.

"Said he knew you from college and had met me once before."

A little worried, Chan asked. "What was his name?"

"I think he said it was Allen."

Chan's brain suddenly came fully awake, searching for the name in her memory banks. She couldn't find it. "Listen, Meg. I don't remember anyone named Allen. Don't talk to him again."

"Oh no, it's nothing like that. He really does know you. Said he always knew what a fine psychologist you would make."

Chan sat in silence, still trying to place a fellow student named Allen.

"Don't worry about it," Meg said lightly. "He's completely nonthreatening and he was just saying hello. I wanted to tell you in case you wanted to get a hold of him. He seems like a really nice guy. He even offered me a ride home but I turned him down. I need my exercise."

Chan wished she could relax at her grandmother's reassuring words, but she felt uncertain and wary. "I'm sure I'll remember him. In the meantime, be careful, okay?"

Meg laughed. "Of course. I'll talk to you later."

Chan hung up and sat staring into space. She knew she should remember a college friend, but it didn't surprise her that she couldn't place his name. Lately, she hadn't been as sharp as usual. More and more she found herself lost in thought rather than focusing on her paying clients. Before she could stew over the probable sources of her lack of concentration, her desk phone broke her trance.

"Dr. Brogan?" It was her secretary, Cynthia. Another woman who, like Meg, hated the way Chan preferred to fly by the seat of her pants.

"Yes?" Chan readied herself for the bickering that was bound to ensue. She hadn't finished going over the charts from the weekend. No doubt Cynthia had noticed.

"Michael Gold's here."

Chan fingered her lips in thought. Tuesday wasn't usually Michael's day. "Is he my next appointment?" She hoped not. For more reasons than one.

"No. He's asking to be seen this week."

"Do I have an opening?"

"No, not yet. He wants to know if you'll stay and see him at six sometime this week."

Chan shook her head, frustrated. Usually she wouldn't mind staying for a late appointment, but at the moment she was in no mood for sticking around. "No, I can't," she lied. "Put him on the cancellation list."

She didn't envy her secretary. Michael wasn't going to be happy with the news.

"Okay." Cynthia sighed and mumbled words resembling Chan's thought.

Chan hung up her phone and allowed her gaze to drift to the photographed landscapes on her wall. It was easy to get lost in each photo. Mountains she'd conquered, cliffs she had climbed. She remembered each place and she wished she were standing high on a peak now, surrounded by nothing but the beauty of nature.

As she studied the alluring blue sky in one photo, she was reminded of similar-colored eyes, staring deeply into her, moved by her pleasure. She shuddered and once again felt a pang of loneliness. If only she could find her.

Chan laughed suddenly, realizing how she sounded. But the feeling remained, luring her back to another time when she felt just as alone.

It was completely dark around her, and warm, the air unmoving. She sat with her knees pulled to her chest, breathing deeply. The more air she took in, the better she felt. But with every exhalation, the pain built back up.

She remained like that for hours, her lungs battling for air, trying desperately to hold in the scent of her mother's perfume. Her body trembled as the tears welled and flowed, streaking down her cheeks to drip onto her knees. It had been four days. Four horrible, excruciatingly painful days since that knock at the door.

She and Hank had been dancing with their teenage babysitter, Jamie, to the Bee Gees. Laughing, twirling, shaking about. Pieces of popcorn littered the floor and sofa. The television flashed in silence, drowned out by the stereo. She was happy, smiling widely at her babysitter, thankful that Jamie was finally off the phone and willing to show them some attention. Chan had a crush on the attractive young sitter, a crush she didn't quite understand. She only knew that she felt excited around her, thrived in her attention, and loved it when Jamie hugged her. She could smell her perfume then. And Chan very much liked the way it smelled. It was different from her mother's. Less flowery.

When the knocking on the front door came, they all stopped their movements and froze, like deer caught in headlights. Chan met Jamie's eyes and they communicated without speaking. It was late, way later than she and Hank were supposed to be up. Suddenly alive with panic, Chan grabbed Hank's hand and jerked him toward the stairs. They flew up the steps hurriedly, half excited, half afraid of getting busted. She heard the stereo turn off as they hit the landing. They rounded the corner and squatted, their breathing quick and short.

She looked to Hank and put her finger to her lips. He nodded with wide green eyes that matched his Incredible Hulk pajamas. She positioned herself on her knees and crawled to peek around the corner. Her heart thumped in her chest and she fought back excited giggles as she waited. She wanted to see what all Jamie would say to her parents, especially if they were going to get in trouble. She and Hank had to prepare for that ahead of time, and it would be nice to have a heads-up.

Chan watched Jamie brush the couch quickly, palming popcorn crumbs and depositing them in the large bowl on the coffee table. More knocking came and the teenager pulled back the curtains to glance outside. Chan watched her curiously as her facial expression changed. Her hand came up to her mouth, as if she were upset. Chan swallowed. Whatever was about to happen, Jamie was unnerved, and that made Chan uneasy.

Jamie opened the door slowly, and Chan waited to hear how upset her parents were about the loud music. She knew it had been loud enough for them to hear, so they would know that she and Hank *had been up. Her heart sank. She didn't want to get in trouble again. Last time it had been Hank's purple mustache that gave them away. He had pigged out on Popsicles all night long, the ones that they weren't supposed to eat because they were for her birthday party the next day. He had eaten his fill and then fallen asleep on top of his covers, Popsicle juice ringing his mouth.*

Now, as she heard a low male voice, Chan readied herself for trouble again.

"What's going on?" Hank wanted to know.

"Shh!" She eased out a little farther, trying to hear her father's words. But as the sitter took a step back, Chan realized the voice at the door wasn't her father's.

Two uniformed policemen walked inside, the first one catching her gaze right away. Chan pulled back against the wall, not sure what to think but knowing she was in real serious trouble for the police to have come. She hugged her knees to her chest and willed her Wonder Woman pajamas to give her courage. Could kids go to jail for staying up too late? Did her parents tell on her to the police? Suddenly, she felt like crying. She didn't want to go to jail.

She huddled close to Hank. "It's the police!" she whispered to him.

"The police!" His face was full of fear. "Why are they here?"

"I don't know!"

They sat listening, and Chan nearly burst with anxiety as she heard her babysitter break down into tears. Oh God it was bad, really bad. They were going to jail. Jamie too. She heard footsteps on the stairs, walking up slowly. She closed her eyes, too afraid to move an inch. When the walking stopped, she felt the air move next to her, letting her know that someone was there.

"Chandler?" It was a man's voice. The policeman. She gulped and trembled and looked up into his face. He smiled softly at her, confusing her even more. He removed his hat and squatted down in front of her and looked to both her and Hank. "Is this your brother?" he asked.

She nodded.

"How old are you guys?"

"Five!" Hank shouted out, just like he did anytime anyone asked.

The policeman held her eyes. "And what about you?"

"I'm eight," she whispered.

He sighed and rubbed his jaw. He shook his head.

Chan saw the sorrow in his expression and suddenly she realized he wasn't there to take them to jail. Something else was wrong, but she couldn't imagine what.

"Listen, guys," he breathed, his voice now a whisper too. "I've got some bad news."

Chan pulled her knees tighter, suddenly cold. The man continued and she could tell he was trying not to cry.

"Your mom and dad. They're not going to come home."

"Are they in jail?" Hank asked, concern on his brow.

"No, pal, they're not in jail." Chan watched the small ball in the cop's throat bob as he swallowed. "They were in a bad accident." His hand flew up to wipe at his cheek as a tear spilled.

Chan sat in a daze, her ears heating and filling with fear and panic.

"Did they get hurt?" Hank asked.

"Yes." The man straightened then, into a stand. He held his hand out for Chan, encouraging her to stand. She did so on her own, afraid to touch him, not wanting to feel what he was obviously feeling. If she didn't touch him, then maybe he would go away. Maybe the sadness that surrounded him would go away too.

She stood and looked back to Hank, who rose up eagerly to clutch the policeman's hand.

He led them down the stairs and Chan walked slowly, her heart hammering with a sudden need to see her parents. If the police were there, then the accident must have been bad. Her parents must be in the hospital. She swallowed a painful lump in her throat as she thought of them hurt and alone in the hospital.

They reached the bottom of the stairs and Jamie bent down with tears in her eyes to scoop up Hank in her arms.

More fear surged through Chan. "I want to go see my mom and dad," she demanded, looking up at the policeman.

He didn't answer, but rather looked to his partner. The shorter cop averted her eyes and reported, "The grandmother is on the way."

Chan figured they hadn't heard her. "I want to go to the hospital!" She had to get there. She didn't want her parents to be afraid.

The policeman rested a hand on her shoulder, but she moved out from under it, looking away from his wet, sad eyes, hating what she saw *in them. Noise came from the front door and another person entered the house, a woman older than Jamie but younger than Chan's mom. She wore regular clothes with her police badge on her chest.*

She walked up to Chan and squatted, meeting her at eye level. "Hi. My name is Susan."

She smiled but Chan saw through it. It was a comforting smile, one like her teachers gave when they were trying to calm down a misbehaving kid. Had she misbehaved? Was that why they weren't taking her to the hospital? They had to let her go to them. They just had to!

She pleaded with the woman in front of her and then fell silent as she saw the look that washed over her face. It was worse than the tall officer. Way worse. Her lips quivered and her eyes welled with tears just before the fake smile returned.

"Sweetie." She reached out and touched Chan's arm, and this time Chan didn't move away from the touch.

Instead she was drawn in, hypnotized by the woman's expression. And she knew something bad had happened.

"You can't go see your mom and dad because they got hurt real bad in a car accident."

She got choked up and suddenly Chan knew what she was trying to say.

"No!" Chan shouted.

"Yes, sweetie, I'm afraid so." She tried to tighten her grip on Chan's arm, but Chan yanked herself free.

"No! You're lying. It's not true!" It had to be a cruel joke. It couldn't be true. She had just hugged them good-bye and promised to go to bed on time. They were supposed to come home and somehow catch her staying up late. She was supposed to get in trouble and get grounded from riding her bike.

Hank began to cry and Jamie held him close and began to hum in his ear, doing her best to comfort him. But his gaze remained fixed on Chan. He shoved Jamie away, forcing her to release him, then ran to Chan.

Tugging on her sleeve, he begged, "Where's Mom and Dad?"

She couldn't answer. She looked at the people standing in her home. All of them were silent, all had tears in their eyes. She dropped her head, consumed with a raw burning that rose up and out of her chest.

Hank's crying became loud and wailing. He clung to her and she clung to him, feeling his tiny body rack with uncontrollable sobs.

Jamie approached them, crying, her arms wrapping them in a protective shield. Chan buried her face in the young woman's hair, wishing that there really were such a thing as a protective shield. Wishing that none of this were true.

Grandma Meg soon arrived and held them tight, crying softly along with Hank. Eventually, Chan could take no more and she freed herself from Meg's arms to run upstairs to her room. She jumped into her bed and pulled the covers up over her head.

It was there, under the comforting safety of her blankets, that she first cried. Not just out of sorrow but out of confusion and fear. She couldn't understand what had happened and why. And she didn't know what would happen to her and Hank. She cried and cried, until eventually things grew quiet downstairs. She heard her bedroom door open, and Hank came to crawl in next to her under the covers.

Grandma Meg came in too and tried to talk to her while sitting on the edge of the bed, but Chan couldn't bring herself to speak. Their grandmother seemed to sense that they needed to be with each other and that they needed to rest. She tucked them in with tears still shining in her eyes and left them to cuddle together and fall asleep.

As Chan drifted off holding her little brother, questions continued to bombard her mind. What happened? How? Where?

In the days that followed her questions were answered, and Chan was aware that everything was changing around her. People were coming and going from the house, Grandma Meg said something about lawyers, delivery boys brought flowers.

Her parents were dead, never to come home again. Someone had said they were in heaven and that she would see them again someday. But she wasn't quite sure what or where heaven was. So how could she find them? How could she get to them?

Chan began hiding out in her parents' closet. It was quiet there and she could hide from the people who continued to say silly things like "bless your heart" and "it will be okay" and who wanted to pat her on the head. Sometimes Hank would climb in next to her, holding his Stretch Armstrong doll, and she would slide the door closed, hiding them from the dozens of adults roaming through the house, eating and drinking, whispering about the tragedy and those "poor, poor, kids."

"Why are you sittin' in the closet?" he asked her one afternoon.

"Because you can smell Mom and Dad in here. And nobody bugs you."

He sniffed and began to cry. "I miss Mommy. I miss Daddy too. When are they gonna come back, Chan?"

She stared into the darkness. "They're not coming back, Hank."

"Ever?"

"Ever."

Knocking sounded from her office door, and Chan greeted her next client with a polite smile. The young woman seated herself on the couch as Chan grabbed a pen and flipped open the appropriate chart. Like it or not, it was time to work. Her loneliness, the lingering sense of emptiness, Officer Monroe—all of it would have to wait.

CHAPTER EIGHT

S arah tossed and turned, yearning for more sleep. Morning sunlight edged in around the blinds, softly illuminating her room. The clock on her night table read seven thirty. She had only slept for four hours. To her dismay, her troubling thoughts had continued well after her shift and into the next one. Her only escape had been the book she had read well into the early morning hours, putting it down only when she could no longer keep her eyes open. Reading was usually the only way she could fall asleep. Her mind wouldn't allow her simply to lie in bed waiting for the quiet peace to come. It needed distractions, pleasant, romantic ones. Loves and lives she could safely dream of having.

She rolled onto her back and stared up at her ceiling. Closing her eyes briefly, she tried to relax. At once images came. First of her father, then, of Chandler.

Frustrated, she threw back her covers and got out of bed. She moved to the dresser mirror, where she reviewed her reflection. She stood firm, cut and strong in her white sleep tank and tight cotton boxer shorts. Unwittingly, she raised her hand and ran it lightly up and down the hard bulge of a bicep. She shuddered, not used to touch, whether it was her own or someone else's.

Raising the thin material of the tank top, she skimmed her fingertips across her skin, grazing the edges of her abdominal muscles. Her eyes fell closed as she imagined a woman's touch, Chandler's touch…Her insides flooded with need and then quickly a cold anxiety. She opened her eyes and glared at her reflection. *Why are you doing this to yourself? Thinking this way, and about Chandler.* She knew what it would lead to. Getting all worked up and turned on. Her body tightening and filling with desire. Tightening and filling to the point of near implosion.

The shrill ring of her doorbell startled her, and she glanced at the clock again and wondered who it could be. Maria? Maybe the older neighbor needed something. She trotted into her living room and pulled open the door without checking through the peephole. A gasp escaped her throat as Danielle stood regarding her with cocky ease.

"Well, good morning," Danielle said. "I often wondered what it was you slept in."

Sarah felt her face flush. Anger followed close on its heels. She hated how vulnerable this woman could make her feel. "What are you doing here?" she asked.

Danielle brushed her way inside, looking around and ignoring her question. Sarah stiffened as she caught the scent of her perfume. Her mind and body reacted to its teasing scent, which reminded her of the numerous powerful orgasms she had given Danielle. The control, the power Sarah remembered, stirred her body as Danielle continued to speak.

"I never had the pleasure of spending the entire night with you." She eyed Sarah hungrily. "Or the pleasure of seeing your apartment."

That's because I never allowed it. And now I'm glad I didn't. Danielle's sarcastic tone instantly made her feel judged and intruded upon.

"What are these, movie posters?" She laughed a little as her eyes swept over the numerous framed classic film posters. Movies that, no doubt, Danielle had never seen. They were romantic films, and Sarah knew firsthand just how little the word "romance" meant to Danielle. Not to mention the word "love." No, Danielle didn't believe in love. And she had scoffed at Sarah's belief in such an idealized concept. The notion of someone loving another so much that they would lay down their life for them failed to impress Danielle Turner. She had once told Sarah that it was sick to even think that way.

"What are you doing here?" Sarah repeated, closing the door and resisting the urge to fold her arms. She didn't want Danielle to see how easily she could still be rattled.

Danielle's dark eyes settled on her once again, running up and down her body. She dug in her large leather shoulder bag, retrieving a chocolate brown garment Sarah recognized as one of her uniform jackets.

"You left this at my place." She handed it to Sarah. "I've been meaning to bring it by."

Sarah took it slowly, studying the face of her ex-lover. Danielle hadn't changed much over the past few months. Her skin was tanned, and freckles dotted her forearms and the bridge of her nose. Her five foot eight body stood delicate and thin. Her hair was dark brown, similar to Sarah's but with a different cut. Danielle wore it trimmed around her ears and longer in the back. When she styled the thick waves for work, it looked professional and hardly the bold mullet it really was.

Sarah tossed the jacket on her sofa, knowing by Danielle's tasteful attire that she was on her way into her office. Tailored pressed pants and a matching blouse fit her body perfectly, the blouse showing off more freckles at the base of her neck, leading down the top of her exposed chest. Danielle was a paralegal who claimed to be more intelligent than the attorneys she worked for.

"You shouldn't have bothered." Sarah's voice was heavy and thick as memories stirred her insides. "I have another."

Danielle's dark, thin lips curled into a devilish grin. "Oh, well, it was no trouble." She took a step closer to Sarah. Her eyes glinted with desire. "Besides, I wanted to see you again."

"What for?" Sarah tried to sound tough, uninterested but her emotions swirled in confusion.

Danielle continued to grin, either seeing right through her bravado or knowing her too well to buy into it.

"What for?" she repeated lightly, cocking her head, teasing. "I've missed you." Her long fingers found Sarah's clenched jaw, then tickled their way down her neck, lingering above her chest. "I've missed us."

Sarah struggled to control her racing heart. She was upset at herself for reacting so easily to the woman who had hurt her with harsh, devastating words. Danielle seemed only to care about herself. Now that Sarah knew just what kind of person Danielle was, she no longer wanted to see her, she didn't even want to think about her. She wasn't worth wasting a breath over. "There was no us," she managed through a rough-sounding throat.

Soft laughter floated from Danielle as she took yet another step closer. "Come now. You enjoyed the things you did to me, I know you did." Her hot breath upon Sarah's skin sent lightning bolts of desire through her. "Didn't you?"

Sarah clenched her fists as her inner battle raged on. She closed her eyes, trying to regain some control.

Danielle sighed as she did so, and her hand lightly grazed up and down Sarah's awakening neck. "Yes, you did enjoy it. " The corner of her mouth lifted, hinting at the victory she felt. She knew she had won and was letting Sarah know it. "And now, you want what I want, don't you. You want to fuck me."

The words entered Sarah's pounding ears and stabbed into her mind. Sucking in a shaky breath, she opened her eyes, no longer ruled by reason, but by the powerful need to conquer. She narrowed her eyes as she studied the woman before her. Yes, she wanted her. Wanted to take back the control Danielle had stripped from her, leaving her feeling helpless and alone. She needed to take her, make her come, make her beg.

With the thought of that revenge surging through her, she grabbed Danielle by the wrists and shoved her up against the front door.

Evil laughter escaped Danielle once more. "Yes, baby, take me."

Sarah felt Danielle's body go limp against her and her fire raged hotter and brighter. A violent need to fuck overcame her and she tore at her ex-lover's expensive blouse, ripping it, sending the buttons flying. Danielle's eyes flashed as she laughed again, loving it. Anger nipped at Sarah's throat at the obvious enjoyment, fueling her behavior further.

She stripped the blouse away and pressed into Danielle, biting her neck, determined to stifle the laughter. She heard and felt a sharp intake of breath as Danielle shuddered and then tensed beneath her. A groan of satisfaction escaped Sarah as she bit and sucked on the delicate flesh just between Danielle's shoulder and neck.

Fingers dug into Sarah's back and knotted into her hair. At the same time, she hastily lowered her hands and worked the button of Danielle's slacks. With every noise Danielle made, Sarah responded with firm teeth, silencing her. She didn't want to hear her enjoyment, couldn't stand to. What she wanted was something more, something so dominant it nearly weakened her knees. She wanted to hear her beg.

Sarah groaned again at the thought as her mouth worked the damp, sweet-smelling skin. She nipped her way down, following the trail of freckles to Danielle's white, satin bra. The pants followed the commands of her forceful hands, eventually sliding past Danielle's sharp, crescent hips. As they did, Sarah tugged the bra away from her small, mostly nipple breasts. She heard Danielle sigh just before they were claimed as Sarah's own.

Danielle cried out, arching her back up and away from the door. Her fingers tightened against Sarah's scalp, painfully pulling on her hair. Sarah thrived on the pain and forced the panties down Danielle's thighs, until they fell and pooled loosely around her ankles.

Then, with a flash of white-hot heat, Sarah pulled her mouth away and looked hard into the dark eyes before her. She saw the need and hunger splintering the irises; Danielle was a mere cry away from voicing her desires and seeking what she craved. Sarah fought back a smile. Yes, this was what she wanted. She was so close to getting it now.

With assured purpose, she gripped one of Danielle's smooth, firm thighs, hoisting it against her hip, opening and exposing the wet, glistening core of Danielle's desire. Another flash of desire lightened the dark eyes and, in turn, heated her own skin.

"Tell me," Sarah whispered, trailing her free hand up, grazing the moist skin of Danielle's inner thigh. "Tell me what it is you want."

Danielle writhed against the door, her breath quickening as Sarah's hand neared her flesh. "I want you to fuck me," she said, her voice still strong and confident.

Sarah focused on the pulsing vein in her neck, watching it spill need into her blood. Carefully, she eased her fingers up, outlining the slick, swollen lips, making Danielle gasp.

Sarah knew she was aching, knew she was wanting it. Painfully so. Her yearning was warm, wetting her flesh thoroughly, and Sarah knew she had probably been wet the moment she stepped foot into the apartment. Yes, she had been thinking about it for a while. A long while.

Sarah warmed inwardly and decided she wanted to hear it for herself.

"You've been wanting this for a while, haven't you?" Her fingers smoothed up and down Danielle's lips, trailing very carefully to just inside them, not quite touching the stiff and pointing clitoris.

Danielle jerked at the teasing fingers. "Yes," she whispered.

"How long?"

"A while."

Dissatisfied with the response, Sarah flicked her thumb across the small but very demanding clitoris. She felt its stiff prominence and knew the direct contact would rock through Danielle. "How long?" she asked again, loving the control, allowing it to feed her like a drug. She grazed her thumb across the tiny root again, causing Danielle to bump her head against the door.

"Weeks," Danielle finally managed. "I've been wanting it for weeks now."

"You've been thinking about me for that long?" Satisfaction ran through her like a strong current, her thumb strumming, once then twice.

"Argh yes!" Danielle cried out. "I can't stop thinking about it!"

Sarah chuckled softly, running her thumb around the full flesh, rubbing against its side.

Danielle bit her lower lip and shook her head.

Sarah continued to play her carefully, knowing exactly what to do. She wound around and around the clitoris, winding it up like a toy, filling it with blood. Tighter and tighter, fuller and fuller, until it pulsed, desperate to erupt.

"Oh God, please." Danielle fastened her eyes on Sarah.

"Please what?"

"Fuck me."

"Fuck you?"

"Yes, fuck me!"

Sarah grazed the tip of the shaft repeatedly, bringing Danielle closer and closer to orgasm. Then, just as she felt her tense, she lowered her hand and plunged inside, where she was deep and tight and hot.

Danielle exhaled her vulnerability over and over again with short wails of pleasure, letting Sarah know just how in control she was. Danielle only expressed herself during sex, and even then it did little to reveal her soul. But Sarah didn't care now. She didn't care if Danielle had a soul at all. No, all she wanted now was her need. And she had it. Had it wrapped tight down against her hand.

"Is this what you want?"

"Mmm, yes." She could hardly speak, Sarah was thrusting into her so powerfully, ramming her tight against the door, holding on to her leg, ensuring her position.

"I can't hear you."

"Yes! Yes! I want it. Want you to fuck me."

Sarah felt the hard, full need for control burst inside of herself. As it fell and spread through her like the afterglow of a firework, her insides lit up and warmed. She had it now. Had what she was after. Elated and satisfied, she pulled her hand from Danielle and watched as she nearly fell. Sarah released her leg as well and took a step back.

Danielle staggered, her eyes wild and confused. "What, what are you doing?" She stood looking at Sarah, her body covered with sweat, her bra resting in an awkward angle against her chest.

"Get out," Sarah coolly demanded, holding her eyes.

"What?"

"I said, get out," she repeated firmly.

Danielle studied her a moment and then, trying to save face, gave a little laugh. "I should've known." She reached down and tugged up her pants as she spoke. "You never could—"

"Thanks for the jacket." Sarah interrupted, bending down and tossing Danielle her torn blouse.

Danielle caught it with surprise and then adjusted her bra to cover her breasts. She smiled. "It's a good thing I know you so well. I brought an extra one." She shot Sarah a sly grin.

Without bothering to pull on the tattered remains of her shirt, Danielle opened the door and stepped out into the morning light in her slacks and white bra.

Burning with anger once again, Sarah slammed the door in her face and turned to rest against it. Danielle had known she would give in. Had known it all along.

Bitch. Sarah shoved away from the door and walked to the bathroom, suddenly desperate to wash the woman away, something she knew would be near impossible to do. She could wash away her scent and the feel of her, but she could never wash away her words.

You're an idealistic dreamer, and one who runs from the physical passion she fantasizes about! You're a fake, Sarah. A fake.

Sarah turned the water on as hot as she could stand it. It beat down, stabbing her skin with heat. She allowed the stream to punish her flesh, let it blast away any and all traces of her ex-lover. After she scrubbed her body she turned the water to cold and gritted her teeth as it pelted her hot skin. She stood for a half an hour, refusing to move, refusing to let Danielle win. When she began to shiver uncontrollably she finally killed the water and stepped out. She had done this many times before in her life, washing away the touch of someone else. It was a ritual she knew well, and sometimes, by pretending that her body was like a chalkboard, that anything on it could be erased, sometimes, that thought alone was the only thing that got her through.

She patted herself dry carefully with a soft white towel, combed through her hair, and stared at her reflection in the mirror. Danielle's scent and any reminder of her touch might be gone, trailing down the drain in her shower, but her words replayed. She could despise Danielle and hate everything she stood for, but the truth was that some of the things Danielle had said rang true. That was what angered Sarah the most. She did indeed live in a fantasy world.

Angrily, she turned and stalked into her bedroom. She threw herself down on the bed and stared, hard and cold, up at the ceiling. Her eyes refused to blink and her mind refused to give in. Why couldn't she let someone in? Why couldn't she attempt the love and passion she dreamt about? For as long as she could remember, she had avoided opening herself up completely and exploring a part of herself she knew existed. A part that longed to love and be loved. A part that would enable her to share and experience true intimacy with another.

She closed her eyes and breathed deeply. As her troubled mind searched for answers, it drifted back to her first love, back to Amy.

Sarah had been six foot tall at age seventeen, her hair long and dark, her body fully developed, that of a beautiful young woman. She was popular at her high school, and not through any doing of her own. She was quiet and driven and always politely declined when a boy asked her out on a date. Her goals were her top priority and took precedence over everything else, including a social life. Even though she kept to herself and rarely went out with her peers, there was one person who could get and hold her attention. Amy Chaplan.

Sarah was sitting in history class, frustrated at her teacher, when Amy first walked into her life. She walked in like a fresh spring breeze, hair cut short and too many earrings. She stopped promptly at Mr. Klein's desk and cocked her head.

"Excuse me?"

Mr. Klein was sleeping, snoring just like he always did after he gave them an in-class assignment. He had exactly four months and three days until he retired with full pension, and he obviously wanted to save his strength for the golf course. He jerked awake, and the majority of the students laughed. Sarah watched intently and then gave a smile of her own as the new student continued.

"Sorry to stir you from your, er, nap, but the office told me to come here."

Mr. Klein snatched her hall pass and slid on his reading glasses to examine it.

"I can go tell them they've made a mistake," she offered lightly.

"No, no. You're fine." He studied her over the lenses. "Sit down in the back there, next to Sarah. Sarah, raise your hand." He crumpled up the pass. "Sarah will get you up to speed. She's my number one student."

The young woman turned around and rolled her eyes before she fastened them to Sarah. Sarah lowered her hand and immediately felt her face heat. The new student slid into the neighboring desk and Sarah caught herself looking at the exposed flesh beneath her torn jeans.

"What the hell is his problem?" she asked, clearly unimpressed with Mr. Klein.

Sarah shrugged. "You want the short or long version?"

They both watched as he removed his glasses and leaned back in his chair to fold his arms across his chest. His eyes fell heavy once again and closed.

"Neither." She looked to Sarah again and grinned. "I'm Amy."

"Sarah."

"Yeah, I know."

She stood and scooted her desk closer to Sarah's and then sat down again. Sarah caught her scent and flushed, confused by her reaction.

"Okay, Sarah. Fill me in."

They were friends from that moment on. They shared many of the same classes, and Sarah found herself spending more and more time with her. Especially after school. Every day Sarah looked forward to hanging out at Amy's house well into the evening. She hated going home, and Amy's mother worked so most of the time they had the house to themselves. They did their homework, gossiped, and often even made dinner together.

People began to comment to Sarah on how much more she smiled, how she seemed happier. What was going on? Did she have a boyfriend, was she dating? Sarah simply grinned and shook her head. She knew what was making her happy, but she didn't understand exactly why. Amy was her new best friend, and that would make anyone happy, wouldn't it? She thought about how nice Amy looked in her tank top, how good she smelled when she first arrived at school. Those thoughts always brought on butterflies but she forced them away.

One Friday, Amy called her mother at work and asked if Sarah could sleep over. Sarah was near giddy at the thought of spending a whole night alone with Amy. She called home and relayed the plans, though her father sounded too messed up to even realize who he was talking to. She hung up the phone and relaxed, content and comfortable for the first Friday night in years.

"Maybe we should go to your house to get some beer." Amy raised an eyebrow.

"No way! I'm not going home unless I have to."

"Come on, it can't be that bad. Your parents party all the time, how can that be bad?" She chomped on her gum and her blue eyes danced playfully.

Sarah swallowed hard as she thought of her home life. The drunken madness, the mess, the loud laughter and radio. And Scottie. She cringed and fought off angry tears.

"I'm not going home." Her voice was stern, her throat burning.

Amy's face softened and she quickly rounded the kitchen counter. "Hey, I'm sorry." She brushed Sarah's cheek, causing her to inhale and glance away. Her heart hammered like a rabbit's.

"Are you pissed off at me?" Amy looked concerned and her hands held Sarah firmly.

Sarah shook her head. "No, I'm just, it's just..." She couldn't find the words, and Amy pulled her in for a hug.

Sarah shuddered against her, her heart racing and her mind reeling with craziness. She wanted to feel her bare skin, touch her lips, and hear her sigh. She wanted to hold her so tight that nothing could ever come between them. She wanted Amy for now and for all eternity.

"I just want to be with you," she said.

Amy released her and smiled. Sarah resisted the urge to trace her fingers up her neck to the numerous necklaces and chokers she wore. When she lifted her eyes, Amy turned her head quizzically.

"Sarah?" She took a step closer and reached for her hand. Hers was warm and soft and inviting. She didn't wait for Sarah to respond. She lifted Sarah's hand to her mouth and breathed upon it slowly, delicately, intentionally.

Sarah gasped and tried to pull away, afraid. Amy held on and held her eyes.

"Don't be afraid," she whispered. "Do you really want me to stop?" Her lips followed her hot breath, kissing Sarah's knuckles, fingers and eventually her inner wrist.

"Oh God." Sarah's entire body pulsed and pounded. She wanted to run, she wanted to hide, but more than that she wanted to remain.

"Tell me." Amy dropped Sarah's hand and stood very still. Her eyes held her magic, her mystique. She was like a spell, a wonderful spell, and it had been cast on Sarah.

"I don't know," Sarah breathed. "I don't know anything."

"Come on." Amy reached for Sarah's wrist and led her down the hallway to her bedroom.

Sarah had been in there many times, and she loved everything about it. The way it smelled, the colors, dark purples and blues. To Sarah, it felt like the home she never had. She could lie in Amy's bed forever.

Amy switched on her stereo and lit two large candles on her dresser. She turned off her bedside lamp and lifted her shirt up over her head. Sarah glanced away, startled and strangely aroused.

"Sarah?" She moved to stand directly before her. Her hands eased Sarah down onto the bed. "I'm undressing and getting ready for bed." She pushed down her jeans and then raised Sarah's chin with a finger. "Don't you want to watch?"

Sarah stood, alarmed. Amy laughed softly and pressed her back down. Sarah tried to look away from the matching black panties and bra, but Amy wouldn't let her.

"See this?" She dropped her head and ran her fingers over her abdomen, where several horizontal cuts were healing above her panties.

"What is it?" Suddenly Sarah was concerned and worried. Tentatively she reached out, needing to feel the wounds for herself, wanting and wishing that she could heal them.

"Sometimes, when I get upset, I cut myself." Amy confessed her secret lightly, as if everyone in the world did the same thing.

Sarah met her eyes, confused. "But why?"

"It's just how I cope." She held Sarah's hand and kissed it softly once again. "But you, Sarah. You make it all okay." She bent down and stroked Sarah's face. "Do I make you feel like that?"

Sarah nodded. "Yes. You do."

Amy pulled her up gently and they stood, a breath apart in the candlelight. "Then come lie with me."

She eased back her comforter and removed her bra and panties with Sarah watching intently. Her breasts were small but full, soft and pale. Pale like ivory, like cream. Her nipples were thick, deep and red, the color of a rose. Cream and roses, cream and roses. It was all Sarah could think of. The contrast was so beautiful, and her body was alive and luminous in the candle light, shimmering and soft like satin.

Amy crawled into the bed and ran her hand up her body, keeping the covers down around her feet. "Please, come lie with me. Please."

Sarah stood trembling, fear rocketing through her. Her brain screamed and her heart pounded. Not ever had she been so frightened. Not ever. Scottie didn't even fucking compare.

"I...I," she rasped.

"Come here, Sarah."

Somehow her body followed the command. She took three steps and felt the heat flood her cheeks like it was alive and spreading.

Amy reached for her hand and kissed the fingertips. "You don't have to get undressed. You don't have to do anything you don't want to."

Sarah swallowed. Amy's mouth was warm, wet, awakening. "What do you want?" she asked, desire mounting and slamming throughout her body all the way to the tips of her fingers, melding with the heat of Amy's mouth.

Amy held her eyes, and her lips parted. Sarah felt her knees buckle as she watched the mouth move and declare its desire.

"I want you to touch me." Amy held Sarah's hand and pressed it gently to her chest. "Anywhere."

Sarah dropped to her knees, too weak to stand. Emotion, deep and fierce and overwhelming, rose up from her insides. She had never felt so alive, so wanted, so moved. Her eyes filled with tears. She wanted *to touch Amy, wanted to more than anything in the world. But touch couldn't be how you showed love. It couldn't be.*

"I can't." She pulled her hand away and wiped away her tears, angry, confused. She didn't want to touch Amy like that, like how Scottie touched her.

Amy sat up and moved to her dresser in silence. She put on a nightgown and stood before Sarah holding another. Slowly and without a word, she undressed Sarah. Sarah's breath shook in her chest as the gentle fingers removed her clothing. She resisted the urge to run and fought off tears as the gown was placed down over her head. Amy took her hand and led her to the bed, where they both lay down. Amy pulled the covers up over them and then snuggled into Sarah. She held her close and kissed her temple.

"I love you, Sarah," she whispered.

Sarah clenched her eyes, moved, safe, home. "I love you too."

After that, Amy never asked her to touch her again. When Sarah spent the night they cuddled up close and fell asleep in each other's arms.

Their time together didn't last long. Amy moved away the week before their senior year began. They wrote each other a lot at first, and Sarah thought she would die without her. Time and time again she begged her parents to pay for the bus trip to go visit her, but they refused. Eventually, Amy's letters stopped coming and eventually, Sarah had to move on with her life. Without Amy. Without anyone.

❖

Chan bent down and laced up her sneakers. Straightening, she stretched out her arms and chest and bounced on her toes. The spring weather was warm and soothing, accompanied by a gentle breeze. A perfect evening for a run.

Pushing on her Oakleys, she started off on a trot to warm up her muscles. She rounded the base of the mountain, kicking up dirt in her wake. As she approached the entrance to the dirt path, she gained speed, ready for her physical high. Most days she rode her Harley to the mountain, which helped to milk some of the tension from her core. But since she knew she shouldn't ride at the urging of the law, her body screamed for some sort of release as she flew up the mountain trail.

The terrain was rough and uneven, switchback after switchback. Her calves tightened as she pushed on, feeling as if they would pop. Her body worked like a well-oiled machine as her heart pumped the drug she craved, the drug she needed. Her eyes focused intensely on the trail and her lungs breathed in the surrounding blooming desert.

Another runner approached from ahead and Chan automatically moved to the right side to let her pass. Settling into a steady pace, she was startled when the oncoming jogger stepped in her way and called her name.

Chan slammed to a stop and nearly tumbled on a loose rock. She angled back and got her balance, trying to catch her breath. The jogger spoke again before Chan could place her.

"Chandler?" The accent was thick and Spanish.

Chan propped her hands on her hips, agitated. "Yeah?" she breathed, shaking out her feet, anxious to continue her jog.

"Why you no call me?"

Chan looked up, recognizing her face. The Latin woman stared at her curiously as Chan tried not to gawk at her olive-skinned body, which was scantily clad in running shorts and a sports bra.

"Uh, hi." Chan had first met the woman on this trail and should've expected they might run into one another. She scowled inwardly as she remembered the numerous messages the woman had left recently on her cell phone. "I'm sorry, I've been so busy at work." It was true, she had been busy. But not too busy to return a phone call.

Despite the unreturned calls, the woman smiled and stepped up to embrace Chan in a lingering hug. Chan's pulse quickened as she felt the sweat from her warm body.

"Is okay." She pulled away. "Come to my house now." Her brown eyes were hungry and determined, looking Chan up and down. She reached up and tugged her ponytail loose, shaking her thick mane free upon her shoulders. "I miss you, Chandler."

Chan swallowed and realized she was holding her breath. "I can't."

Her libido churned like an angry monster, but she didn't want to see the woman again. Fuck her, yes. But see her, no. And Chan knew at this point she couldn't have one without the other.

"Why?" The woman frowned and reached up to stroke Chan's face.

"I can't. I'm just so busy." She shuddered with desire and backed away, knowing she needed to flee. Just like she had done countless times before with countless other women. "I'll give you a call." She started trotting again, careful not to keep eye contact.

The woman didn't respond, merely stood watching as Chan gained speed and fled up the trail.

Chan heard her call out in Spanish but she didn't turn. Her legs kept moving as she pushed the woman from her mind. It was rude to treat her that way, but she had to do what she had to do. The woman wanted more than Chan could give. Chan was saving her pain in the long run.

With that convincing thought comforting her, she continued her run and again felt the sweet release of adrenaline well before she reached the top. Once there, she stopped only briefly to raise her arms in a soothing stretch. The sun was setting and she took in the beautiful outskirts of the city, dimming with the approaching darkness, yet softly glowing from the lingering rays of the sun.

She panned the ground down below and focused on her vehicle, where the Latin woman stood scribbling on a piece of paper. Chan watched her with worry, concerned she might be considering damaging the Durango. Chan knew firsthand that there were few limits when it came to a woman scorned.

The woman finished her writing and moved to tuck the paper under the windshield wiper. Chan walked to the edge of the mountain to get a better view. To her relief, the woman glanced around and walked away, disappearing around the bend. Chiding herself to be more careful with future lovers, Chan picked up her pace and jogged back onto the trail. All the way down, that thought replayed in her mind. Future lovers. A face kept reappearing, remaining, insisting. The only face, Chan realized, she wanted to see. The face of Officer Monroe.

As she hit the bottom of the mountain where the trail flattened out, Chan slowed, moved by the thought of the mysterious cop and wary of the lingering former lover. She eased into a brisk walk and rounded the corner, a little unsure as to what lay ahead. Was the woman still there, waiting, watching, wanting to talk? Her SUV came into view and Chan felt relief wash through her when she saw no one nearby. She fished out her keys and unlocked the door with her remote. Casting a quick, nervous glance around, she retrieved the letter on the windshield and climbed inside, unfolding the paper only when the doors were locked safely around her.

Written in large letters were the woman's phone number and a simple plea. *Por favor, call me.* Chan sucked in a shaky breath and crumpled up the message, tossing it aside as she started her vehicle. Her mind reeling, she pulled away from the mountain and noted that a blue sedan did the same behind her. When it finally turned in a different direction, she relaxed and headed home, comfortably basking in the afterglow of her hard run.

CHAPTER NINE

S arah sighed and switched off her truck. She sat for a moment, soaking up the warmth from the sun as it heated her vehicle. She was surprised she had come, especially after her unsettling encounter with Danielle the day before. But here she was.

She stared at the sign on the door of suite number four through her windshield. Desert Mountain Professional Group. Her fingers rapped the steering wheel. A quick glance to her wristwatch let her know she was fifteen minutes early, just as requested by the secretary who'd made her appointment. Another sigh, this one longer and deeper.

You can do this, Monroe. Show some guts, for God's sake. Her heart hammered in response as her mouth and throat dried. *This will be good for you. In a lot of ways.* She gave herself a quick look in the rearview mirror and grimaced at her inner voice as she stepped out of the truck.

Tired of the negative feelings and of fighting within herself, she walked up to the door and readied herself for the appointment. Inwardly she tried to relax, knowing how difficult it would be to have to confide in a complete stranger. She couldn't do it with anyone else, close friend or lover. How was this going to be possible?

As she opened the glass door, she thought of Danielle and her hurtful words. *Damn you, Danielle. I am okay. And I'll prove it.* She knew she shouldn't be keeping her appointment solely out of spite, but at the moment she didn't care. She went with it. Whatever it took to get and keep her butt inside.

The woman behind the partition gave her a soft smile. Sarah approached and lifted the pen and clipboard with trembling hands.

Embarrassed, she lowered them quickly back to the counter and scribbled her name for the two o'clock appointment. The secretary retrieved it and after highlighting her name asked her, "Do you know which doctor you're seeing?"

Sarah had to clear her tight throat before she could answer. "No."

The secretary wheeled her chair back to rifle through some files. Sarah waited anxiously, her nerves on edge. Maybe this was a mistake. Maybe she should run now while she had the chance.

"We just need you to fill out these forms." Another polite smile. A clipboard came across the counter and Sarah took it carefully, already studying the questions before she sat down. As she wrote, her mind jerked, still nervous with anticipation. Her hand flew across the page, hastily answering some very unsettling questions.

Do you feel "dirty" during sexual intimacy?
Have you ever been abused, sexually or otherwise?
Are able to reach orgasm?
Are you able to bring yourself to orgasm?

When she'd reached the merciful end, she rose and returned the clipboard. The secretary stacked the papers neatly and put them in a file. Sarah returned to her seat and heard her talking from behind the partition, letting a doctor know that the two o'clock was here. She looked around the empty waiting room. Obviously they were talking about her. She clenched her hands together in her lap as the secretary, holding her file, walked down the corridor and disappeared into the second door. A quiet couple had just emerged. Sarah shifted, knowing she was next.

"Ms. Monroe?" The secretary was back and looking at Sarah with raised eyebrows. "You can go on in now. Second door on your left."

Breathing shallow, Sarah stood and willed her legs to hold her. She walked slowly, having to convince herself to take every single step forward. The door was cracked open and she paused a moment, unsure. Raising a hand, she took a big breath and gave a soft knock.

"Come in," a female voice replied.

Sarah pushed open the door, stepped inside, and heard a soft gasp. As the door slowly swung shut behind her, she glanced up and froze. An audible noise escaped her as well when she saw Chandler Brogan standing behind the desk, staring right back at her.

Chandler. The one woman she couldn't get from her mind.

"Sarah?" Chandler asked, holding the file in her hand.

Sarah's body suddenly came back to life and she hurriedly reached for the door, her skin on fire.

"Wait! Sarah!"

Sarah froze, her hand gripping the doorknob almost too tightly to turn it.

"Wait!" Chandler said again, whispering this time, reaching out for Sarah's arm. "Please."

Sarah stood very still, her chest rising and falling with a shock like none she'd ever felt before. "I didn't know," she finally managed, sounding and feeling like she was about to break. Her voice was low and tight and she didn't trust it enough to continue.

"I didn't either." Chandler held up the chart. "I just got this."

"Did you read it?" Sarah burned a stare into her. Oh God, this was so much worse than anything she could've imagined.

"I didn't have time. I started to, but stopped as soon as you walked in."

Sarah felt Chandler ease up her grip. She met her eyes but only briefly. At least she hadn't read the chart. She didn't yet know.

"Please, come in and sit down."

Sarah remained standing firm.

"It's okay," Chandler encouraged.

Sarah wavered slightly and then walked slowly into the room. She would look ridiculous if she ran. Like it or not, she had to face what was before her. She followed Chandler to the couch and sat slowly, feeling extremely exposed. "The name on the door is Desert Mountain Professional Group," she said, rattled and confused. "They never told me the name of the doctor I would be seeing."

Chandler sat down and nodded, seemingly understanding how this could've happened. "I'm sorry." She held up the file once again. "I was supposed to go over my patient list, but as you know, things…come up." She gave a soft smile.

"This can't work," Sarah replied quickly, ignoring the comfort and understanding resonating from Chandler's eyes and from her words.

"What can't?"

"This."

Chandler studied her and seemed to think for a moment. "Well, that depends." Her eyes met Sarah's. "If we continue to see each other outside the office, then yes, you will need to see someone else professionally." Her cheeks reddened. "But if we don't continue to see each other privately, then I can counsel you. Assuming, of course, that you would want me to."

Sarah couldn't bring herself to speak. Thoughts of their encounter, as well as the way Chandler was looking at her, consumed all logic. She gazed down at her hands, barely able to believe her bad luck, yet at the same time strangely elated to see Chandler.

"The way we left things the other night, I assume you have no desire to keep seeing me on a personal level," Chandler said.

Sarah stiffened but refused to look up from her hands. Her pulse raced rapidly, so much so that she could feel it throbbing in the vein on her temple. Her confidence was gone, vanished with the color she felt draining from her face, leaving her feeling helpless. She didn't know what to say, what to do. There was so much Chandler didn't know and that she didn't want her to know. She would be just like Danielle. Hateful, judgmental. It couldn't work. Nothing could. It didn't help that she was fiercely drawn to the woman. Even now, amidst all this, Sarah could hardly bring herself to look at her for fear of staring.

The gorgeous tomboy she had pulled over on her bike looked even better than she remembered. Gone were the worn, well-fitted jeans and muscle shirt. Covering her body instead were a sleek pair of light gray dress slacks and a formfitting sleeveless white blouse. Her short brown hair was styled, her eyelids brushed with light makeup.

The transformation into a tastefully dressed, career-oriented woman overwhelmed her, and she knew then that Chandler, like herself, had many different layers. Not only was she a passionate woman in bed and a wild woman on her bike, she was intelligent and a professional. And that was sexy as hell.

Sarah swallowed her raising desire and noticed that Chandler was studying her as if she too was trying to grasp all that was happening. "I can't treat you," Chandler said, her voice like velvet to Sarah's ears.

Sarah nodded, filling with relief. At least the uncomfortable situation was coming to an end. She could run home and hide and debate whether or not she would ever show her face in the world again.

Avoiding eye contact, she responded, "Then I should go." She tried to stand, but Chandler stopped her.

"No. I'm not finished," she said, forcing Sarah to remain seated. She softened her grip and stroked Sarah's palm. Sarah reacted instantly to the gentle touch, and she felt Chandler shudder and heard her voice become thick and husky in response. "I would like to help you."

"I thought you just said you couldn't." Sarah rose again, this time breaking the contact between them. *I have to get out of here.* She felt more confused than ever, not only by her own feelings but by Chandler's words as well.

Chandler rose beside her, desperation on her face. "I can't help you here, as your doctor."

"I don't under—"

"I can't help you on a professional level." She touched her arm, and Sarah nearly died once again from the feel of her. "But I could help you as your lover."

Sarah felt cold with terror. *She knows.* "You did read the chart!" The words were gruff and accusing, forced through clenched teeth. She didn't need another damn know-it-all in her bed, telling her she was messed up.

"No, no!" Chandler denied emphatically. "I mean, I started to, not knowing it was you, but I stopped."

Sarah tore her arm away and marched to the door, anger and shame surging through her. "If you didn't read it all, then why else would you think I needed your help as my lover?" She gripped the doorknob tightly, whitening her knuckles.

"Because you're here, aren't you?" The comment startled Sarah, and when she hesitated briefly, Chandler continued, "I don't exactly see patients who claim they've got mommy issues or want to jump to their death because life is just too damn hard. I'm a sex therapist. That's it. That's all I do."

Sarah turned the doorknob and pulled. When she spoke her voice was softer, but beaten. She was exposed. Exposed for all to see. First Danielle and now Chandler.

"You're right. I guess it is obvious why I'm here." She brought her eyes up to Chandler's. She could feel the pain and sorrow in them harden into indifference and she knew Chandler could see it too. "Sorry to have wasted your time."

She moved to exit but Chandler stopped her once again.

"Wait." Chandler held the chart out to her. "This is yours."

"Aren't you going to read the rest of it?" Sarah asked with a cynical tone.

"I can't. You're not my patient."

Sarah took the chart carefully then, as if it were fragile.

Chandler whispered her final words. "My offer stands. Anytime."

Sarah gripped the chart and stood even taller. She looked past Chandler, refusing to meet her gaze. She could no longer allow herself to feel. It was too dangerous. Summoning all her dignity, she said, "That won't be necessary," and walked out the door, leaving Chandler to stand alone, gazing after her.

CHAPTER TEN

Chandler slammed her Durango to a halt and hurriedly climbed out. She was late, but it wasn't the first time and was unlikely to be her last.

"Goddamned dishwasher." She tugged open the rear door and grabbed her thick briefcases. Of course it wasn't the dishwasher's fault; her mind had been elsewhere, making the already difficult task of concentrating that much harder.

Kim, a friend and colleague, had called her to talk about Michael Gold. It seemed that the troublesome patient was not only rubbing Chan the wrong way by expecting her to see him without notice, but he also happened to be Kim's smothering ex-husband, a minor fact he'd left out when he began seeing Chan a couple of weeks ago. Of course, with Kim being her friend, Chan couldn't keep seeing him. Not only did it bring up ethical issues, but it didn't feel right to her. Something about Michael left her wondering what his real intentions were in seeking counseling.

He continuously tried to control the conversation by avoiding questions he didn't like and overemphasizing issues that made him the victim. Nothing seemed to be his fault, and when he did take responsibility, it was almost as if he only said what he thought she wanted to hear. It didn't come across as genuine. She could almost see his mind working out ways to manipulate each session, especially now that she knew who he was. He bragged constantly about his virtues as a husband and as a lover while insisting that the women in his life just didn't appreciate him.

Now that Kim had told her about his refusal to let go and his violent temper, Chan suspected an agenda. Most likely he was using her to get to his real target, his ex-wife. Remembering sessions where Michael had openly admitted to wanting to beat the shit out of any man who laid a hand on his woman, she felt uneasy and worried for Kim. According to Michael, he was still married and seeing a therapist to work out some personal intimacy issues. If he was that delusional or that willing to lie about his marriage, Chan knew he was dangerous. She also knew that he was a black belt in Tae Kwon Do and that he used steroids and frequently picked fights to prove his machismo. He was a man confident in his physical ability, a short fuse just waiting to be lit. She could only hope that Kim would be able to get a handle on the situation. She hoped for all their sakes that it would happen soon.

And then there was Sarah Monroe. It seemed the mysterious woman was in her head to stay. It had been a couple of days since the office visit that had shaken Chan up from the inside out. She had been surprised at first to see Sarah again, but then she had been startled to see Sarah the way she was, all tense with anxiety and deeply rooted pain. The kind of pain that Chan knew could only be hidden for so long.

Chan could still see that pain in her eyes, the panic on her face, the fear at being exposed. The confident woman who had taken Chan to new sexual heights was somehow gone, almost as though she had never existed. She felt for Sarah, not just as a care provider but on a deeper level. It had hurt her to see that kind of torture and pain in her eyes. It left her feeling desperate to reach the stoic woman. Chan had even been tempted to chase after her, to make her see that she could help her. That she wanted to help her. Having let her go, she found herself stuck with way more questions than answers.

For the first twenty-four hours, a naïve part of her thought that Sarah might actually call, willing to take her up on her offer. But the phone didn't ring and Chan had to accept that it never would. So why was she still thinking about Sarah Monroe when no other woman was able to hold her attention for longer than a few hours? The question made her uneasy. So, too, did the pain she'd glimpsed in Sarah. She wondered what the woman's story was and almost wished she'd read her file thoroughly. But she couldn't continue to think about it now.

Hurrying up the concrete walkway, she pushed her thoughts about work and the tall cop aside.

A large strawberry planter filled with beautiful blooming snapdragons and pansies helped to bring her attention back to the here and now. Refocusing, she rang the doorbell, already hearing the voices and laughter of women coming from within. She knew what they most likely looked like, along with the kind of lives they led. White, middle class, straight. She hated to assume or stereotype, but anyone who had done as many of these functions as she had tended to expect certain things. And Chan prided herself on making accurate assumptions when it came to people.

Curious as to whether or not she was correct, she quickly turned back and noted several other average newer sedans parked along the street in front of the house. Even though her assumption was winning out, she grimaced, usually preferring to arrive before most of the women did so she could set up properly.

The door opened and a blond woman in her late thirties answered with a pleasant smile.

"Hi," Chandler said. "Sorry I'm late."

"No problem. We're all excited!" The blonde smiled and laughed as if waiting for Chandler to do the same.

"Okay, that's good." Chan offered, forcing a smile of her own. "Excited is always good."

"I'm Lynne, by the way." The woman moved to the side to allow Chan in. She had on a sundress and trendy, strappy sandals. *White, middle class*...Chandler pushed her thoughts away.

Lynn's positive attitude radiated, and Chan welcomed it, remembering why it was she always enjoyed doing these parties. Around her, the hyper chitchat of married, straight women buzzed. The nicely dressed women humming around the living room and kitchen were busy setting out hors d'oeuvres and napkins while talking away aimlessly with one another. A thick candle burned on the coffee table, tickling Chan's nose with the strong scent of cinnamon. She breathed deep and relaxed.

Turning her back to the chattering women, she lifted her briefcases up onto the counter and opened them. An energetic woman in a yellow blouse immediately appeared at her side, introducing herself as Nicky, tonight's hostess.

"Is there anything you need, anything I can help you with?" She gave the same friendly, yet very platonic female smile Chan saw endlessly at these functions.

"A glass of water would be great," Chan said and began to remove her goods from their cases.

Nicky glanced at several of the multicolored dildos Chan was setting up and moved away, clearly unsettled. Chan recognized the type and guessed that the hostess probably knew very little about sex overall. More on the conservative end with little interest in sex, she was hosting the party at the behest of a wilder friend who, for whatever reason, couldn't. She probably had missionary sex with her husband once a month or so, without reaching orgasm most times. But she wanted to seem hip in front of her friends, so she was trying her best to hide her discomfort.

Chan eyed the woman's friends again, noting their similarity to one another. She wondered if Nicky had any gay friends, or even knew anyone who was openly gay. Unlikely, Chan decided, pondering how the more conservative woman felt about homosexuals. Chan relished the fact that she was at the helm in these situations and was free to discuss whatever she wanted when it came to sex, regardless of people's long-held beliefs. She was there to educate and open their minds, and she loved it.

She continued displaying her props, examining each dildo before standing it on its base. She had placed them all in the dishwasher to clean them, just like she always did before every presentation. While these particular ones weren't for sale, the women at these parties loved to handle them, and a few even slipped them in their mouths as a joke. Keeping them clean was a matter of common sense and safety. She emptied the first case and moved to the other. She laid out the numerous vibrators, some of them cordless, some of them phallus shaped, some of them unbelievably tiny. Several of the ladies stopped their chitchat, coming to stand behind Chandler as she worked. The chatter quickly turned into gasps and giggles as Chan calmed and focused, truly feeling in her element now.

Her excitement had grown and she was prepared for the next two hours. There weren't many things she enjoyed more than educating women about their bodies and their sexuality. In her practice she encountered so many, too many, who were ashamed of their genitals and afraid to ask for pleasure. It was the reason she had started doing these private parties, to teach women what they should already know and be comfortable with.

Chan glanced up and gave everyone a friendly smile as she finished. She unveiled the three-dimensional diagram of the female pubic region, grabbed her bag full of lubricants, and looked to Nicky for direction. Her hostess appeared to be flustered once again as she realized what Chan held in her hand.

"Everyone." She spoke up, her voice high pitched and markedly nervous. "If we could all gather in the living room."

The dozen or so women immediately followed the suggestion and filed into the adjoining room, where they sat on the various sofas and folding chairs that had been brought in for the party.

Chandler carried her diagram and bag of goodies over to the main couch and set them down on the coffee table next to the cinnamon candle. She smiled inwardly, remembering her similarly flavored lube and just how many times she had licked it up off someone. And then, seemingly from nowhere, a pang of yearning swept in, quickly clouding her mind. Bright blue eyes stared into her, burning her soul as they watched as she came.

She eased herself down on the sofa and fought to keep Sarah from her thoughts, but the strong, sexy cop kept reappearing, torturing her to no end.

Her attention was refocused, however, when Nicky's nervous voice rose above the excited hum.

"This is Dr. Brogan," she announced, placing Chan's glass of water on the coffee table, her eyes careful to avoid the large polyurethane vagina that stared up at her. "Everyone please make sure your name tags are on so Dr. Brogan knows who you are."

The women all voiced various hellos and a few laughed like nervous schoolgirls. This group all batted for one team and one team only. Not only were they straight, but as she looked around at the group of soccer moms and middle-aged married women, Chan knew they were straitlaced as well and not likely the type of women that experimented.

She glanced down at herself, conscious that she was dressed nicely, but in her black slacks and matching pin-striped gray and black blouse she was not nearly as feminine as the females surrounding her. Her jewelry was the same as always, platinum, tasteful, yet somewhat bold, not remotely similar to the choices these women made. Most wore their nails long and painted, with average-size diamonds on their wedding fingers, their hair highlighted and styled just so. Chan tried to relax, knowing that while she was in her element with the knowledge she had, she wasn't a part of this group. Never had been and never would be.

She sipped the water to wet her palate. Then, making sure that all the ladies were seated and ready, she began, a knowledgeable minnow in a room full of clueless sharks.

"Okay," she breathed out, returning her glass to the table as she organized her thoughts. *Vagina, clitoris, G-spot, some info on anal pleasure. Then on to orgasms, masturbation, and toys.* "Welcome, everyone. My name is Dr. Chandler Brogan. And for the next two hours we'll be talking about female sexuality." She picked up the model, turning it for all the women to see. "Now, the first thing I would like to discuss is the vagina." The women whispered and shuffled, a few giggling nervously. "Most women aren't even aware of the power that they have in their vaginal region alone." More snickers.

Chan stood then, knowing that she needed to hold their attention and guide them into a zone that many found embarrassing or uncomfortable. She'd discovered long ago that women came to these parties for many different reasons, including peer pressure, and it wasn't wise to assume they were all at ease with the subject matter. Even though she knew this party was being thrown with a bachelorette theme, she still needed to be prepared for those guests that came out of obligation rather than fun. Her eyes traveled to two elderly women in the back who looked a bit apprehensive, and she began.

"I assume everyone knows where the clitoris is?" She walked slowly around the room, meeting the eyes of all who dared to look at her and her handheld vagina. Of course she knew that most if not all knew where their clitoris was, but she was treading lightly, giving the women a brief introduction. "It's here," she said, sliding her finger along the distended shaft. More than a few sets of eyes darted away, their discomfort more than evident.

Sighing with frustration, she returned to the sofa, realizing she would have to use one of her old tricks. She had seen this all too often: women and the shame they held in regard to sex. She placed the model on the table and dug into her goodie bag.

"Let's start off with some fun," she declared, holding up a handful of sample lubricants. "The things we're going to discuss tonight might be a little uncomfortable for some of you. We're going to talk about vaginas, penises, orgasms, et cetera. I'm not here to make anyone feel uncomfortable, so if you would rather not be here…" She motioned with her hand toward the exit. No one moved as she watched and waited.

"Okay then, what I've got in my hand"—she held up a tiny orange packet—"is flavored lubricant." This won some more interesting remarks. "I have all different flavors." She rifled through the pile. "Orange, strawberry, cherry, grape, *cinnamon*." Chan's eyes rested on Nicky, the hostess, who blushed profusely. Smiling, Chan said, "Some of them—like the cinnamon, for example—produce a warming sensation when applied." Some oohs and ahs floated in from the crowd. "They're lots of fun and I have plenty of samples here, but only for those who can come up with the dirtiest, crudest words for sex."

She raised her eyebrows for emphasis. "For instance, I'm going to start with the word 'vagina.'" She pointed quickly at a thick-waisted brunette who sat staring like a scared deer. Reading her nametag quickly, Chan instructed, "You, Susan, think of a word for vagina."

The woman stammered, looking around wildly.

"Don't think, just say it!" Chan encouraged. "Hurry!"

Susan met her eyes and jerked to life as Chan pressured her. "Pussy!"

Laughter erupted around the room as Susan's face lit up and she smiled, regardless of the heat in her cheeks.

Chan praised her quickly. "Pussy, yes, excellent." She tossed Susan a purple packet of flavored lube. The woman juggled it, her reflexes not so quick. Chan moved on, hoping to keep up the momentum and the energy. "Quick, you." She looked to the woman seated next to Susan. "Julie. What's another word?"

The woman paused, unsure. "You mean for vagina?"

"Yes, quick, hurry! Not pussy, but…"

"Cunt?" she asked, obviously unsure, squeezing her shoulders up.

"Cunt! Beautiful!" Chan tossed her a pack of lube as some of the women clapped. "What's another one? Come on, anyone. I've got a whole bag here." She shook the bag as she looked around the room. Someone spoke up from the back.

"Coochie!"

"Coochie wins a prize!" Lubricant began to fly across the room as Chan continued, encouraging the women to speak up, unafraid. The ladies, in turn, began to relax, calling out anything and everything they could think of as Chan tossed packets into the air.

"Cooter!"

"Fuzzy clam!"

"Pu-nonnie!"

Her eyes fell upon the two quiet ladies in the back, the only two yet to give answers. They were older, perhaps in their seventies, and she thought for a moment that if anyone was likely to get up and leave it would be them.

Aunt Betty, according to her nametag, sat with her large purse clasped in her lap, and the other woman looked completely ashen. Chandler figured they had expected more of a bridal shower–type gathering, and she hoped they weren't as uncomfortable as they appeared. The room grew painfully silent as Betty, the woman with the purse, stared Chan down.

"Little man in the canoe!" she declared as Chan braced herself for a voice of disapproval.

She nearly fell over with relief and Betty grinned proudly and shrugged her shoulders as laughter and applause rocked the room. Chan slid a hand into the pocket of her slacks and laughed softly at Betty's choice of words. Everyone was relaxing now and she was thrilled, but there was still one woman left who hadn't given a response: Betty's friend, Dorothy. The older woman fiddled with her dangling earring while Betty nudged her with an elbow. Dorothy bit her lower lip, which had a generous helping of bright lipstick.

"Come on, say something!" Betty encouraged her.

"I don't know!" she quickly retorted.

"Don't give me that. You used to cuss like a sailor."

Dorothy seemed about to protest, then thought better of it. Instead, sitting up straighter as if it helped her gain strength, she said, "Mud flaps!"

The two best, most unique answers of the evening had come from a pair of unassuming elderly ladies. Chandler was not entirely surprised. She'd discovered long ago that appearances were not always reliable indicators of sexual awareness or behavior. Tickled pink, she laughed along with the other women as Dorothy stood up and began prancing around proudly.

She stopped in front of Chan and held out her hand. "Where's my prize, girlie? Make it the red, the kind that tingles. Fred and I are gonna heat things up when I get home."

More laughter ensued as Chan obligingly unloaded a handful of the cinnamon, which Dorothy cradled carefully and gleefully back over to her chair, where she dropped them in her purse. With her hands on her hips, Chan waited patiently for the laughter to die down. Everyone seemed to be relaxed and feeling fine, their faces glowing. She felt good too, the best she had all week.

Taking a deep breath, she said, "Okay, now that we've all heard and learned"—she looked to Betty and Dorothy with a grin—"some terms for the vagina, let's learn a little bit more." She pointed to the clitoris. "We all know that this is the clitoris. But can anyone tell me what it does?"

She glanced around. Most of the women were shaking their heads. Chan pressed on. "Why is it there? What's it for? Certainly it must have a biological reason, right?"

A woman from the front spoke up, "I don't know, it just feels good."

"She's exactly right." Chan responded, tossing her another lube. "That's it, ladies, that's the answer." She glanced back down at the model. "This little bundle of fleshy nerves is on your body for one purpose only. For pleasure."

"You mean it doesn't do anything else?"

Chan folded her arms across her chest. "Nope."

"Nothing at all?"

"*Nada.*" Chan could almost hear the wheels in their heads turning as they took in the information. "The clitoris is there solely for your pleasure." She began to pace as she spoke. "Now I ask you, how many of you have been taking advantage of this? I mean, we are the only sex that has such a gift."

"What about the penis?" Julie piped in. Chan merely smiled.

"What about it?" she continued before anyone could answer. "Think about it a minute. The penis has functions other than those of just pleasure. It ejects sperm, as well as urine." She paused, then continued. "Without the clitoris could we still procreate? Could we still urinate?"

They all nodded their heads in agreement.

"Now that you know a little bit about this great, wonderful gift that's nestled between your legs, let's talk about the fun we can have with it." She moved around toward the vibrators that sat displayed on the counter behind the sofa.

"Some of you have had clitoral orgasms, some of you have not. For some of you, it's the only way you can climax." She held up one the smaller vibrators. "And even though we are all the same in that we have similar body parts, we all have different preferences. Some of us like a lot of clitoral stimulation, while others don't. I like to think of it as a doorbell. You don't necessarily have to push the button hard and directly in order to make it ding. But then again, sometimes you do."

"So you're saying it all depends on what kind of doorbell we have," Lynne said. The room chuckled at the analogy.

"Exactly. With me personally, if someone immediately goes to ring my bell hard and directly, they get kicked across the room. I can't handle it." Chan noticed that all eyes were trained on her. She smiled, glad that she was reaching them. "That's why it's important for you to experiment, play with your bell, learn what it is that you like and don't like. Ring your own—" The doorbell chimed at that exact moment, startling Chandler, causing everyone to laugh.

"Sounds like someone wants to do it for you," Betty let out, clapping her hand on her knee.

Their hostess rose to leave the room, but a male voice sounded from the other side of the house, along with the deep barks of a dog. "I'll get it!" he called out, bringing his wife to a halt.

She seemed relaxed now and her eyes were dancing as she returned to her seat. "Please continue, Dr. Brogan," she encouraged politely.

Chan met her smile. "Thank you, Nicky, I think I will."

CHAPTER ELEVEN

Sarah stood at the door and squeezed the bottle of wine in her hands. She glanced around and noted all the cars on the street. A neighbor of Dave's was, no doubt, having a party. A blue sedan backed into a space between two cars a few doors down and she watched automatically, certain the driver had miscalculated and was about to slam into the car behind him. To her surprise, he managed his way into the tight spot, but instead of getting out of the vehicle and heading for the party, he remained in the driver's seat, engine off.

She watched him for a moment more, curious. But when he put his cell phone to his ear she turned her attention back to Dave's. Laughter drifted out from inside the house, and her heart rate picked up as she realized that her invitation to dinner might not still be good. She hadn't spoken to Dave since Monday, when he had confronted her about her behavior. But she had talked herself into showing up for dinner, wanting to make good with her friend. And to be more honest, to force herself out of her apartment and force her mind away from Chandler Brogan.

She felt the nauseous burning of shame rise up again as she thought about their uncomfortable meeting. How could she have been so stupid as to think that going to a shrink would solve her problems? What Chandler must think of her. Her thoughts were stifled as the door swung open and Dave stood looking at her in complete astonishment. "Sarah."

He opened the door farther, showing off his basketball shorts and worn T-shirt. She knew by the look on his face that he hadn't planned on her showing up. Killer, his chubby bulldog, immediately trotted out with excitement and began sniffing her boots.

"I'm sorry, Dave. I took a chance that dinner was still on." She felt awkward, but more than that, she was concerned. He must be really pissed at her if he had thrown away their plans.

"No, no," he said quickly. "I just thought you wouldn't show, not after what happened on Monday and all…"

"No big deal." She held out the wine, her peace offering, while trying not to step on the bulky, wiggling bulldog. "I see that you have other plans." She heard more laughter from inside. She swallowed against her raw throat as the loneliness made itself known again. "Please, take this and I'll see you later."

Her eyes threatened tears as she waited for him to accept the bottle. She wanted, needed to leave before the pain grew inside. What was wrong with her? Why did she care if Dave made other plans? Had other friends?

"Oh hell no! You're staying." He tugged her inside and eased the door closed with Killer already trying to latch to her leg. "Thank God you're here, I was about to go crazy!"

Puzzled that he was suddenly whispering like a little boy who had secretly stayed up late, she shook Killer from her boot and moved a few paces into the hallway. Keeping her voice low, she asked, "Why, what's going on?"

"Nicky's hosting one of those, ya know, sex toy parties."

Sarah stared at him a moment in disbelief, then her throat loosened and the sadness that had threatened to break like a gathering thunderhead dissipated. Cracked up by not only his words but by his uncomfortable expression, she laughed out loud.

"Shh!" he insisted, leading her farther into the house. "Killer, no!" he commanded his pet. The bulldog released her leg, enabling her to walk.

"Are you serious?" She fought the laughter but couldn't hide her smile. Nicky was wilder than she thought, and she couldn't pass up teasing Dave over it. No one else would've been able to. "Not keeping up your end in the bedroom, eh, Houston?"

She laughed again but was suddenly silenced as she heard a familiar voice. Her ears homed in as her mind placed it. Suddenly, her entire body grew tight and she found that her mouth was too dry to swallow as she turned to the living room, her emotions downshifting yet again.

The voice was low and smooth, humor lacing every word. Sarah crept up to the wall just as she had as a child and laid her hands on its surface as she imagined who was on the other side.

"Listen all you want," Dave said, stepping up past her. "I'll go get you a beer." He walked off into the kitchen, leaving her alone at the wall.

Barely able to breathe, she peeked around the corner. Her insides burned as her eyes swept over the wonderfully delectable body of Chandler Brogan. The doctor stood confidently, holding her audience completely captive as she talked about the small vibrator in her hands.

Sarah drew in a quick rush of air as Chandler made reference to her personal use of the device and how she had derived pleasure from it. She held up a curved attachment, explaining how it would nestle up against the G-spot as well as the clitoris to give any woman immense pleasure.

The psychologist shifted her stance then, and Sarah jumped back behind the wall. She leaned against the cool surface, listening intently as her heart continued to thud. Chandler. It was her. She was here. God, was she ever. Sarah peered back around the corner to take in her outfit. Desire tightened her muscles and squeezed her heart. Mesmerized, she didn't even bother to fend off the slobbering dog at her feet.

"Here ya go." Dave was back next to her and she nearly yelped with surprise. He didn't seem to notice, though, and kept talking. "Yeah, Nicky's had this party planned for weeks. I forgot about it when I invited you over. But then, I didn't think it mattered much because I didn't think you would actually show." He took a swallow from his bottle as he watched the crowd of women.

Sarah continued to stare, unable to tear her eyes away. She had been trying her damndest to get Chandler Brogan out of her head, but now that she was in front of her, nothing else mattered. She wanted her. Wanted her just like she'd had her before. Writhing with pleasure, completely submissive, taking, willing, trembling. But Chandler knew. She could see right through Sarah's façade now. She knew the confidence and control were not real. It was just the way she hid. The realization broke Chandler's spell at once and Sarah glanced down, noticing for the first time the ice-cold beer in her hand. Then Chandler spoke again and her body reacted at once, perking up—fevering, needing to see her, to touch her, to taste her.

"Christ, Sarah." Dave frowned. "You look like shit."

Sarah felt herself heat, not from his words but from the ones pouring out of Chandler.

"I know." She took a nervous swig of beer. She knew she must look pale and drawn. Which was funny considering how dark and full she felt on the inside. Full of the confusion, anger, resentment, and loneliness that had consumed her until she saw Chandler. Now she felt a yearning and raw attraction so strong, it nearly left her breathless.

"Come on, let's go back to my office."

Sarah hesitated, not wanting to leave the wall. She wanted to hide behind it, to be protected by it as she listened and watched. From the safety of the barrier she could have Chandler, imagine being with her all over again without risk of exposing herself.

"You don't actually want to stay and listen, do you?" Dave raised his small, curious hazel eyes to her.

Sarah stood taller, shaking the overwhelming feelings from her head. "No, don't be ridiculous."

Her ears straining to hear every word Chandler spoke, she followed Dave down the hallway to his office, a small room that contained a desk, a bookshelf, and two easy chairs facing a television. The station was tuned to ESPN, where Dave had apparently been watching professional bowling.

He plopped down in a recliner and swallowed more beer, then said, "Make yourself comfortable."

Sarah sat but couldn't relax. Her mind and body screamed to be back with Chandler. But Dave didn't seem to notice as he reclined his chair, his athletic-socked feet pointing to the ceiling.

"Killer, no!" he commanded the pelvic-thrusting dog and made sure he went to the corner to lie down. Then, satisfied, he burped softly, excused himself, and asked, "So how you been?"

Sarah sat poised in her chair, her black cowboy boots aimed toward the door. "Fine." Her voice was flat and uninterested and she wished he would stop talking so she could hear Chandler better.

"Yeah? I was a little worried after our last conversation." He fidgeted with the remote, upping the volume a little so he could hear the commentary.

Sarah glanced around the room and took in the pile of neatly stacked bills that sat on the desk, the framed, signed basketball jersey on the wall. Books ranging from Tom Clancy to John Grisham to the biography of Chuck Yeager filled the shelves. A military photo depicted a young, fresh Dave, right out of high school, ready to serve his country in the Marine Corps. She herself hadn't gone that route, choosing instead to go to Arizona State to get her bachelor's in administration of justice. Then she had gone on to apply to the Department of Public Safety. Law enforcement was all she had ever wanted to do. It was her life.

"So you doing okay, then?" He sipped his beer.

"Can't complain." She gave him a half smile as she lied.

"Can't or won't?" He knew her well.

She smiled again and studied her beer bottle. "Won't."

"How are you feeling? Any better since we spoke?"

Sarah shrugged and straightened her white long-sleeved blouse. The silver snaps were undone to her chest and the sleeves were loosely rolled, showing off a couple of leather bracelets adorned with white shells. "Yeah, I'm good."

Dave scratched his head and eyed her outfit. "You didn't have to get all dressed up on my account." He cracked a smile.

"I didn't." She pulled a sip from her beer and raised an eyebrow his way. "I did it for Nicky."

Both laughed for a moment before a serious look washed over Dave and he turned down the television. He stared at his hands for a moment, obviously in thought. Even Killer perked up to watch him, seeming to sense something.

"Listen, Sarah," he said, still not looking up. "I meant what I said the other day, about you telling me anything." He glanced her way quickly before focusing back on the beer bottle resting in his lap.

Sarah rubbed her palms on her fitted, faded jeans, unsure what he was getting at. Laughter filtered in from the other room, and once again she wished she were privy to it.

"I know you said you're not dating..." His hazel eyes held hers. "But if you were..." He searched her face and she could tell he was nervous by the way his voice trembled a little. "Would it be a woman?"

Sarah held his eyes. He was finally asking. After years of easing around it, or hinting his suspicions. She thought calmly before she answered and realized that had her heart not been raging for Chandler, she might have put him off once again. But with her desire flaming hot, she knew it would be difficult not to speak the truth. Even if she was intensely private, a part of her told her it was time to trust Dave and let him be what he was—a friend.

"Yes," she said simply and softly.

Dave studied her face for a moment, obviously a little shocked at her blunt answer. He no doubt expected her to dance around the question, like she did most times he asked her something personal.

"Okay," he finally breathed and then relaxed back against his chair. "Thanks for telling me." He reached over to pat her leg affectionately. Laughing, he joked, "Just stay the hell away from my wife. You're a hell of a lot better looking and probably way better in bed than me."

Sarah laughed with him and allowed herself to breathe deep and relax. She had never experienced that kind of love before, and she felt it radiating pleasantly through her. She had no idea it would feel so good to reveal her sexuality. Her parents had always been too focused on themselves to pay her much attention. From as early as she could remember, she had been on her own and alone in the world. Even worse, when she'd really needed their protection, they had failed her.

Dave's acceptance reached her heart as she realized that he really did care. He cared for her just as she was, and that was all that mattered. She studied him and cleared her throat, knowing what she had to do. It was time to tell him about her intentions. With all that had transpired over the past few days, she was surprised to find that the FBI had somehow taken a back corner in her mind. As she readied herself to speak she yanked it to the fore.

"I need to tell you something," she said, her voice sounding stronger than she felt. She was worried about how he would take the news. Her superiors knew, but she was pretty sure no one else did.

Dave glanced over at her. "Yeah? Something else?" he teased her with a smile.

"Yes."

He turned down the television. "Shoot."

Sarah folded her hands together nervously. She was surprised to find that she was more nervous over this than she had been about her sexuality. "I'm thinking of leaving the department."

"What?"

"I've applied to the FBI."

He hastily switched off the television and thought for a while before he responded. "I know."

Sarah stared at him. "You do?"

He nodded, licking his lips. "They contacted me a few weeks ago."

"Why didn't you say something?"

"Because you hadn't. I just figured you would tell me when you were ready."

She sighed. "I'm sorry. I should've told you sooner."

"It's okay. Just be glad they got to me before that incident with the convicted rapist."

She swallowed with difficulty. Dave truly was a good man. He had waited for her to bring up the FBI in her own time—and had the FBI come to him after that incident, she knew he would've been put in a tough spot. But she also knew he would've done the right thing and told the truth. He was a noble man. Again she acknowledged just how lucky she was to have a person like him as a friend.

His forehead crinkled in puzzlement. "Where did this come from? I mean, why?"

"It's always been my goal."

"All along you've been planning on going?" He sounded hurt.

"Yes."

"Why now?"

Sarah looked away at the question. "I just think it's time."

They sat in silence for a long while. Dave was obviously searching for words that were hard to find. "You're my friend, Sarah. I'll support you no matter what." He sighed. "I'm going to hate it, though. You being gone."

Instinctively he patted his thigh and gave Killer a whistle. The furry bundle of muscle swaggered up to him with a wagging tail. Dave stroked him softly, taking comfort from the one pal who never left his side.

"Thanks," Sarah managed, knowing she had hurt him.

"Yeah, yeah." He waved her off playfully. "Don't start crying on me, Monroe. I know you're going to miss me too, but there will be no crying." He smiled and they both laughed softly.

"I'll try to control myself," she teased. Maybe things would be okay after all. Maybe she wouldn't have to hide forever. She thought of Chandler again, and the sense of freedom collided with her desire. If it could happen with Dave, then maybe, just maybe...

She sat back and imagined herself approaching Chandler. What would she say to her? What would Chandler do? Her mind flew with the possibilities as Dave settled in his chair next to her. More than once her heart encouraged her to stand, to go back into the living room to where Chandler was. But her brain kept her frozen in place, telling her to at least wait until the party was over.

An hour or so went by, Dave speaking to her from time to time, switching the channel from a basketball game and then back to bowling. She answered him vaguely, keeping her focus on Chandler. Eventually, more loud laughter and applause drifted down the hall and Sarah could tolerate no more. Rising from her chair, she took the empty beer bottle from Dave's hand.

"I'll go get us another." She slipped out of the room, leaving Dave to enjoy his bowling. Slowing as she approached the wall to the living room, she leaned in and stole a peek from around the corner.

Chandler had her back to her as she spoke. "It can help if they wear a condom, or even two, to help desensitize their pleasure. Also if they are prematurely ejaculating, have them masturbate before sex."

Sarah studied the women hanging on Chandler's every word. Some were even scribbling down notes.

"That should help hold off the orgasm he will then have with you. But the most effective way to help ensure a longer erection is communication. He has to be willing to say 'stop' when he feels himself getting close. It won't be easy for him and it does take practice. He can practice on his own or with you. If he's at all concerned about your pleasure, then he should be willing to try."

"What if he won't do these things?" a woman near the back asked.

Chandler sighed at the question. "If he's unwilling and you are not gaining the pleasure that you should as his lover, then I would suggest some counseling. No one wants a selfish lover, and frankly I don't think anyone should put up with it."

Sarah retreated at the words, resting her back against the wall. Was she selfish? No, she had pleased Chandler, several times. But she hadn't allowed Chandler to please her. Was that selfish?

Another woman spoke up from the living room. "Is that why they say that women are the only ones who can really please another woman?"

Sarah perked up again and eased her head around the corner, awaiting the answer.

Chandler chuckled softly and slid her hands into her pockets. "From the knowledge I have and from what I've heard, women are more apt to focus more on pleasing their partners rather than themselves. It doesn't matter if their partner is male or female. Women, by nature, are givers, pleasers. Can a woman please another woman better than a man? If you want my opinion, I would say yes. Women know what they want and know how to give it to another woman. And it pleases them greatly to do so. But it's really all in what you prefer. If you like the feel of a five o'clock shadow, a hard chest, and a stiff prick, then you should go with that. Find a man and work with him, teach him. But before you can expect him to please you, you have to know enough about yourself, know what you like and be willing to voice it." Chandler paused, apparently waiting for another woman to speak.

"Why would a woman use a dildo? I mean, why do lesbians use them if it's men they want to get away from in the first place?"

"I will answer that question generally." Chandler began to pace, and Sarah took a step back, careful not to be seen. "Both sexualities, gay and straight, enjoy the use of dildos. Mainly because they offer what the real penis cannot...everlasting firmness and control. And that's pretty important for the majority of us who like penetration. Not to mention the fact that you get to pick your own size and color."

Sarah smiled to herself as the women laughed. Chandler was great with the crowd, and she suddenly felt left out. She wanted to know Chandler, wanted to laugh at her wit and revel in her mind. Surprising jealousy overpowered her as she thought about it. If she wanted to be with Chandler, and experience her on all levels, then what was she doing hiding behind a wall? She took another step, cementing herself to the ground. She wanted to get closer and was suddenly unwilling to listen to the side of herself that was afraid of being exposed.

She focused on Chandler as a soft-spoken blonde toward the front voiced a question, one that hit home with Sarah. "What if you can't orgasm? How could you tell your lover what you wanted when you really just don't know?"

"This is more common than you think." Chandler glanced around the room. "I'll tell you what I suggest to my patients…" She paused then as if lost in thought, and Sarah wondered if she was thinking of her.

She wished she could be sure just how much of the chart Chandler had read. Realizing then that she'd inched farther away from the wall than she'd intended, Sarah started to move, but Chandler's light green eyes locked with hers and she stumbled a little, completely startled.

"What are you doing?" Dave asked in her ear.

Sarah jerked but did not move her eyes from Chandler's. Dave sighed loudly, as if the sex therapist had won over the last woman in the house and took the beer bottles from her hands to head into the kitchen.

"Doctor?" a woman asked. "Dr. Brogan, are you okay?" Chandler shuddered visibly, then seemed to do her best to regain her composure.

Sarah's body tingled; she felt like it was ready to float away. Chandler had seen her; she no longer had to hide. She could watch and listen freely, relish her very presence. She was amazed that she felt no fear, no anxiety. Only freedom. And desire.

"Yes, I'm sorry." Chandler eased a hand through her brown hair. "With women who have difficulty climaxing, I tell them to"—her eyes rose to Sarah's—"masturbate."

The women all shuffled a little and whispered. Sarah felt her face flush, but not from embarrassment. Her body hardened where she stood as she felt the caress of Chandler's gaze and her words.

"A woman has to learn from her own body." Chandler continued, her voice lowered to a smooth suggestion, "If she cannot bring herself to orgasm, then how can she expect someone else to be able to do it for her?"

"But what if you've tried and you just can't?" the same woman asked.

"I would suggest trying different ways." She walked to the counter that bordered the kitchen, where she met Dave's eyes. Chandler smiled at him as she lifted up a nozzle connected to a long cord.

"Like this, for example." She held it out for the women to see. "Water pressure has long been a friend to women. And with this adapter, you don't need a Jacuzzi or a special tub. You simply twist the adapter onto your sink faucet, climb in the bathtub, and with this nozzle, you can control the pressure and pattern of the spray, directing it right to where you need it most." Chandler handed it to the woman who'd introduced the topic and encouraged her to pass it around.

"Another suggestion is to find the right vibrator. Shop around, experiment. You may find that the combination dildo/vibrator works for you, or just a powerful steady vibration in general. As you can see here, there are dozens to choose from. Try the warming lubricants, set the mood by reading a racy book or watching a sexy movie. Sometimes it helps to please your partner at the same time. You, in a sense, gain pleasure by pleasing them. Go slow. Painfully so. Touch each other for five minutes with only your fingertips, avoiding the erogenous zones. Then move to kissing. These deliberate actions will help to awaken your libido."

She walked back over to the coffee table, her eyes straying to Sarah again. "And if you still cannot reach orgasm, I would suggest getting some counseling." Her voice became softer, as did her expression, and Sarah felt Chandler reach out to her, just like she had before. "To orgasm means to be able to give up control, to let yourself go. And if you can't do that, even with all the pleasure in the world, then I would say there are some underlying reasons."

"Like what, for example?" another woman asked.

Chandler glanced down away from Sarah to face the group as a whole. "Like psychological reasons, such as sexual abuse."

Sarah stared at Chandler's profile and willed herself to remain calm. Chandler was bright and passionate and obviously very compassionate; that was evident in the way she spoke and related to these women, these strangers. Sarah refused to turn away.

"It takes a lot of work to help a patient deal with their abuse, but it can work. There is hope. But it has been my experience that the patient must be willing to let it all out, to face every last demon and literally relive the abuse before they can move past it. If they can do that, they can heal. They can then allow themselves to be touched without the face of their abuser reentering their minds."

Sarah felt her stomach clench and she reached out to lean on the corner of the wall. It was as if Chandler knew. As if she could see into her soul and witness firsthand the abuse she'd suffered. Sarah's mind spun as emotions tangled with reason. But before she could make sense of all she was feeling, Dave was back at her side.

"You okay?" He placed a hand on her shoulder, forcing her to look over at him.

She raised a weak hand to fend him off. "I'm fine. Just got a little dizzy there." She glanced back at Chandler, who continued to speak but watched her with a worried expression.

"You're probably hungry," Dave said. "Christ knows I'm starving." He patted his stomach.

He looked like he wanted to escape as Chandler concluded her session with some of the physical reasons why a woman might not be able to climax. The women all rose to buzz around the room. More than a few shook Chandler's hand and offered their thanks. Sarah knew she should look away but couldn't. Her common sense told her to go with Dave, who was shifting impatiently from one foot to the other, but she was drawn to Chandler, and as long as the woman was near, she wanted to remain as close to her as she could get.

"Please, help yourselves to the sex toy catalogue where you can place your orders online or by phone," Chandler lifted her voice to announce. "And please don't forget to take the samples of lubricant, warming gel, and information on the research being done on the physical aspect of the female orgasm."

All smiles, Nicky said good-bye to her departing guests, then approached Sarah and Dave, apparently not noticing the intense stare Sarah was giving the guest speaker. "Honey, I didn't know Sarah was coming over," she chided her husband playfully.

"I screwed up," Dave confessed. "I forgot you had this little… party happening and invited her to dinner." He handed Sarah a fresh beer, which she took slowly, not really wanting it.

"How are you, Sarah?" Nicky asked as she waved to the last of her departing friends.

"Fine. Good, actually." Sarah tried to hide her distraction with a polite smile as her eyes found Chandler again. This time the psychologist was gliding toward her with confident ease.

"Officer Monroe," Chandler greeted with a wide grin.

"You two know each other?" Nicky exchanged a surprised look with her husband.

"Yes." Sarah barely managed to get the word out. Consumed by her fierce attraction, she was lost in eyes of green. Even if she had wanted to, she doubted she could find her way back out to be able to participate in social niceties. All she could think about was Chandler. Her hair, her eyes, her smile. The deep richness of her laugh. She was amazing and she had no idea the effect she had on her.

"She pulled me over about a week ago," Chandler filled in, seeming to sense her discomposure. "For speeding."

All three laughed and Sarah found herself sipping her beer as a way to appear calm.

"She gave you the ticket, then?" Dave asked, as if already knowing the answer.

"Oh yeah, she gave me the ticket." Chandler's eyes burned with intensity. "One I'll never forget."

Sarah swallowed wrong at the words and began to cough. The beer burned a trail down her throat. Nicky studied the both of them with her smile intact. Her face did little to hide her curiosity, but she shifted her attention as one of her lady friends reappeared at the door, car keys in hand.

"Who's got the blue Mazda sedan? You're blocking me in."

Both Sarah and Chandler shook their heads, and Nicky said, "Will you please excuse me?"

She gave her husband a look and he hastily excused himself, saying, "I better go help direct traffic."

They both headed out the front door, leaving Sarah alone with Chandler.

"What a pleasant surprise, Officer Monroe," Chandler immediately said, taking a step closer, one hand in her pocket. "Did you enjoy the show?"

"It was very informative," Sarah replied, raising her bottle to her mouth slowly, as if she were completely relaxed. But the beer did little to douse the flames in her body.

"That's what I like to hear." Chandler's eyes laid caressing kisses up and down Sarah's body, then with a sly grin she shook her head. "It's too bad you're not into me, Officer Monroe"—she took another step closer, her breasts touching Sarah's beer bottle, lightly grazing her fingers—"because you are by far the sexiest woman I have ever seen at one of these parties."

Sarah felt a hot flash in her chest as Chandler spoke. She laughed softly but a bit nervously as Chandler continued.

"No, I'm serious now. I'll have you know, before you walked in, I had my sights set on Betty over there." She indicated one of the two elderly ladies hovering in the hallway as they stuffed lube samples into their purses.

Again Sarah laughed, and this time the nervousness was gone. She took in Chandler and allowed herself to be affected by her. By her words, her scent, the feel of her body so close. The fear and exposure she had felt in the psychologist's office was all but forgotten.

"I bet she's pretty good in bed," she teased, her desire way too powerful, restoring her confidence.

Chandler met her eyes again and her smile weakened a little as she licked her lips. "Pretty good doesn't cut it when you've been with the best." The words were spoken softly, for Sarah's ears only.

"I know what you mean," she whispered in return, completely entranced. She felt Chandler tremble next to her in response to her words. But before Chandler could speak, Dave interrupted.

"Sarah, and you too, Doctor, you're welcome to stay, of course." He clapped his hands together with anticipation, eyeing them both. "Steak sound good?"

Slowly, Sarah pressed her shoulder just behind Chandler's and eased her hand out to stroke her back. "Actually, Dave, I'm not going to be able to stay."

Chandler audibly took in a deep, shaky breath, and grinned. The glint in her eyes made it clear that she welcomed the touch and caught Sarah's meaning. "I really should get things packed up here," she said, moving to the counter to put away her display.

"You sure you can't stay?" Dave asked Sarah, obviously disappointed.

"Some other time, Dave. I promise." She handed him her beer.

"Did you really pull her over?"

"Yes, I really did." She couldn't help but smile, knowing he was working furiously to make sense of what he was seeing. His eyes constantly darted back and forth between her and Chandler.

He caught her grin and his expression changed at once. "And now you want to follow her home…to make sure she doesn't speed again."

"Something like that." The grin stung her cheeks as she tried unsuccessfully to repress it.

Dave laughed and gave her a pat on the back. "Go help her and get out of here."

Sarah moved at once, thanking him and crossing the room to help Chandler with her briefcases. They said their good-byes and exited hurriedly, leaving the world and everything in it far behind.

CHAPTER TWELVE

Chan tried her best not to stomp on her gas pedal and fly home. Her body stirred with excitement while her mind reeled with possibilities. Sarah remained in sight in the rearview mirror, arousing her every time she glanced at it, making her insides flutter all wild and crazy. She still couldn't believe she had run into the mysterious cop yet again. Her longing wish to see her again had come true.

She continued to speed down the highway, too excited to slow down. She wondered briefly if Sarah would give her another ticket. She laughed, truly unsure what the by-the-book cop would do. Who was Sarah Monroe really? The officer had already surprised Chan by willingly agreeing to follow her home.

When Chan had looked up to see her at the party, she was at first completely shocked, but then her shock had turned to fear. She had been afraid Sarah would run. It was to her great amusement that Sarah had remained, not only listening to every word, but apparently captivated.

Chan steered off on her exit and slowed her truck. She thought of Sarah's visit to her office and her problem with sex. She had briefly glanced at the chart just before she walked in. It seemed Sarah couldn't bring herself to orgasm, whether alone or with another. Chan would have to be mindful tonight and not allow herself to get carried away. Sarah needed her and her knowledge. And Chan was willing to do anything to help her.

She pulled into her garage and waited for Sarah to stroll up, much like she had done nearly a week ago. As the cop moved, Chan's breath quickened with the sight of her, all confidence and control. Even though she knew one of the secrets the woman held, it was still difficult to see past the strength of her exterior.

"Hi," Sarah said, low and smooth as a grin stretched across her face.

"Hi." Chan smiled back, fighting her body's need to melt as memories of their previous encounter overtook her. Sarah had taken complete control of her, something Chan wasn't used to. The sex had been beyond hot. She never knew being submissive could be so incredible. Would it be that way tonight? Or would Sarah ease up, embarrassed because of her appointment?

Sarah stood before her and glanced back at the open garage door, answering Chan's question with her self-assuredness. "You better close that."

"Why?" Chan questioned, playfully curious. Her voice trembled slightly, betraying the depth to which she was moved by her visitor and her close proximity.

Sarah reached out and wrapped a possessive arm around her waist, tugging her to her. "Because your neighbors will never leave you alone again if they see what I've seen."

Chan pushed down some saliva as her eyelids fluttered against the intense blue-burning gaze. She was amazed at how quickly Sarah had regained control and gone from a nervous, resistant client to a pleasantly intimidating and dominant woman.

Before Chan could manage to speak, Sarah leaned in and nipped at her neck while whispering in her ear. "If anyone saw you like I have, watched you come, watched your face, heard your cries of pleasure, they would forever be yours. They would be willing to do anything for you."

Chan shuddered as the hot breath tickled her ear and her heart. Pushing herself back a little, she held Sarah's eyes. "What about you? Are you willing to do anything for me?" The question had many different elements to it, and she waited with nerves on edge for an answer.

Sarah stared back in serious thought and Chandler felt her firm, powerful body give ever so slightly before she spoke. "I would."

Chan nearly collapsed with desire and what she recognized as the white-hot flame of passion. She clung to Sarah's strong arms, unconsciously drawing on her strength. "You would?"

Sarah nodded. "I am willing." She lowered her gaze. "I just don't know if I can."

Chan held on tight and felt the cop tremble. As she studied her, she felt herself once again moved by Sarah, differently than ever before, stronger, deeper. She allowed herself to stare at Sarah's face. Her bronzed skin seemed to glow in the dim light, awakened by heat of passion and powerful desire. Her eyes were splintering sapphire, cut from the stone on a stormy winter's night. The halo ringing her pupils seemed to encircle Chan, holding her suspended in time. It was a moment she knew she would remember forever.

She knew there were pains that had been hidden deep from everyone, including Sarah herself. Would she ever let Chan in? Sexually? Intimately? Sex would be a start, but what secrets did the pain represent? More importantly, were the pain and secrets something Chan was ready for? Sex was one thing, but emotions were another.

"We better shut that garage door, then." Chan smiled softly and took Sarah by the hand to lead her inside.

Sarah followed her in silence into the kitchen, where the light from the living room drifted in a warm glow just like it had before.

"Make yourself at home." Chan moved to the fridge, searching for something to ease her dry throat. Picking up a beer, she turned, finding Sarah settling in on the sofa. "Can I get you anything?"

Chan took a sip and let the liquid soothe her throat, worn and strained from the two hours of constant talking. While the beer doused the flames in her throat, her nerves were still afire with Sarah's presence. The tough yet pain-yielding cop seemed to stir everything inside her—desire, curiosity, submissiveness, excitement—a feat no one had accomplished before.

"No thanks," Sarah replied.

Chan walked to her, sipping her beer slowly. A meow came from the back door as she set the bottle on the coffee table. Mitote was home and no doubt hungry. She moved to open the door and was once again surprised to find it unlocked. Mentally scolding herself for her carelessness, she allowed the cat to scuttle inside.

"You have a cat," Sarah stated rather than questioned.

Chan closed the door and watched him as he began to strut, tail high in the air. "Whenever he chooses to claim me." She sat down on the couch and Mitote followed, jumping up into her lap. As she stroked him, she glanced over at Sarah and noted her apprehensive look. "You don't like cats?"

"I really don't know. I've never had a pet."

"Never?"

Sarah shook her head. "They're too messy. I don't think I could handle that."

Chan could understand Sarah's reasoning. For someone who valued control as she seemed to, it made sense. She thought of Donna then, and inwardly cringed. Was Sarah too much like her ex? Both were confident, both seemingly very much in control of what went on around them. Chan remembered the iron fist with which Donna ran her household. Nothing was permitted to be out of place, not even for a second. And if it was, there was hell to pay. Chan could only hope that Sarah wasn't as bad.

"They're very relaxing," she offered, trying gently to get Sarah to relax a little. "Very soothing." As if he understood her words, Mitote walked the short distance to where Sarah sat and nuzzled her hand. Chan laughed softly at Sarah's wary expression. "Do you want me to take him away?"

Sarah eyed the cat and tentatively raised her hand to pat him on the head. Mitote ate it up, stretching his head and body under her hand, purring loudly as he did so. Appearing to gain confidence, Sarah stroked him down the length of his back and smiled slightly as he raised his rear in the air. "No, it's okay," she replied. "What's his name?"

Chan smiled, very much liking the softening look in Sarah's eyes. "Mitote."

Sarah glanced up. "Meh-toe-what?"

"Mitote. It means 'the fog.'"

Puzzlement remained on her face.

Chan laughed and explained. "The fog that clouds our vision, keeps us from seeing what's really important in life."

Sarah continued to stroke the charmingly demanding cat, obviously deep in thought. "So the fog is like stress?"

"Yes. It's all the little things that we worry about that, in the scheme of things, really aren't that important."

"I see."

"I named him that to remind me to stop every once and a while to see through it."

"Has it worked?" Sarah raised an eyebrow.

"Sometimes." *Though not lately.*

Mitote, having got his fill of physical affection, jumped down and trotted into the kitchen. His cries of hunger demanded that Chan rise and feed him. As she scooped out some dry cat food from the pantry, her concern went back to her guest. "Are you sure I can't get you anything?"

There was a lengthy pause and Chan almost thought Sarah hadn't heard her. Just as she was ready to ask her again, she heard her voice, deep and throaty and almost directly behind her.

"I am thirsty."

Chan felt the strokes of the words on her back. They caressed her, softly, like a warm breath kissing her bare skin. Chan turned, her skin tingling and desperate for more. Sarah stood next to the counter with her hands at her sides and her blue eyes blazing.

"Beer?" was all Chan could think to say as her body reacted to Sarah's stare.

The cop moved with deliberate purpose, tugging Chan in for a wild, passionate kiss. Chan felt her insides surge with powerful adrenaline and then go limp with exertion, as if Sarah were feeding from her, pulling out all her energy. With the kiss she relented, giving in to Sarah's raw strength, letting her lead the way. Finally, with Chan's seeking hands clinging to her blouse, Sarah pulled away.

Her breathing was quick and hot as she stared hard into Chan's eyes. "I could kiss you…" she breathed, obviously searching for words. "I want to kiss you…" She yanked Chan back into her arms. "I don't ever want to stop."

Chan felt herself sway in Sarah's arms. She didn't know how to respond. The confession was a complete surprise and something she somehow knew Sarah didn't do often, if ever. The mysterious cop was igniting every last cell in her body with her passionate gaze, kisses, and words. *You're unbelievable, an enigma…Are you really real? So wonderfully powerful and yet passionate. How could someone with such obvious feeling have problems with letting go?*

As the thoughts played out in her mind, she reached up to touch the warm, soft skin of Sarah's cheek. The feel of her, delicate and beautiful, anchored Chan. Sarah was real. And she was here.

"Eternity, huh?" Chan half teased, half tested.

Sarah pressed her lips together. "Something like that," she whispered and Chan saw the heat rise in her cheeks.

She was embarrassed and Chan nearly swooned, completely endeared and moved by the innocence she saw. Sarah searched her face, and as if she saw the recognition in Chan's eyes, she moved in again and enveloped her with another dominant kiss. Chan knew it was Sarah's way of moving beyond the intimate moment. She understood, and her body thrummed as the kiss continued.

Sarah's long, talented tongue probed her mouth with obvious thirst. Chan moaned with delight, her hands finding the back of Sarah's neck just as Sarah's found her backside. Then, with skill and ease, Sarah hoisted her up and carried her to the couch in the living room. She sat Chan down carefully and lowered herself to her knees before her. She pulled on Chan's lower lip as their mouths separated.

"When I heard your voice tonight, something inside me sparked to life," Sarah said as she slowly unbuttoned Chan's blouse. "I can't explain it, but I had to see you. I had to lay my eyes on you again." She paused and looked deep into her eyes. "And my hands." She eased the blouse open and gently lowered it from Chan's shoulders.

Nearly speechless, Chan confessed her fear. "I thought I would never see you again."

Sarah removed the blouse and laid it on the couch next to Chan. She raised up a bit to kiss Chan's neck, causing her to shiver with excitement.

Clinging to her once more, Chan continued to speak. "I'm glad you're giving me a chance." She meant it, and she hoped Sarah would understand just how much. Despite her raging libido, Sarah's feelings were first and foremost on her mind.

"We should take it slow." Sucking in shaky breaths, she felt awakened by Sarah's hungry kisses and caresses.

"Shh." Sarah bit and nuzzled the delicate flesh just below her ear. "Don't think about it."

Strong hands pulled Chan until she was standing. Sarah seared a stare up at her from her knees, and Chan's legs quaked with anticipation. The button of her slacks was opened with quick ease as the cool night air touched the bare skin of her abdomen and shoulders. Her head swam with desire as Sarah lowered her pants in a fluid motion, pulling them free of her now-shoeless feet. She stood before the cop, her skin alive and chilled with goose bumps, yet burning and craving like that of a being starved of touch.

"What about you?" she managed to rasp as Sarah's fingers eased down her satin panties. Everything was happening so quickly and so wonderfully. She loved the feel of Sarah's breath on her thighs, the delicate strokes of her fingertips as she undressed her. She didn't want it to stop, but she had to think of Sarah.

"I'm fine." The panties were removed and tossed over Sarah's shoulder with a grin. "Take off your bra." Her hands ran fiery trails up and down Chan's thighs, making her shake with need.

"But…you…you haven't undressed." She had to grip Sarah's shoulders in order to maintain balance. It was happening again, she was quickly losing control. She shuddered with arousal, shuddered with weakness. She couldn't fight it; her head felt too warm, too heavy.

Sarah gripped her wrists, gaining her full attention. "I told you, I'm fine." She leaned in to place light kisses on Chan's legs. "Now, let me watch as you take off your bra."

Serious, intense blue eyes stared up at her as her own excited and nervous fingers unlatched her bra. Sarah's vein pulsed in her neck and Chan saw her jaw clench as she removed the material, releasing her pale breasts.

"Yes," Sarah purred up at her. "Beautiful. Now, sit down on the sofa."

Chan hesitated slightly, too stirred to think clearly. Sarah was still her concern but she couldn't imagine arguing with her. Instead, she did what the cop wanted and willed the rest to fall into place. This, she convinced herself, was what she wanted too.

Sarah knelt down in front of her once more, pulling Chan gently to the edge. With deliberation, her fierce eyes never leaving Chan's, Sarah spread her legs and used her right hand to stroke up her thigh to her awaiting flesh.

"I want to take you, Chandler. I want to take you over and over again." She licked her lips as her hand crept closer. "Do you want me to take you?"

Chan trembled and nearly cried out as the hand found her, wet and willing. The long fingers rimmed the outside of her aching flesh, careful to avoid the clitoris, adding more fuel to her raging fire.

"Yes." The answer crawled up from her belly as it clenched with every move of the fingers.

"Say it," came the demand. "Tell me you want me to take you." The fingers dipped down into her vagina where her satin pooled, waiting. But instead of diving in, they came back up, wet with arousal to stroke the sides of her swollen shaft. Chan groaned and jerked as the pleasure shot through her.

"Mmm…I want you to." She jerked again, grabbing the teasing wrist, holding it to her.

"You want me to what?" Sarah whispered, low and smooth, continuing her deliberate strokes. Chan closed her eyes and exhaled as she writhed and jerked. Another moan escaped her as Sarah demanded more.

"Tell me." She raised her other hand then as Chan opened her eyes. With her left thumb, she rubbed the exposed head of Chan's clitoris as her other fingers squeezed and stroked the length of the shaft.

"Oh God!"

"Tell me, Chandler. Say it." The assault continued and Chan bit her lower lip, the pleasure pushing her beyond her threshold.

"God…take me…I want you to take me," she breathed out, begging.

As the words were spoken, Sarah stiffened with harnessed strength and lowered her right hand. With one fluid motion, her fingers slipped inside of Chan, a hot, searing sword of pleasure. Chan cried out and arched her back, her swollen, flesh alive and hungry. Sarah thrust into her forcefully, leaning up against Chan, sucking her breasts, pinching the nipples with her teeth.

"Yes," Sarah cooed, kissing and licking her chest. Her left arm moved to Chan's hip, supporting, holding, demanding. "Do you want to come?"

"Yes." Chan opened her eyes, realizing with surprise that they had been shut. She looked down at Sarah and her pleasure increased, moved by the very sight of her. "I want to kiss you." She voiced her own demand.

"You want to kiss me while you come?"

"Yes." Chan clenched her teeth as she answered, dangerously close to exploding as the fingers worked her, fucked her, hitting her G-spot just right as she rode them.

Sarah lifted her face and braced herself against Chan, careful to keep her fingers thrusting. Chan reached out and grabbed Sarah's head, bringing Sarah's mouth up to her own. The kiss was ravenous, dangerously fierce. Chan claimed Sarah with her tongue, her lips, her teeth. Biting, probing, sucking, unable to get enough of her.

Sarah kissed her back just as hard, groaning up into her, audibly turned on by the feel of Chan's nails on her scalp. As Chan felt the wet, hot velvety tongue of her lover against her own, she came.

The orgasm rocked through her like an enormous volcano followed quickly by a soul-shattering earthquake. Her mouth, her hands, her vagina clung to Sarah, refusing to let go. She wanted to consume her, in every way possible. Her body shook and pulsed as the climax reverberated through her and ultimately through Sarah. As the last wave crested and then flattened to sweep ashore, Chan relaxed and then fell limp against the other woman.

Sarah sat still, bracing her. Chan pulled her bruised mouth away and released her grip on the dark hair. Panting, she flopped herself back against the couch, her arms heavy and tingling at her sides.

Sarah lowered her backside to rest on her feet, but kept her fingers nestled up deep within Chan. "I can still feel you throbbing."

Chan laughed weakly. "That's because I'm not done with you yet."

"No?"

Chan opened her eyes slowly to meet a sea of churning blue. "No." Sitting up, she lowered her mouth to Sarah's, gently kissing her on the lips. "You, Officer Monroe, are one hell of a passionate lover."

"Think so?"

"Absolutely." Again Chan wondered what it was that ailed this warrior of a woman.

Sarah broke eye contact and leaned in, turning her fingers over inside of Chandler. The movement felt hot and full, causing Chan to gasp.

With a serious look upon her near-perfect face, Sarah whispered, "I need to taste you."

She glanced up and Chan was shocked to see something different in her gaze. Gone was the fierceness, the conquering fiery blue. The pale yellow halo she had seen before was more prominent, shining outward to warm Chan's bare skin. The look was calming, warm and something else. Caring. A quick spark startled her heart.

Sarah pressed her fingers into her then, holding the emotions captive, stroking them from the inside out. Chan watched in awe as her beautiful face softened and burned at the same time. Her high cheeks brushed with the color of desire, her lips pursed with deep pink fullness.

The intense pleasure urged Chan to toss her head and groan with need, but she couldn't tear her eyes away from the face before her. Sarah was watching her, reveling in the pleasure she was giving. Every gasp, every whimper that escaped Chan's throat seemed to be a gift given in return.

Chan reached out and held the face that was touching her heart. Inside her chest things were happening—there was fluttering, there was heat, there was a tightening. As the new feelings grew, she took Sarah's lips with her own. She needed to feel them, needed to press against them and breathe against their fullness.

The kiss was soft, yet hungry. The taste and smell of Sarah lured her, called to her, so much so that she felt she would die if she didn't breathe her in. Chan held her tighter and kissed her harder. She couldn't explain what was happening or why. But she wanted Sarah, from the inside out. Not just wanted her—needed her.

Nearly breathless, she pulled away and looked deep into her eyes once again. Sarah gazed up at her, her own breathing quick and hot. There was no sly grin, no mischievous playfulness in her eyes. And when she spoke, a ragged whisper, there was no conquering dominance in her voice.

"Chan."

It was all she said. All she had to say.

Chan stroked her face as their eyes melted into one another, much like their breath had done seconds before. Warming, swirling, mixing, becoming one. Chan shuddered again, moved beyond all words. All words with the exception of one.

"Sarah." It was a plea. A begging, an insistence that the other woman immediately understood as their mouths met yet again.

They kissed, long and hungry, wet and hot. A brief precursor to what was to come between her legs. Sarah thrust into her, paralleling the movement of her tongue. Chan felt her fingertips turn over where they stroked the back side of her tightening wall. The sensation was phenomenal, and Chan couldn't help but cry out.

She tore her mouth away as she tensed and arched her back and pelvis, unknowingly trying to consume Sarah's hand. Sarah let out a groan as she watched Chan writhe atop her fingers. Her eyes bore an intensity Chan had never seen before as she lowered herself to Chan's reddened clitoris.

Chan heard her own sounds. They were quick and throaty, the pleasure unbelievable. Sarah's mouth was hot and fierce, soft and hard against her flesh. She felt the sweet blissful pressure leave her suddenly and she looked down. Sarah was looking up at her again with incredible passion, and Chan felt her breath steal from her chest as Sarah spoke.

"Watch me, Chandler. Watch my mouth take you."

Chan swallowed and focused on Sarah's face, watching as it moved toward her center again. Sarah's breath was hot and teasing, as was her tongue, which extended to lick around Chan's clitoris. The sensation increased when Sarah's tongue flattened to lick her slowly up and down. Every time it passed over her clit, Chan shook with the need to come. Her hands clung to the chestnut mane. She needed more, would die for more. She tangled her fingers in the thick hair, trying desperately to hold Sarah to her.

The cop groaned in pleasure and responded by placing her entire mouth up next to the wet flesh. Chan watched as Sarah devoured her, sucking her. It felt so good. So goddamned good. Her body rocked in pleasurable motion, shoving itself in undulating waves against Sarah. Chan held fast to her head and clenched her eyes, unable to keep to them open any longer. Her mind and body became one, elevating to a level beyond her physical being. She felt free, she felt bright, she felt alive. And then suddenly, just when she didn't think she could feel any better, she did.

The orgasm crashed down upon her with such great force she nearly shattered. It tore through her, rocking her like a tiny vessel consumed by giant waves at sea, and she held on to Sarah for dear life. As she rode it out, she tensed and shook and shuddered, all the while using Sarah to stay afloat in the stormy seas.

In the distance she saw light piercing through the fog that hung over the sea, beckoning her home, along with a smooth, calming voice calling to her. As she stilled, she opened her eyes to try and focus on the beacon of light. Her lighthouse.

The fog around her dissipated and the sea pulled back from shore, leaving her on solid ground. The lighthouse was the living room lamp; the voice, Sarah. The cop sat before her, stroking her legs, smiling softly up at her.

Holy shit. Chan raised a trembling hand to her temple. Sarah had done it again. Somehow, she had managed to take Chan to new heights. To shake her very world with one incredible orgasm after another. But Chan knew, even as she thought it, that it went beyond the physical pleasure. It went beyond the orgasm. It was deeper. It was meaningful. She blinked slowly at Sarah, who glowed with warmth as their eyes met. It was intimacy.

Chan continued to study her, amazed and moved. She was unbelievable. The whole thing was unbelievable and surreal. She had spent her entire adult life studying all aspects of sex. And yet here she sat, baffled by something she had never known before. Something so strong and overwhelming, yet untouchable; it didn't exist in a world where she could wrap her hands around it.

Intimacy. Yes, she knew the word. Knew it well enough to know that this even went beyond that. It was more. Chan felt her chest tighten with emotion. She shook her head, trying to clear her mind of the powerful realizations. But she found it difficult to do so with Sarah staring up at her, all confidence and sexiness, laced with deep, purring passion and yearning.

Not to mention the fact that she had just experienced two soul-altering orgasms that obviously had pushed her emotions dangerously close to the surface. Though it had never happened to her before, she recognized it for what it was. She had read about women who often cried after a good orgasm. Now, for the first time, she understood how that could happen. Swallowing back the rawness she was feeling, she eased herself very carefully from the couch to the floor in front of Sarah, their noses nearly touching. She swallowed back the burning of emotions and willed herself to regain some control.

Sarah's fingers were still inside her and she felt the heat from them as they turned once again. Sarah looked at her with waves of dark blue churning desire. She was still obviously turned on, and her look of sensual wanting fanned Chan's fire yet again.

Chan shook with helpless pleasure as she felt the fingers pushing up and in, curling. She reached out, desperate to feel her heated skin. She stroked Sarah's face, nearly overwhelmed with her beauty, her presence. She was suddenly overcome by an urge to voice her thoughts and share her feelings but she bit them back, too afraid. She wasn't afraid of Sarah, she was afraid of herself. She fought off the stirring feelings and concentrated instead on pleasuring Sarah, on giving back to her.

Taking in a deep breath, she relaxed and began to gyrate against the firm fingers as her own moved to unbutton Sarah's blouse.

Sarah tensed and Chan slowed, meeting her eyes. She wanted Sarah to feel. To feel all that she felt.

"Relax," Chan said softly. "Just think about how I feel and the pleasure you're giving me."

Sarah exhaled a long breath and nodded.

"Help me do it," Chan encouraged.

Her hands trembled as they joined Sarah's to fan open the blouse. The strong woman wore a pale satin bra, contrasting against her darker skin. The muscles in her shoulders, arms, and abdomen were hard and etched, contracting with each movement. As Sarah thrust into her, Chan saw her pectoral muscle pulse just above her bra. She was an incredible specimen of a human being, the closest to perfection Chan had ever seen.

"You're breathtaking." Her throat tightened again with emotion just as a hint of red darkened Sarah's cheeks. "And you feel so good inside me." She sighed as she moved. "I want to feel you too."

Chan cupped her face and then grazed her fingertips down her neck. "Put your fingers with mine." Chan's hand rested at the base of Sarah's neck.

Sarah shuddered and raised her hand to rest next to Chandler's.

"Now," Chan whispered, "touch yourself."

Sarah touched her own skin lightly and Chan's fingers quickly joined Sarah's, encouraging, leading. Together they moved slowly, awakening, caressing, and exploring down below Sarah's neck to her chest. Chan leaned in to kiss her, to follow the path of their fingers.

Her skin was warm brown sugar to Chan's lips. She inhaled, her senses alive and stirring with all that Sarah was. A mixture of different scents made her dizzy. Shampoo, hot skin, and an alluring masculine cologne. She eased their fingers down over Sarah's bra to her stomach, where she felt her muscles contract.

"You feel so good," she whispered. "Can you feel? Do you feel how beautiful you are?"

Sarah nodded, seemingly unable to speak, but her eyes spoke volumes, churning in a hurricane of hungry blue.

Touching her, feeling her, inhaling her ignited Chan's arousal once again. She thrust against the powerful hand and held Sarah's eyes as their fingers continued to delicately stroke. "Are you okay?" she asked, making sure.

Sarah nodded again.

"Does your touch feel good?" Chan rocked into her, the pleasure mounting.

"Yes," Sarah rasped.

Chan felt herself tighten inwardly at the response. *Yes. Yes.* Sarah's words. Sarah. "I'm going to come again," she declared.

Her budding orgasm was different. It was deeper than she had ever gone within herself before, and she had to let Sarah know. "I'm going to come because of you. You feel so good to me."

As the last word crept from her throat, she exploded within. Arching her back and neck, she groaned as it took hold of her like a giant gripping hand. It squeezed her—held her tight as she pulsed within it and then fought to be free of it—suspended in time, despite her writhing, despite her pleas. And then, just as powerfully, it released her.

Her entire being went limp. She raised her heavy head and offered Sarah all she could manage at the moment. A lazy grin.

The cop stared at her, eyes softening and hazing. She was moved and aroused and feeling deeply. Chan could see it in her just as she saw it within herself. Even if she couldn't explain it.

Chan eased herself off Sarah's fingers and placed a leg on either side of her, straddling her as Sarah sat lotus style. She waited patiently, hoping Sarah would speak. When she didn't, Chan became slightly worried.

"Are you okay?"

Sarah didn't nod this time, but rather glanced away and swallowed slowly. Chan stroked her cheek and felt her own throat go raw at the emotion hanging thick on the air. "Hey," she whispered.

Sarah turned and pinned her with her intense gaze. "I'm okay." She hesitated for a moment. "I've…It's just that I've never…felt like that before."

"You want to talk about it?"

Sarah tugged Chan closer and nibbled on her neck, stifling any further conversation. "Let's just do this instead." Her mouth moved up Chan's neck to her jaw, awakening her skin with goose bumps.

Chan trembled and couldn't resist voicing her desire. "I want to make you come now."

Sarah responded with a quick breath and a shudder. Chan felt the muscles in her strong body tense with excitement. She met Sarah's mouth, but didn't kiss her, instead lingering there, teasing. Sarah leaned into her, trying for the kiss, but Chan refused, her way of taking control. She blazed a hot trail of kisses down Sarah's neck, devouring her scent, her skin, eliciting small cries of pleasure from Sarah.

Relishing the response, Chan traced their intertwined fingers down the firm skin of Sarah's chest to her satin-covered breasts. Her desire got the better of her, beating back her patience, and she pinched through the material, kneading the nipples. Sarah stiffened beneath her and Chan groaned, caught up in her own desire.

She looked to Sarah for another kiss, but froze as she saw a look of fright on her face. Panicked, she asked, "You okay?" and watched helplessly as the arousal that brushed Sarah's cheeks vanished, leaving in its place a pale fear.

Sarah seemed to stare right through her, lost in another, obviously very dark place.

"Sarah? What is it?" Chan knew and she was afraid to ask, but she had to. She reached out to trace her jawline, but Sarah flinched and grabbed her hand, stopping her.

"I need to go." The words were cold and firm, mirroring her look.

Chan crawled from her at once and got to her feet alongside her as Sarah stood up and shoved her arms back into her shirt.

"What's wrong?" Chan's panic receded as a new feeling overcame her. Fear. Fear of the pain in Sarah's eyes. Fear that she had caused it. "I thought it was feeling good."

"It was."

"Then what is it?" Chan looked at her with pleading eyes, hating how desperate she was suddenly feeling and sounding.

Sarah walked briskly to the front door, where she paused. She turned and looked at Chandler, who was nude and hugging herself against the chill that had washed into the room.

"It stopped," Sarah said.

"What stopped?"

"The good feelings."

Chan's mind flew. *She was feeling good as long as we were doing it together. And as long as she was touching me. Of course. As soon as that stopped, something dark overcame her. The focus solely on her was too much.*

Desperate to get her to stay, Chan said, "I understand." She tried reaching out to touch her, but Sarah dodged her hand and grabbed the doorknob. Chan spoke again, pleading. "Wait, please. I know—"

"No," Sarah said flatly. "You don't understand."

"I do, Sarah. More than you know." Chan saw the pain in her eyes, and her voice hitched with emotion. "It doesn't have to be like this. I can help make it go away." She saw the demons clouding Sarah's eyes, and she wanted desperately to fight them head-on, to force them from Sarah's life. But she wasn't going to get the chance.

"I'm sorry," Sarah said. "But it doesn't ever go away." She opened the door and stepped out into the black of night—a place where her own darkness, it seemed, seeped out and melded into it, making her right at home.

CHAPTER THIRTEEN

It doesn't ever go away. Sarah jogged to her truck, needing to escape, needing to flee. Her wall was crumbling fast and her breath shook in her throat as she started the vehicle and caught one last glimpse of Chandler standing at her front door, hugging her creamy breasts, watching her leave with anguish on her beautiful face.

God damn it. She threw the truck into gear and peeled away as fast as she could. Her body trembled as her mind raced. Chandler had gotten in. Somehow, the woman had penetrated through her lifelong barriers, threatening everything she knew, everything she was. It wasn't supposed to ever happen. She should have never let her touch her. But dear God, it had felt so good. Chandler made her feel alive.

No. It was a mistake. She was just shaken up right now. More vulnerable than usual. That was all. She would push Chandler from her mind and go on with her life. Get things back to normal. She would go to work for the FBI, exercise, and refocus. And everything would be fine. Sarah met her own eyes in the rearview mirror.

Normal. She hastily wiped away a pooling tear and forced back her pain, shoving it down her raw esophagus and into her chest, where it shook with every breath. The faces of her past entered her mind, reminding her that she had never known what normal was, no matter how hard she tried to pretend.

Clenching her steering wheel, she sped up, anxious to get home, needing to go faster. Her thoughts drifted to what she soon would have to face, causing panic and fear to rocket through her. Could she do this? Swallowing back the biting tears, she willed herself to be okay. She was grown now and nothing could hurt her. And yet he was. He was hurting her right now. Everything was. Ever since the phone call she had received weeks before.

She hadn't spoken to her parents at great length for almost ten years. So it was quite a shock in itself when she answered and heard her mother's voice on the other end of the line. The older woman sounded weak, beaten.

"Roy is sick," she had said. "He's dying. It's cancer."

When she heard those few words, Sarah's life had suddenly whirled into a tailspin. Feelings she had forced down deep years ago came screaming back up to the surface. Her childhood, her parents, Scottie. They all resurfaced and bobbed in the wake of her mind, unsinking and unrelenting.

"Your father wants to see you. He doesn't have much longer." But Sarah couldn't bring herself to go, finding numerous reasons to put it off. But it wasn't going away. Even if he died, her past would still be there. Waiting for her to face it.

She grunted with anger and hardened her body as she flew down the road.

Once home, she slammed her truck door shut and stormed up the stairs to her apartment. Her hand trembled as she tried to insert the key. She stopped herself and straightened, taking in a deep breath. She tried to convince herself that she wasn't falling apart, that she was home now and everything was in her control.

Steady enough to unlock her door, she pushed her way inside and secured the entryway behind her. She stood in the dark, in no mood for the light. Her heart hammered loudly in her ears as her eyes adjusted to the lack of light. Her keys clanked against the countertop as she navigated with ease to the fridge, where she gulped at some bottled water. She was so damn thirsty, but its chill was not near strong enough to rid her guts of the churning and burning.

As the water stung its way down, she concentrated on her breathing. Out of the corner of her eye, a blinking red light got her attention. She bent and pressed the play button on her answering machine. Her mother's voice once again spoke to her, slamming all that she was running from right into her face.

"Sarah, it's me." Long, shaky sigh. "It's any time now. Please come soon." A soft click ended the recording.

Sarah set down her water bottle and leaned on the counter with one hand. She suddenly felt dizzy with emotion. Mechanically she raised her other hand to wipe away water from her mouth. She paused, though, as a scent caught her attention.

Chandler. Yes, just think about Chandler. Nothing else.

She rested her fingers on her lips. She could still taste her, still smell her. Her heart rate kicked up as she remembered the feel of her, clenching and tightening, holding her deep inside. The lovemaking was earth shattering and mind altering, just like it had been before. Chandler was wild and free, passionate and sensual. And the way the woman touched her...

Sarah closed her eyes and remembered Chan's hands and mouth on her, awakening her. She had been lost in a world of soft pleasures and hazy moans, pleasing Chandler as Chandler pleased her. Never before had anything felt so good, so right. And for the briefest of moments, she had thought it would last.

She lowered her hand and stared into the darkness as her mind continued. The wonderful feeling, the connection with Chandler, the passion, it was all so powerful and overwhelming. Then she thought about the way she had felt inside. Like every last bit of her being had been touched and awakened for the first time. Not just her skin, not just in a physical sense. But her soul.

For the first time she understood what it meant to be truly touched by another. Just like in the books she read and the movies she enjoyed. Finally, she had found it. And it was more than any word could ever describe, more than any scene a movie could capture. She had found it and felt it, and just when she thought she could fly with the weightlessness it brought with it, it ended.

It had only teased her, letting her know what she had been missing all along. It had shown her and then disappeared, vanishing into the darkness that was her past. The darkness. Forever lurking, waiting, cruelly riding on the coattails of Chandler's touch, hiding in the shadows, watching as Sarah felt and found what she had been searching for. And just as she lowered her wall to feel the exquisiteness that was Chandler, it struck. Suddenly Chandler's fingers were not Chandler's. They were his. Touching her, using her, tainting her.

Sarah fought down the nausea that was quickly rising from her stomach. She took another sip of water and as she caught the scent of Chandler again on her fingers, she lost what little control she had left. The plastic bottle flew across the room to a destination she could not see but was able to hear. The splat was loud and quick, enraging her even more. She needed more of a result to represent what she was feeling inside.

Anger, cold and fierce, hot and overwhelming, surged up through her. Why couldn't she let Chandler in? Why did it have to be this way? Raising her hands to her head, she grabbed her hair as Scottie's face filled her mind once again. He was laughing at her, toying with her, loving that he could still control her, even now. And there was no one to stop him.

"No!" She reached out and began knocking everything off the kitchen counter. The movement and the crashing noises fed her, encouraging her to keep going. The more she destroyed, the further he would go from her mind.

She moved violently, as if possessed, tearing her way through the darkness, wrecking anything she bumped into. Images and thoughts soon faded as she raged on, acting on feelings alone.

All of her adult life she had been in control. Neatness, perfection, punctuality, all of it. All so she could keep the demons away. But what good had it done her? Not one bit of good. Now the past was back and destroying the neat little life she had worked so hard to build. It was useless, all of it.

She shoved some houseplants off of their corner stand and heard them shatter on the tile floor. Dirt would be everywhere, but she didn't care. The dirt was everywhere inside her, no matter what she did, no matter how she ran her life. She was stained. Forever.

Trembling with anger, she bent down and scooped up the cool soil and remnants of the clay pots. She crushed them in her hands, welcoming the pain, bleeding into the dirt that marked her internally. It fell from her hands in grainy clumps disappearing into the dark abyss of the floor.

Thin bars of light lit up her miniblinds, showing her the grays and blacks of her hands. A loud banging came from her door and she could hear her neighbor shouting, calling her name. Like a zombie, she walked to it and pulled it open slightly.

"Señora, are you okay?" Maria, her neighbor questioned with a thick Spanish accent.

Sarah squinted into the light from her landing.

"I'm fine." Her voice was forced and tight.

Maria stared back at her with silver strings of hair springing out from her tight bun, which wound like a black and white snake on top of her head.

"I heard noises. Like banging." Her eyes widened. "Are you sure you're okay?"

Sarah raised an unsteady hand to her forehead. "I'm fine, I just got a little angry…"

"*Ay, Dios mío*! You're bleeding!" She reached for Sarah's hand, but Sarah recoiled.

"I just got a little angry and threw some things around. I promise there won't be any more noise, okay?"

Maria's eyes remained large and alarmed. "I will go, then. But if I hear anything else, I will come back and I will bring Arturo. 'Cause this is not like you, señora."

She gave her neighbor a weak smile and Maria continued to eye her warily as she walked away to return to her apartment across the landing.

Sarah eased the door closed and rested against it. She suddenly felt exhausted as she flipped on the light. Her small apartment lay in ruins. Her framed movie posters had been torn from their place on the wall, glass candleholders lay shattered.

She walked slowly to where one of her lamps rested next to the end table on the floor. Placing it back in its position, she stepped through the dark soil from her plants and eyed her kitchen. Broken coffee mugs littered the floor, along with her toaster and spice rack. A few oranges rested close to the dining room wall, slightly disfigured from their thud against it.

She took it all in numbly, her body and mind too weak to care. As she moved through the mess she had to remind herself to breathe. That act too had become difficult.

Leaving the enormous mess behind her, she moved down the hall to her bedroom. She was tired and felt like melting into the bed. Kicking off her boots, she flipped on the small bedside lamp. Her reflection in the dresser mirror startled her to a standstill.

The woman she saw was a stranger, a woman weak and pale, tattered and torn. Her hands were covered with dirt mixed in blood, oozing blackberry. Her white shirt was filthy, her arms scratched and bruised. She looked up as she began to tremble again. The eyes she saw were full of pain, dead with cold, pooled with the past. This stranger terrified her, angered her. This wasn't who she was. This wasn't who she was supposed to be. But the image wouldn't go away. It kept staring back at her, insistent.

She bent down and picked up her boot. There was only one way to get rid of the beaten woman. With all her might, she smashed the heel of her boot into the glass, distorting the image into a spider's web of cracks. She stared at the woman who had multiplied into dozens of small wedges and slowly lowered the boot. It was useless. She couldn't escape her. As the realization hit, she dropped the boot and began to cry. The sobs came in giant, burning waves, consuming her from the inside out.

This was it. This was who she was. Nothing she ever did would change it. The cries continued, rocking her weak body, stinging her face. She collapsed down onto the bed and curled into a fetal position as her filthy hands raised to blend with hot tears. Having not been released for a decade or more, the sorrow conquered her and stomped on any remnants that remained of her wall until finally, she drifted off to an exhausted sleep.

CHAPTER FOURTEEN

D r. Brogan?" her secretary Cynthia queried over the intercom. Right away Chan picked up on the distress in her voice. "Yes."

"Your three o'clock is here."

"Thanks." Chan reached automatically for the client file. It wasn't there.

Just as she sighed with irritation, there was a knock and Cynthia slipped into the room. "Looking for this?"

The unease on her face tempered Chan's relief at the sight of the missing file and she realized who her three o'clock was. Michael Gold. *Great. Just what I needed today.*

She thanked Cynthia and fingered her throbbing temple as the secretary breezed out. Gloomily she flicked through the chart. She'd been thinking about the problem this client presented. If he was genuine in his search for help, she would refer him to another therapist. But if, as she suspected, he had an entirely different agenda, this appointment could get ugly.

She was about to summon him when the door swung open after a quick knock and Michael entered the room softly. "Good morning, Dr. Brogan." He pushed the door closed behind him, his expression one of smug confidence.

Chan reached for a pen as she eased back in her chair. "Hello, Michael."

He sat down on the couch, perched on the edge, resting his briefcase in his lap. She retrained her eyes on his chart and made a note that yet again this client had ignored boundaries.

"I thought we talked about waiting for permission before you come in," Chan said. She knew Cynthia would not have told him to come in; her secretary avoided Michael Gold at all costs.

He cleared his throat, crossed his ankle over his knee, and stretched his arms along the back of the couch to either side. His standard, self-assured sitting position showed off the steel toes on his cowboy boots. Michael was a tough guy through and through. And he wasn't afraid to show it in the way he dressed and the way he carried himself. He could kill a man with his bare hands if he chose to, and he wanted everyone to know it.

She had heard firsthand of his temper and she had hoped never to be witness to it. Not only did he enjoy picking fights, according to Kim, he raged when he didn't get his way. Throwing things, destroying things, manhandling her. It was behavior that worried Chan deeply. She had known Kim for years, and it saddened her to discover just how unhappy and violent her marriage had been. And it wasn't over. The nightmare her friend had lived continued to this day with Michael following her, damaging her property, and harassing her.

"I saw Cynthia walk out and I just assumed you were ready for me," he said, completely lacking sincerity.

Chan set down her pen and sighed inwardly at the lack of progress she had made with Michael. He was a control freak and a know-it-all. No one got the better of him. He did things his way and her calling him on it was nothing more than a minor annoyance for him. It didn't bother him, and he didn't take her seriously. She decided to take the bull by the horns.

"I spoke with Kim last week." She studied him, studied his masculine haircut and the bulging muscles under his tight-fitting polo shirt, waiting to see a spark of recognition on his lined face. Nothing. He merely raised an eyebrow.

"And who is Kim?"

Damn it, he was cocky. He shifted a little, eyebrows high, waiting for her to answer. Then he fished out a cigarette from his jeans pocket and inserted it in his mouth as his other hand searched for his lighter.

Chan cleared her throat, annoyed. She had told him a million times. "There's no smoking."

He paused and looked at her with practiced surprise. "Right. Sorry." The cigarette dangled from his lip, unlit. "What were you saying? Something about a Kim?"

"Let me clarify." She smiled, challenging him. "Your ex-wife."

He shrugged and tried to look calm with the cigarette still clinging to his lower lip. "What does that have to do with me?"

"Why don't you tell me?"

"I don't know what you mean."

He wasn't going to budge, and she was growing tired of his games. She could tell she was getting to him, because his hands returned to fold over his knee, rather than resting with devil-may-care nonchalance along the back of the couch.

"Michael, I can no longer see you."

This got his attention and his face reddened. But he kept his voice calm. "Why is that?" he wanted to know. Finally the cigarette was plucked from his mouth.

"Because you failed to tell me that your wife is really your ex-wife, the one you've been blaming all your sexual performance problems on. You also failed to mention that she happens to be my friend and colleague."

His eyes narrowed. "That's not my problem."

"Oh, but it is. You see, it's a problem for me, and that in turn, makes it a problem for you and me. It would be unethical for me to continue as your therapist."

"If you two are such great friends, then you should've known who I was."

Chan sighed, trying to keep her calm. "You knew damn well that I didn't know you. That was the reason why you chose me." Kim had kept her maiden name, and Chan had never met Michael until he showed up as her patient. "But that's not the point. The fact is that you are the ex-spouse of my colleague. Therefore, it is in everyone's best interest if I longer see you. I can refer you to someone else."

He uncrossed his leg and leaned forward, his face etched in anger. "I came to see you because I'm having problems getting it up."

"Which you continue to blame on your ex-wife, a woman I see every day, a partner in this practice."

"Are you saying you're incapable of helping me?"

Chan refused to rise to the bait. "No, I'm saying I will not help you to continue to harass your ex-wife. Which is what you've been doing." She watched as he squeezed his hands together, the knuckles whitening. "She told me all about the stalking, the reports to the police, the vandalism."

He rose to his feet and glared down at her. "My ex-wife will tell any story to get sympathy. What's it to you? It has nothing to do with what goes on in this room between you and me. " The veiled threat underlying his remarks was unmistakable. Michael Gold thought he could intimidate her exactly the way he'd intimidated Kim throughout their marriage.

Keeping her face and tone neutral, she said, "I'm sure you're aware of the restraining order Kim is seeking. Once it is executed, there's no way I can continue to see you."

"This is bullshit!" He raised a fist and shoved it down against his thigh. Spittle flew from his mouth. "She can't do this! You're my therapist, I came to you for help!"

"And your therapy is going nowhere, according to your own accounts. So this is probably a blessing in disguise. There are many other good professionals out there, and I'd be happy to recommend one."

"You're the one I picked. You're supposed to be one of the best."

"You could've chosen from countless others, Michael. You picked me for a reason." She kept her eyes trained on him as her heart pounded with fear.

A wicked smile crept up on his face. "That's right, Dr. Brogan, I did pick you for a reason."

"To get to your wife?" It was what she suspected, and she wondered if he was upset enough to admit it.

"No. I picked you because you're a dyke. I picked you because you're probably the one sleeping with her. You're the one who probably ruined my marriage!"

"What!" Chan flew out her chair, anger displacing her fear. "You're nuts!"

"Am I?"

"Get the hell out of here," she seethed.

He stalked to the door, eyeing her with cocky menace, yanked it open, and then slammed it shut behind him.

Chan picked up the intercom phone. "Cynthia, don't even talk to him. If he doesn't leave, call the police. I won't be seeing him again."

"Chan, hello."

Chan spun quickly to face her friend and colleague, Dr. Kim Richards. "Hi, please, come in and have a seat." She motioned with her hand and then brushed back her hair, still rattled from the visit from Michael.

"I heard Michael causing quite a ruckus." Kim settled into the sofa and looked at Chan with obvious concern.

"You heard correctly." Chan's hands were still trembling and she rubbed them together, embarrassed.

Kim sat forward, noticing. "Are you okay?"

"Of course, of course. He just scared me a little."

"I'm sorry," Kim sighed. Her gaze drifted past Chan to the wall, where she stared in silence before dropping her head. "I'm hoping to get that restraining order to go into effect tomorrow."

"This isn't your fault." Chan consciously slowed her breathing. "He's the one making the choice to behave this way."

Kim looked up but said nothing. Chan noticed the dark circles under her eyes and realized the usually professional-looking woman wasn't wearing any makeup. Her face looked drawn, distraught. Her dark hair was streaked with a few strands of gray.

"I still feel responsible. For him coming here."

"We both know why he did that. To get close to you. To shake you up by showing up at your place of work."

"He did a damn good job, didn't he?" Her voice cracked.

"Only if we let him." Chan gave her a warm smile, her own heart finally calming down. "He said something to me today. Something that concerned me."

Kim met her eyes. "Oh?"

"He said that he suspected we were having an affair."

Kim stared at her and then shook her head in confusion. "You and I?"

Chan nodded.

Kim rubbed her neck. "He's completely lost it. I mean, he's really going insane. No offense, Chan, but come on! You and I?" She pegged Chan with her eyes.

"I know, I know. I told him he was nuts. It only angered him more. He said I was probably the one who ruined your marriage. That I was the one you were having an affair with."

"Jesus, Chan, this is really scary. He's targeted you now." Kim sagged back into the sofa.

"Why would he think that?" Chan asked. "I mean, is there any reason he would?"

"No, of course not! I've never said anything about you, other than the usual." She fell silent and cupped her chin in her hand.

"But there is someone," Chan stated softly. "Someone else in your life." Chan could see it written on her face. Kim was afraid, but not just for Chan or for herself.

"Yes."

"Can you talk about it?" Chan crossed her leg over her knee, truly worried for her friend.

"I haven't told a soul, yet Michael somehow knows."

"Sometimes it doesn't take words. You're well aware of that."

"Yes."

"Does this person know of your current situation with Michael?"

"Yes, he knows. He wants to…"

"Beat the hell out of him?" Chan finished for her.

"Yes."

"That's not good."

"No, it isn't. I just don't know what to do. I mean, how long do I have to keep seeing him secretly? I'm divorced. Why can't I be allowed to move on?" Her questions were angry and rightfully so. "Michael's been openly dating, so why can't I?"

"Why don't you?" Chan knew the reason but she was trying to help Kim sort it out.

"Because I'm terrified of him! And I hate myself for being afraid. For playing this cloak-and-dagger shit just because he can't get over the failure of our marriage."

Chan breathed deep. "I think, as unfair as it truly is, that you've done the right thing. It's obvious that he's a loose cannon. I think it was wise to get the restraining order before you proclaim your new love for all to see."

"I only hope it works." Kim's voice quivered slightly. "He's made a mess of my life." Tears pooled in her eyes and she wiped at them angrily. "He flattens my tires, bugs my phone, goes through my garbage. He even has his brother and his crazy friends try and follow me when I leave the house."

"My God. That's no way to live."

"I know. I know. I think it's finally getting to me. I don't sleep, I'm always on guard."

"You've done the right thing by reporting him. Maybe it will take the law getting involved to finally stop him." Chan watched helplessly as she wiped away more tears. "Kim, you know, if you ever need anything, I'm here." It was all she could do.

"Thanks." Kim forced a weak smile. "I really appreciate your support."

"Call me anytime. If you don't feel safe at home, come stay with me. I would rather him think we're sleeping together than you feeling afraid in your own home. In the meantime, I've told Cynthia to call the police if he comes anywhere near the building."

"Good idea." Kim stood and wiped her face with a tissue. "I'm sorry about all this, Chan," she said, combing through her hair with her fingers, regaining her composure.

"No need. Just be careful."

Kim pulled open the door and offered a tired smile. Her words, however hit home. "Thanks. You be careful too."

CHAPTER FIFTEEN

Sarah focused on the road with an intensity she could only describe as a calm determination she had never felt before. Not over her family, not over her job, not even over the FBI. The mission was new and surprisingly simple, and so was the reasoning behind it: Chandler Brogan.

Somehow, the woman had seeped through cracks that Sarah didn't even know she had. Now, instead of just her father and Scottie haunting her mind, Chandler was there as well, and the competing forces were raging a battle inside Sarah's head. Chandler fought tooth and nail against the villains of Sarah's past, reminding Sarah of the incredible feelings she had experienced with her.

She very much wanted those feelings in her life. In fact, having felt them, she could no longer conceive of her life without them. She wanted Chandler, and that meant Scottie would have to go. Thus, the mission.

It was new in that she had never thought she would muster the nerve to actually do it, and simple because all she had to do was walk right up to him. Her blood seemed to move with the same calm determination she felt. She was in a zone, completely focused, yet completely unfeeling. This was how it had to be done.

She knew where he lived and had for some time. She pulled her truck up across the street and killed the engine, her eyes settling on the house number. She had driven by the house countless times before. Not with the intent of facing him, but because she needed to see where he lived. She needed to see that he was still human and mortal and not the powerful demonic figure in her mind.

As she sat watching, she wondered what it was she intended to say. She thought ahead and pictured herself looking into his heartless eyes and confronting him about the abuse. Her heart beat a little quicker, but again she realized she wasn't panicked. It seemed her inner turmoil had brought her beyond all that, leading her instead along the path of present reality. This very moment, the house in front of her, it was real. Her fear and the demon in her head, while seeming very real to her, didn't belong here in this neighborhood. They belonged with the abuse, in the past.

She waited, her gaze straying past the overgrown grass and weeds that protruded through the short chain-link fence that encased the front yard. No vehicle sat in the drive, no welcome sign on the porch.

A mailman moved along the sidewalk with his stuffed bag in tow. He stopped at the rusted old mailbox and deposited a few envelopes. The door to the house opened and an older woman in a faded floral smock and white sneakers stepped out, patting her permed salt-and-pepper hair. The mailman gave her a wave and a smile and headed off. Suddenly, Sarah wondered if she had the right house. Maybe Scottie had moved.

With an adequate excuse to flee, she surprised herself yet again by remaining. It was time. And nothing and no one could interfere with this newfound destiny. Desperate to make sure she had the right place, she eased down her window.

"Excuse me?"

The woman turned, showing off her dark brown eyes and a smile that revealed extremely white dentures.

"I think I'm lost. I'm looking for Parkview?" Sarah knew it was a few streets down, but the question brought the woman closer, allowing Sarah a peek at her mail. The top envelope was addressed to Scott Phillips. She had the right place.

"You go up to the end there and turn right," the woman instructed, pointing. "I think it's a couple of streets down. Not far. You can't miss it."

"Thank you."

The woman nodded and watched as Sarah drove away.

Sarah turned at the stop sign as directed and cruised slowly around the block. As she eased back down Scottie's street, she saw more movement from the front door. She pulled over well before she reached the house and switched off her engine. The woman had deposited the mail and reappeared, pushing a middle-aged man in a wheel chair. Sarah sat very still trying to focus on his face. It didn't take longer than a second to recognize him.

Leaving the truck, she walked slowly down the sidewalk and paused in the neighboring yard, shielding herself behind a tree. The woman parked the wheelchair and covered the man with a light throw blanket. She spoke to him, loud enough for Sarah to hear.

"I'll come back out to get you after *The Price is Right*." She patted his shoulder and walked inside the house.

With the sun shining on him, Sarah got a good long look and gasped at the sight of his emaciated face. He looked so much older closer up. Motionless, he stared down at the ground. A sense of panic tried to ignite in her gut, but there wasn't enough fuel. She could feel rage burn as it so often had. He wasn't the same. Time had changed him. So had events.

She knew what had happened to him. Ten years earlier, she'd devoured the newspaper reports. Scottie had been brutality attacked by a man yielding a claw hammer. The assailant had jumped out at him from behind the bushes in front of his house, and Scottie had barely survived, suffering from serious damage to his head. The perpetrator, a young man who was caught a short time later, claimed Scottie had sexually assaulted his girlfriend. Charges were never brought against Scottie, but the young man was convicted and was currently serving out a lengthy prison sentence.

Scottie, it seemed as she studied him, had avoided prison but had suffered the ultimate punishment anyway. He was trapped in a crippled body, unable to move, unable to abuse. She watched him blink and wondered if anything was left of his mind. She wasn't afraid, but she felt kind of sick. This was the man who had taken her innocence and scarred her for life. It was hard to believe that now. His hands, bony and pale, curled at the wrists. His hair was still thick, but threaded with gray. It was wavy and sticking up slightly in several areas, probably resting over the patched remains of his skull.

She stepped out from behind the tree and walked slowly up to the edge of the porch, needing to look into his eyes. Her heart thudded wildly as she came to a standstill in front of him. She set her jaw and felt all sorts of emotions birthing within. A part of her wanted to lash out, to beat the hell out of him where he sat. But she couldn't. Not just because he was helpless, but because it wouldn't do any good. The man before her wasn't the one she wanted. Not physically, anyway. Frustration, anger, and determination made her speak.

"Do you remember me, Scottie?" The sound of her voice surprised her, deep and strong, while her body began to tremble. She bent down into his line of sight. "It's me. Sarah Monroe." He didn't move but she didn't stop. "Don't you remember your 'pretty little Sarah'?"

His head slowly raised and his eyes shifted toward her. Vengeance flamed up her throat, so much so that she thought she could breathe fire with her words. She waited for his gaze to settle on her face before she said anything more. And then as she saw a glint of recognition in his drooping eyes, she spoke.

"That's right, you son of a bitch. It's me." He groaned. She continued. "I wish I could say I've come for your soul. But I can't. That belongs to a higher power." She laughed, strange sounding and excited, as she saw the recognition in his eyes flicker with something else. Fear. He was in there. Trapped, just as she'd thought.

She wanted to pound him to a pulp, but she laughed again, realizing he couldn't get much worse than he already was, unable to stand, to walk, to escape. She tried to imagine how it must feel. He was probably terrified. Helpless and afraid of what she might do. She had all the power. The realization thrilled her.

The screen door opened and Sarah took a step back as the woman she had seen before approached, looking confused. "Can I help you?"

It was obvious she recognized Sarah from their earlier exchange but she couldn't make sense of her current presence.

"No. I've found what I was looking for."

The woman's confused expression gave way to apprehension. "You know him?"

"You could say that."

The woman took a step back, her face tight with fear. "You're not her, are you? The girl whose boyfriend attacked him?"

"No. I'm another one."

"I see. Is this the first time you've seen him?"

"Yes." Sarah held her eyes firmly and saw the woman's expression slowly cloud with sadness.

Scottie groaned again and tried to move his fingers. The woman stepped up and placed a comforting hand on his shoulder. "I have a pretty good idea what you're looking for."

"I found it," Sarah said. "He's in there."

"Yes, yes he is. But he's not the same. He's not the man he once was." She bent down next to him and took his hand. "I've been taking care of him since the…attack. I knew him before that, though. I'm his cousin Ilene."

She took in an audible breath. "I always knew he wasn't the best man he could be, but I had a hard time believing some of the things people said he'd done."

Sarah felt a flicker of anger at her words. "What he did to me, I remember it like it was yesterday. And it haunts me, every single day."

"I believe you," Ilene responded calmly. "You aren't the first one who's come looking for him, either. There's been others. They came right after the attack. Guess they must've read about it or something."

Oh God. Sarah felt a wave of cold dizziness. She reached out and braced herself against the wall of the porch. Had there been others because she hadn't told? It hadn't been long after her eighteenth birthday that Scottie was attacked. She breathed a little easier. If she hadn't been the last, there couldn't have been many others. There wasn't time.

"They come looking for him," Ilene continued. "I think it made them feel better to see him like this."

"I can imagine."

Ilene watched her guardedly. "You seem to want something more."

"Don't worry, " Sarah said dryly. "I'm not here to hurt you."

"Like I said before, he's not the same. He's in there, but what's left is a tortured soul. A fragile man who cries out in the middle of night, scared to death of the darkness."

"I know the feeling," Sarah responded, her voice still cold.

"Then I hope you know that the peace you seek is something he will never find. He knows who he was, he remembers, he relives. He cries, he feels, he fears."

Sarah straightened, watching Ilene stroke his undeserving hand.

"He can't hurt anybody anymore. He only hurts himself now, with his mind."

Sarah allowed herself a long look at his gaunt face. A tear pooled and fell, traveling down the lines of his skin. He groaned again and fixed his eyes on her.

"He knows who I am," she said.

"Yes." Ilene paused, studying Sarah. "Believe me when I tell you that he's paying for his sins. In this life and eventually, beyond."

"I can see that."

For several seconds they stared at one another and Sarah wondered what his cousin would do if she reached out both hands and strangled him. Would she stop her? Sarah clenched her jaw. She couldn't summon the long-held vengeance and desire to do it. It would take a ruthless detachment that she didn't have. She squeezed her fingers into her palms and looked away.

A hand fleetingly touched her arm and Ilene said, "I hope you find your peace." She kicked up the brakes and rolled the wheelchair slowly backward.

Sarah stared at Scottie's tortured face until it disappeared with his crippled body behind the door. "I do too," she whispered. "I do too."

❖

Sarah rinsed her face with cool water and returned to the sofa. She felt weak, drained, beaten. She eased back down and eyed the envelope. Was it what she wanted? For years, she had wanted nothing more than to join the FBI and move far away, leaving her past far behind. But now she wasn't so sure. After seeing Scottie, after looking into his eyes—into his soul—and seeing the suffering and fear, she felt strangely numb. Any anger and desire to take her own revenge had vanished, its hindering weight left on that front porch with the man trapped in his waking nightmare.

So what would she be running from now? She thought of Chandler. A part of her wanted to run from the woman, to hide her true self. But as exposed as Chandler made her feel, she also made her feel alive and willing to do anything to feel that way with her again. Sarah pondered her options, truly confused. Something had changed, and with it, so had her choices. Chandler Brogan was no longer a person she knew she would have to let go of. With the darkness and plague of Scottie vanishing from her chest, maybe there was room for love, room for Chandler. Maybe she could fill that empty space with light and warmth. Maybe she could be safe with another person at last.

Her eyes felt heavy and she allowed them to close, finally accepting all that she was feeling. Sleep seeped in, warm and soothing, promising the peace she longed for.

CHAPTER SIXTEEN

A fierce wind beat steadily against Chan's tight chest, mirroring the hurt she felt deep inside. She relaxed a little as the roaring of her Harley soothed her inner turmoil. With a flick of her wrist, the machine sped up and she rode on, once again as one with the motorcycle, as one with the road. The sun was setting behind her, warming her back as she steered on toward her destination. The speed fed her need, pushing all that bothered her to the back of her mind. She had gone too long without it, and now her addiction demanded control once again. She had been foolish to think that she could go without pushing the limits, that sex could take its place.

No, not just sex. But Sarah. She laughed aloud at the thought. Sarah was the main reason she was riding tonight. Sarah was enough to make her forget about speeding through the night, if only she could have her. It was the aching that was getting to her. The goddamned craving. And jealousy. Three things she had never experienced before. The sex must've truly been amazing to drive her so crazy. But that was all it was, right? Sex. So why was she so driven to push Sarah from her mind by pushing the limit?

Because with Sarah, the sex had been more. The realization smacked her hard in the face, merging with the wind. She thought about the statement and no matter which way she examined it, she knew it was true, whether she wanted it to be or not. The intimacy she had felt wasn't going away, it wasn't something she could just forget about. Sarah wasn't just another one-night stand. Chan had feelings for her, feelings that unsettled her. She *cared* about Sarah.

Chan remembered her face, the flush of desire on her cheeks, the depth in her eyes. She remembered the way Sarah trembled beneath her fingers. So strong in body but so fragile inside.

With the thoughts still eating at her, she slowed her bike and pulled into Hank's driveway. If there was one person who would understand her disorientation, it was Hank. As she climbed off the bike and tried to clear her mind of Sarah, she was thankful for his dinner invitation. Hopefully, he wanted to ride.

She gave the door to his new, costly home a soft knock and pushed her way inside. Grandma Meg saw her first, smiling warmly and approaching from the kitchen. She gave Chan a peck on the cheek and her shoulders a squeeze. Chan had been in such a daze she hadn't even noticed her car parked out front.

"How are you, love?" Meg asked.

Chan managed a smile regardless of her wayward thoughts. "I'm okay. How are you?"

She had noticed recently that her grandmother looked tired and wondered if she was eating right. She wondered if she was lonely. Not for the first time she felt a small pang, knowing that the woman who had brought them up wasn't getting any younger. She had taken Meg for granted most of her life, and she knew that had to change.

"I'm perfectly fine, as usual." Meg raised her hand to tilt Chan's face toward her own. "But you don't seem okay. Your eyes are full of troubles."

Chan turned her head, resisting the pressure from her hand. Her grandmother could always read her, and the accurate assessment brought a flood of emotion dangerously close to the surface. Not wanting to let her feelings overcome her, Chan moved away and headed farther into the house, asking, "Where's Hank?"

"I'm not sure." Meg followed, still examining her with concerned intensity. They entered the kitchen, where Kelly, Hank's wife, was stirring a pot at the stove with one hand and holding the phone to her ear with the other.

"Kelly won't let me help," Meg remarked. "We're just supposed to make ourselves comfortable."

Obviously hearing their discussion, Kelly turned and gave a friendly wave. She ended her phone call with a promise to call back later and approached Chan for a brief hug.

"Hank's out back." She motioned toward the back door. "Why don't you go tell him I'm almost finished in here?"

Chan nodded and walked to the sliding door. She eased it open, thankful for an escape from her grandmother's knowing eyes.

The yard was vast, at least two acres in size, with the back half completely covered with mounds and mounds of packed dirt. She smiled. Hank had made his own practice run. Catching the unmistakable sounds and smells of meat sizzling over a fire, she walked to the edge of the large patio, noticing the onset of nightfall. They'd been invited for a family meal, but her insides were in no mood for food. Antsy, and wanting to get on the road, she stepped up next to her brother, who was busy flipping the smoking steaks.

"Hey, sis." He smiled.

"Hey yourself." She smiled back and slid her hands into her pockets. "This is quite a surprise." She glanced around his well-kept yard and beautiful pool, taking in just how much he had matured since his marriage a few months before. The house was a huge change from his large, bachelor apartment, the one he'd shared with a few wild daredevil friends over the years, too content to worry about getting another place. Racing bikes paid handsomely if you were good, and until now Hank had spent his money on toys, vehicles, and partying. Kelly was causing big changes in her brother. He was twenty-nine and finally growing up. She wondered how long it would be before he grew a mustache and love handles and started spending all his time on home improvement rather than raising hell.

"A surprise?" he asked.

Her gaze fell back upon him, spatula paused in midair. "This." She motioned with her hand. "You cooking, inviting us over." It was different, a start to his married life, a start to the new ways she predicted.

Hank laughed. "I guess it is a change. I bet you and Meg don't know what to think."

Chan nodded. She knew what was to come. It wouldn't be a surprise to her. Still, she wondered about the riding. Surely he wouldn't give that up. She looked up into the sky and again noted just how quickly daylight was dimming. "I was hoping we would have time to ride before nightfall."

Hank lifted the steaks up off the grill, sliding them onto a large plate. "You rode your bike?" He seemed surprised.

"Well yeah, I thought that was why you invited me over."

He set down the plate and faced her. "I thought we weren't going to ride again for a while. You know, since the law—"

"Oh come on, Hank. I already paid my ticket, it's been almost two weeks—"

"No," he interrupted, not letting her finish.

"No what?"

"No. I'm not riding."

"What?"

"You heard me." He closed the lid to the grill.

"Yes, I did, but I'm convinced I didn't hear correctly. I thought I heard you say you weren't going to ride." He couldn't mean it. She wouldn't accept it. This was so unlike him. Nothing and no one told Hank no, not when it came to riding. She searched for a meaning, a root. "That cop actually scared you?"

"No. But she did open my eyes a little."

Chan glanced away, suddenly afraid Hank would see just what all the cop had done to her. She shoved Sarah to the back of her mind as he continued.

"I was hoping the fear of getting arrested would open yours as well."

Chan scoffed. "I'm not going to get arrested. She was bluffing."

"Then what about getting killed? Does that scare you?"

Chan straightened at the words. She could feel her eyes widening as she took stock of her brother, this changed man before her. It was Kelly. Kelly had done this. Sure Chan had expected the young bride would change her brother in many predictable ways. But convincing him to stop riding? It was unbelievable.

"Where is this coming from?" she demanded. "Since when do you worry about shit like that?"

He sounded like Meg. Maybe that's what this was all about. Meg had gotten to Kelly, and now they both were after Hank, his new bride no doubt sick with worry over his wild riding.

"Look if it's Kelly, I understand, I'll talk to her."

"Chan." But she kept on, convinced and willing to do anything to get her partner back, her brother, her best friend who rode alongside her on the wings of fate. "Chan!"

She stopped then, startled. Hank stood staring at her, his hand gripping the spatula with obvious stress.

"Kelly's pregnant."

"What?" She could barely comprehend what he was saying.

"I'm going to be a father."

Chan stared up at him in complete surprise, desperate to find the little brother who had forever chased after her, willing to do all that she dared. But he was gone. What stood before her now was a married young man, a responsible young man, a man about to become a father.

"I don't know what to say." She looked away, unsure and completely shocked.

Why was she so surprised? This was what young married couples did. They started a family. But all she could think about was herself and how this was going to change their relationship, how it already had. It pained her, all of it.

"Congratulations would be a start." He gave a soft smile and released his grip on the spatula.

Chan shook her head. "Of course." She met his eyes. "Congratulations." She wished she could say the word with more conviction, but it just wasn't in her. She felt torn and overwhelmed. The changes she had been ready for didn't include this, and she was having trouble accepting it right away. "This is why you won't ride," she whispered.

"There are other things in life," he replied, taking her breath away once more. The Hank she knew as well as she knew herself would never have said such a thing.

Dismayed, she asked, "Is this…forever? You're quitting?" She was referring to his career as a motocross rider as well as his leisure riding.

"Yes. Eventually. I'm going to start backing off a little. Stick around home a little more."

"What will you do, I mean, after the riding?"

He shrugged. "I don't know. Get a job."

It was all coming at her so fast. She could barely keep up with his words. Hank, a job? A suit-and-tie-type job? No way. How could he give up riding? He was pro and it paid him well, better than well. Especially when he won. Sponsors ate him up, paying him huge sums to wear their gear, ride their bikes, and wear their T-shirts.

He seemed to read her mind and her questions. "We have enough to live off for a while. But eventually, I'll do something else." He paused. "I was thinking about getting a real estate license. The valley's booming…"

She zoned him out, refusing to hear anymore. It wasn't Hank, it didn't even sound like him. None of it seemed real to her. "What about that new chopper you just bought?"

The memory of their last ride blew through her, leaving a hollow sadness. She needed to remind him of it, remind him that he just got that bike. Why would he do that if he really wanted to stop riding?

"I didn't buy it. It was a gift," he clarified.

Chan ran a wary hand through her hair, recalling that one of his sponsors had it made for him as a bonus. Hank had been given numerous gifts like that over the years. The realization shot down and sank her last floating hope at reaching him. He hadn't actually bought it, hadn't put the thought into its creation. He had other things on his mind. Hank was settling down. Not just in a physical sense, but emotionally as well. She had just been too blind to see it.

"So you're never going to ride with me again?" It seemed so ludicrous to just give it all up. Couldn't he see how crazy he was being?

"I never said that."

"Then what are you saying? Because I'm confused." Her growing anger was evident in her tone.

"I will ride with you, but not anytime soon. And never like we did last time. It's too dangerous."

Chan started to speak but changed her mind. No words were coming. Hank, though, had more to say.

"I wish you would stop too." He reached for the plateful of food and moved to stand directly in front of her. "I want you to be around. To be in my kid's life."

"Who says I won't be?"

His eyes became very serious. "If you keep riding like you do, the speeding, the weaving…I'm afraid you'll get hurt."

"Since when are you afraid of anything, Hank?"

"Since now, Chan. I'm going to be a father. I can't afford to go out daring the devil anymore. I have a child to consider. My son, or daughter, has a right to a healthy father." He paused and then continued softly, "I wish you would stop to think about that too."

Chan felt her body stiffen. So much was happening. Her brother was changing his ways and his life, and he wholeheartedly expected her to do the same. But she couldn't. She needed to ride. It was the only way she could handle problems, put things in perspective. When she was riding nothing else mattered; she was free.

"I'm sorry, but I can't," she said. "I see your point, but I don't have your responsibilities."

"Really? So you think Meg won't need us when she's too old to care for herself. You don't think anyone else cares about you?" His tone had changed and he sounded like he did when Sarah had pulled them over—impatient with her stubborn attitude and wild ways. He moved past her and yanked open the door. Just before he stepped inside, he faced her and said wearily, "At least start wearing a helmet."

Chan shoved her hands firmly down into her pockets and stepped inside after her him. As she followed him in silence into the kitchen, her mind flew with all that she'd been told. She understood why Hank was hanging up his riding boots. He was obviously concerned and afraid; he had a new life he was responsible for. But Chan thought he was overreacting. It was one thing to be a little more cautious, but to quit altogether out of fear? And to expect her to do the same? No way.

She noticed a few uncomfortable glances between Hank and Kelly. Meg seemed to feel the tension too and busied herself retrieving silverware from a drawer. Suddenly Chan felt like an outsider. She knew they—all three of them—would agree and insist that she stop riding. It would be even worse now that Meg had someone on her side.

Feeling trapped and anxious, she said, "I'm not feeling too well." All three raised their eyes to hers in surprise. "I don't feel much like eating, so I'm going to take off."

She had to get out, to escape the worried stares and inevitable disappointed shakes of the heads. Her legs carried her to the door quickly, leading her outside into the dim evening. She straddled her bike with her heart beating madly in her chest. She suddenly realized she was afraid of her own family's judgment and concern. Hank jogged after her and spoke before she could crank her engine.

"Chan, wait." He held on to one of her handlebars. "I only said what I did because I love you."

She sat very still, startled once again by his words.

"Please, come in and have dinner."

She licked her dry lips, her emotions swirling in a churning sea of confusion, shock and fear. It wasn't just Hank and all that he had said. It was everything. Her life, her loneliness, Sarah. She shook her head, upset at herself for letting Sarah Monroe back into her mind.

"I can't stay. I've got too much on my mind tonight. I wouldn't be good company." There was no way she could stay and sit at the table with that heavy silence she knew would be there, hanging so low over them. She would suffocate.

Accepting defeat, Hank hung his head and stepped back, allowing her to start her powerful bike.

She eased out of the drive and gave him one last look. "I'm sorry," she said again and swallowed the burning in her throat.

She sped away, leaving her brother standing alone.

CHAPTER SEVENTEEN

S arah awoke from a deep, sound sleep to find herself on her sofa. She pushed herself up and rubbed her face. Her place still lay in ruins. She squinted against the harshness of the sun blasting in through the bars of her miniblinds in bright, piercing rays. Her sensitive eyes focused on her hands, where a large, thick envelope rested. She had found it hours ago, amidst the many letters and papers on the floor. It was her notification of acceptance into the FBI. She had been so preoccupied the past several days, she had failed to notice it when bringing in her mail. Now, as she read and reread it, she felt numb. It was as if it no longer meant anything to her. Maybe it didn't. Maybe nothing would ever matter again.

Moving slowly and stiffly into the kitchen, she tugged open the fridge for something cold to drink. Her reality seemed hazy, thick and warping. The hours that passed seemed like seconds, clearly evident in the way her stomach growled angrily and her thirst caused her to down the rest of her milk from the plastic gallon. She wiped her mouth with the back of her hand and replaced her phone back on its charger. She plugged it back in, vaguely remembering that she had tugged it from the wall.

It rang right away and she let it, waiting as her answering machine picked up. It was Dave. He was worried about her and wanted her to call him. He hadn't heard from her in days and she had even called in sick to work, something she had never done before.

Sarah groaned. She didn't feel like talking to him quite yet, didn't know how to answer the questions he would no doubt ask. Avoiding the inevitable, she continued to clean for about an hour or so, her mind constantly working. With Scottie faced and dealt with, she thought about her father. She had put her mother off yet again, and now she wondered what the next call would bring when it came. As if it knew her thoughts, the phone rang again, slamming panic through her.

This time she snatched it up, but she was too afraid to say hello.

"Sarah?" The voice was familiar but was not that of her mother.

Sighing with relief, she responded, "Yes?"

"It's Danielle." At once Sarah's insides hardened. "I have some news."

"What?" Her jaws tightened in angry confusion. News? What the hell was she talking about?

"I've met someone new."

Sarah breathed in a powerful breath, startled by the phone call itself, not the news. Regardless, it was a breath Danielle obviously heard.

"Yes, she's lovely. And phenomenal in bed."

As Sarah tried to get a grip on what was happening, Danielle continued talking, taking full advantage of her silence.

"She's passionate, sensual, and the noises she makes when I fuck her…" She laughed a wicked-sounding laugh.

"You've…slept with her?" The words came out before Sarah could stop them. She was thinking aloud.

More laughter. "Many times!"

Sarah felt her brow furrow. "Then what the hell were you doing begging for it from me?"

The irritating laughter stopped. But Danielle spoke quickly, her tone nonchalant. "I only came by to return your jacket. But when I saw how hung up you were over me, I couldn't very well tell you no, now, could I?"

"You could've mentioned her." Sarah's temple began to pound.

"And shatter your heart even more?"

"My heart isn't shattered."

"It seemed that way to me. The way you got upset during sex…"

"I wasn't about to give you what you wanted. I wasn't about to let you use me again."

"Use you! Is that what you think?"

"I don't think it, I know it," Sarah said through clenched teeth. "Why do you think I refused to let you come?"

More laughter flowed over the line. "I'm the one who left! I had obligations and I allowed myself to get caught up in your pain—"

"Save it!" Sarah pulled the phone from her ear, having heard enough. Danielle could still set her nerves aflame, and Sarah hated herself for that. She gripped the phone so hard her knuckles whitened.

"Sarah, Sarah, are you okay?" Danielle questioned with mock concern. "I hope I haven't upset you."

Sarah narrowed her eyes. Upsetting her was the purpose of the phone call. Revenge for the other morning. But she wasn't going to let Danielle get the best of her. She slammed down the phone on its charger and stood there for a moment, furious, then she marched into the bathroom and twisted on the shower.

While Danielle's words fueled her rage, it wasn't what she was solely concerned about. As she stripped and stepped into the hot stream of water, only one thing went through her mind.

Chandler Brogan.

❖

With an astonishing amount of newfound energy, Sarah soon found herself sitting in her truck contemplating her next move, just as she'd done the day of her counseling appointment and the day she had gone to find Scottie. Cringing at the embarrassing thought of the appointment, and the shameful and exposed feelings it caused to surface, she wrinkled her brow and studied Chandler's house.

It appeared to be quiet, the garage closed, the wind chime hanging by the front door singing its song with the evening breeze. The street was nearly bare, with the exception of a sky-colored sedan parked just down from Chandler's driveway. The car registered with her because she had a feeling she'd seen it before. Squeezing her hands on the warm steering wheel, she tried to place it, even wondering briefly if it belonged to someone Chandler was seeing.

For a split second, she glared at the car, then she reminded herself that Chandler had a right to see whomever she wanted. There was nothing between the two of them, so there was no reason for Sarah to feel jealous, if that's what it was.

She stared out the window and tried to settle her nerves. She didn't know why she was here, couldn't even remember the drive over. All she knew was that Danielle's phone call had sent her into a frenzy of fury and action. Danielle's words had hit her hard, and Sarah had immediately thought about Chandler and what it would mean if it had been she calling to report on a new lover. It would kill her.

God damn it. She formed a fist and thumped her steering wheel with frustration. Like it or not, she cared. Not about Danielle, but about Chandler. The more she thought about it, the more it ate at her, forcing up the fact that Sarah didn't really know the woman at all. The realization made her mad. If only she hadn't run from Chandler. If only she had given her a chance. Maybe she would know her better. She wanted to know her better.

She shook her head. From what little she did know, she didn't think Chandler was the type to date one woman exclusively. She was way too passionate a lover and too wild in her ways. But Sarah couldn't bear to think about Chandler having sex with another woman, especially when she relived how incredible being with Chandler was.

With that last thought in mind, she climbed out of her truck and closed the door. The wind greeted her with warm caresses, running through her dark hair, allowing the setting sun to kiss the skin of her neck. Taking a courage-seeking breath, she squared her shoulders and let her hands fall to her sides, trying her best to look relaxed and casual. She strolled up the driveway with her heart thumping wildly and came to a standstill at the front door.

The wind chime spoke its hellos, causing her insides to jump a bit. *Why am I so nervous? It's just a woman. She's just another…* The thought dissipated, finding no ground to stand on. Her nervous hand found the back of her neck where it rubbed beneath the collar of her snug-fitting chocolate brown T-shirt. Regardless of what her pride preached, she knew she couldn't walk away, no matter how hard she tried.

Admitting that truth, she finally reached out and pushed the doorbell.

Its gentle call echoed through the house, distant and faint. Sarah's heart doubled its pace as she realized she didn't have any idea what she would say. What was the reason for her visit? "Hi, I'm here because I'm insane with jealousy at the thought of you with someone else"? She shook her head, upset at herself for not preparing, for not thinking of this on the way over. She shifted her feet and scrambled for something to say. "I came by to see how you were…" No, lame and needy. Chandler would see right through it. "I was wondering if you were seeing anyone else…" No. She flushed with embarrassment. She would sound like an idiot, like a fool.

That's it! She shifted her feet, anxious for the door to open. *I'll just tell her I came to apologize for running out so suddenly the other night.*

Relaxing a little at having found the right words, she rang the doorbell a second time and waited, sure of her words but not completely sure of her motives. After a couple of minutes, her assuredness began to dim as she realized that Chandler wasn't home—or wasn't answering her door, for reasons Sarah didn't want to think about.

All that, the worry, the build up, the craziness. For nothing. Cursing herself, she walked back to her truck.

Night was just falling and the colors of day still lingered, pinks and oranges giving way to purples and blues. Her nerves, along with her thoughts and feelings, were doing much the same—the newly found and fresh mixing with the feelings that had always been there, painting a new and different picture.

She climbed into her truck and put it into drive. As she pulled onto the street, she couldn't resist looking once more at the blue sedan. Did Chandler know its driver? Angry with herself for going there, she gripped the steering wheel and hit the gas. She should never have come here. What in hell was she thinking?

CHAPTER EIGHTEEN

The cool night air beat against Chan's face and chest, easing the pain resonating from her insides. Streaking onto the highway, she made her way over to the far left lane. She needed to speed, needed to leave all her troubles far behind in the slower lanes. Faster and harder, she pushed her machine, lowering her body and holding her bars tightly, until she felt as one with her bike.

Like a glowing ball of light, searing down the highway in a laser line, she and her bike were in a protective shell of wind, connected. Nothing could stop her, nothing could harm her. A car honked at her as she breezed by it. Others sounded still in the wind as she passed them. She glanced up at a highway sign. She had traveled ten miles. She hunkered down again. Ten miles wasn't nearly enough. Faces and words were still hot on her tail, one face in particular.

The siren blared behind her, as if it knew who she was thinking about. Jerking, she clenched her jaw and contemplated speeding up and forcing Sarah to chase her. Anger spread through her as the siren continued its wail. Damn her. Damn this cop for coming into her life. Sarah had corrupted her thoughts, her bed, and her ways. Now she was behind her, no doubt ready to do what Hank had just done, what she'd done the first time they'd met—tell her to stop. Threaten her, even.

Chan wasn't about to let that happen. She pushed on, forcing the patrol car to chase her. Sarah wouldn't see her on a personal level, she wouldn't let Chan help her, and yet she still felt she had the right to tell Chan how to live her life. Well, she would have to catch her first. Blood beat hot in her ears as she pressed on, ignoring the screaming police cruiser behind her. She wove through a few cars and settled back into the left lane.

A loud voice cut through the siren and she turned, sensing the car pull alongside her. "Pull over!" yelled the law.

Chan straightened, startled that the voice wasn't Sarah's. It was deeper, male. She squinted to her right and saw the officer behind the wheel. *Oh God.* Suddenly panicked, she slowed her bike and made her way to the right shoulder, where she skidded to a stop. Fear raced through her as she realized what she had done. She had nearly gotten herself into a high-speed chase. All over some one-night stand. She rested her head in her hand in frustration. Surely she was going to be arrested.

"Step off your bike, please."

Chan did as requested, on shaky, unsure legs still tingling from her ride. She smoothed down her jeans and coughed to shake the fear hardening in her throat. The officer approached her, pulling off his wide-brimmed hat. Tucking it under one arm, he halted in front of her and said, "Dr. Brogan."

"Dave." She recognized his face at once.

"Yes. Dave Houston."

Her fear gave way to nervousness. He recognized her, and she wasn't sure how that made her feel. He was a friend of Sarah's and she didn't know what that would ultimately mean. He obviously knew Sarah from work, but just how close were they? She thought of all the men she knew similar to Dave. He probably knew about Sarah's sexuality but excused it because he saw her as just one of the guys. To him, she probably wasn't even a woman.

She could see his masculinity now as he stared her down. The energy he exuded stirred in with her other emotions, all of them boiled by the heat of anger. She couldn't believe she was thinking of Sarah, a woman who had friends like Dave. "I'm sorry about all this." She motioned with her hands back toward the highway, where cars zoomed by loudly. Her beef wasn't with him and she wanted him to know that. "I thought you were…" She lowered her eyes, suddenly realizing how that must sound.

"You thought I was Sarah?" He caught on, regardless of her attempt to silence the sentence.

Sighing with sudden nervousness, she nodded. "Yeah. Crazy, huh?"

She cursed herself, not needing to look the crazy hotheaded fool in front of him but doing a damn good job of it.

He held her eyes for a long while with his small serious ones. "I won't even ask just what in hell's going on with the two of you," he said. "But this," he pointed to her bike, "has got to stop."

"There's nothing going on," she said.

"Then why did you refuse to stop?"

Chan ran a hand through her hair and lied, "I don't know." *Because I thought you were Sarah. Because I'm so damned angry and jealous and confused, and I wasn't about to give her the satisfaction of pulling me over again.*

"Well, I suggest you figure it out. The way both of you are behaving—"

"Wait." She stopped him. "What do you mean?"

Dave worked his jaw. The lights from the traffic reflected off the sweat on his brow. "Never mind." He looked away, clearly upset.

"Is something wrong with Sarah?" Her heart pounded, but not out of anger.

"Let's just say I wish the two of you would work it out."

What? "Work what out?"

Dave sounded like a man at the end of his patience. "Whatever the hell's wrong. Sarah's avoiding my calls, acting out." He stopped abruptly as if he had said too much. "And you...you're trying to kill yourself out here."

"Sarah and I aren't involved. There's nothing going on." She knew as she spoke that the words weren't true. There definitely was something going on, whether they were seeing each other or not. There was something tangible there, the same something that was driving her mad. But she didn't know what else to say. And what was wrong with Sarah? Was she going just as crazy as Chan?

"Is she...okay?" she asked.

He shrugged. "I've said more than I should have."

He held up a hand and Chan began to think that maybe she had been wrong about him in regard to Sarah. Maybe he really did care. Maybe they really were close friends.

He seemed to calm as well and softened his tone. "If you want to know more, then I suggest you call her."

He placed his hat back on his head in a practiced fashion that let her know he had done it countless times before. "Lay off the speed on that bike," he commanded. "You're lucky I know you." His eyes held hers firmly. "And if I ever see you ride like that again, I'll make sure you never ride again, period."

Having said all he wanted, or all that he could, he walked away toward his cruiser.

"I've tried," she called out after him, causing him to pause and turn. "I've tried to talk to her, but I can't reach her." If he really was Sarah's friend, she wanted him to know that. In her way, in her mind, it was her way of letting Dave know she cared about Sarah too.

He gave her a long, hard look. "If you care about her, then I hope you'll try again."

He climbed back into his cruiser, offering her no more pieces to the puzzle that was Sarah Monroe. As he pulled back on the highway, she slung her leg over her motorcycle and cranked the engine. For a moment, she sat revving it up, letting its power vibrate through her. She could still make out the faint red of his fading taillights. She wished her thoughts and feelings about Sarah would ride off with him and dim into the blackness of the night.

CHAPTER NINETEEN

As Chandler gunned her bike and streaked back onto the freeway, she knew the mysterious woman who had rocked her world wasn't about to leave her thoughts. And it seemed that speed wasn't going to be an option any longer. Not if she wanted to remain out of jail. With her insides tight and tensing, she took the next exit and rode with determination to the only place she could think of that might actually help to ease her plagued mind.

She killed her engine and sauntered up to the door of the small brick building. She could hear the jukebox, smell the cigarettes. Not bothering to run her hands through her hair, she pulled open the door and walked inside. The place was a little more crowded than it had been the last visit—the night she had run into Sarah.

Trying to clear her head, she rested her hand on the bar and ordered a shot of tequila. A young woman sitting and smoking glanced her way and gave a tilted grin, letting Chan know she was interested. Chan thanked the bartender and downed her shot quickly, not bothering with the lime and salt. She turned the shot glass upside down on the counter walked over to the stranger who continued to eye her.

"Hi," Chan greeted her, with a slow grin of her own.

The woman appeared to be in her mid-twenties with wild, blond-tipped hair. Chan ignored the lingering smoke and concentrated on her tanned, toned arms.

"Hi."

"Did that hurt?" Chan reached out and lightly touched her eyebrow piercing.

"Not really." She stubbed out her cigarette and turned on her stool, resting her arm on the bar as she faced Chan.

Chan took in her long board shorts and tight T-shirt with interest and excitement. She lowered her hand from the woman's brow to finger the elaborate sun tattoo on her inner wrist. Maybe she would be able to forget Sarah after all. Even if only for a night.

"What's your name?" Chan leaned into her, wondering how good the young woman was in bed. She was young and fit, and hopefully very energetic.

"Leah."

Chan stroked her arm. "Tell me, Leah, are you pierced anywhere else?"

The young woman smiled again. "You interested in finding out?"

Chan sat down on the stool next to her and extended her hand for Leah's pack of cigarettes. Plucking one out, she waited as Leah struck a match and leaned in to cup Chan's mouth, lighting the cigarette. Chan sucked on it with force, wanting it to top off her new attitude. Her shell had hardened and she was determined to conquer, to leave everything else behind. She blew the smoke out of the side of her mouth while focusing on Leah's bee-stung lips.

Leaning in, she said. "My name's—"

"Chandler." A deep, strong voice came from behind, immediately sending shock waves up Chan's spine. Turning, she sucked in a quick breath and choked on the smoke she had accidentally inhaled.

Sarah stood staring at her with her piercing blue eyes and strong, tall body. "Please tell me that's not your bike outside."

Chan tensed and then got over the shock of seeing her in an instant as anger rose up through her. "It just so happens it is," she countered, daring her to do something about it.

"Speeding, riding like a maniac." Sarah's eyes lowered to look around, searching. "No helmet either?" She returned her fierce gaze to Chan's face, deadly serious.

"Who's this?" Leah queried from behind Chan, obviously picking up on the tension.

Chan forced a smile. "Leah, this is Sarah." Chan set down her cigarette with an unsteady hand. She trained her eyes back on Leah, unwilling to let Sarah's presence affect her. Her temper flared, dying to be unleashed at Sarah's accusing words. Words that assumed how Chan would be riding. Words that were dead-on in accuracy.

"Chandler, will you come with me, please?"

Chan felt a strong grip on her arm. She jerked it away, angry.

Sarah continued, grabbing her again. "I need to talk to you." She pulled Chan up with force, and Leah quickly stood as well.

With anger heating her skin, Chan jerked away again. *How dare she! What gives her the right?*

"Let go of her," Leah said.

Chan glared up at Sarah, unnerved by the seriousness in her face. Suddenly, Dave's words entered her mind. Maybe Sarah needed to talk. Maybe that's what this was about. Sarah was reaching out to her the only way she knew how. She relaxed and immediately felt Sarah release her grip.

"It's okay," she told Leah, appreciating the fact that the young woman was clueless but ready to fight regardless of Sarah's size. "Later, okay?"

Leah gave a hesitant nod and returned to her seat at the bar, gazing after them as Sarah led the way to the back of the small club. Following close behind, Chan tried desperately not to notice how sexy the cop looked in her tight brown shirt and blue jeans with matching heavy boots. Sarah reached the wall behind the tables and chairs, and turned to cross her arms as she waited for Chan to approach.

Chan did so with a light attitude, careful not to show how much she was affected. "Okay, I'm here, so what's going on?" She too crossed her arms and waited. She did her best not to focus on the eyes that were fixed on her face. They were too moving, too knowing.

"You rode here tonight?" The question startled her, even though similar words had just been spoken at the bar.

Chan took a step back, confused and then offended. "What?" *That's what this is about? The fucking bike?*

"I got a call from Dave." Sarah touched the cell phone on her belt and Chan suddenly realized everything.

She couldn't believe it. And here she had actually thought Sarah was going to confide in her. She had actually allowed herself to believe that Sarah was finally going to trust her enough to be real, to open up. The mere thought had brought a rush of longing so strong she was embarrassed by her own gullibility. She held up her hand and tried to walk away, angry, hurt.

"Wait, Chandler!" Sarah's hand found her arm again, stopping her. "Wait!"

Chan spun around in anger. "Fuck off!" She tried to jerk away but Sarah was too strong.

"God damn it, Chandler!" Her other hand came down, clamping Chan's free arm, ensuring that she couldn't get away. Sarah's eyes were wide and her voice strained. "Come here!"

Chan found herself being turned firmly against the wall. Sarah pinned her back to the cool bricks and stared hard into her eyes. Her hands eased up but when Chan jolted to flee again, they bore back down, holding her still. Sarah leaned into her, pressing her powerful body up against Chan's, their warm breath mixing.

"Damn you," Sarah exhaled. Her eyes searched Chan's for answers they couldn't seem to find.

Chan felt her insides go weak as she was held captive by the sexy cop. Desperate to escape the fierce desire that was growing within, she demanded, "What do you want?"

Her answer was given at once as Sarah pinned her tighter and took her mouth with her own. Even if Chan had wanted to fight it, she quickly found that she didn't have the strength. Sarah claimed her hungrily, with quick, forceful assaults of her tongue and possessive tugs of her lips. Chan moaned into her mouth, overcome and overwhelmed. It felt so good, Sarah taking her once again. She kissed her back and Sarah responded by kissing her harder, using her teeth to hold her lips, making sure that she was the one with the control. Chan shuddered beneath her, completely turned on, her body now tense with need.

She felt Sarah's hands drop from her arms and pull away.

"Come on," Sarah rasped, tugging her down a dim hallway to a dark corner near the back exit. "I have to have you."

She slinked up against Chan, once again holding her to the wall. Chan welcomed the feel of her body with another groan. Sarah's fingers unbuttoned her jeans as her hot mouth bit and sucked on her neck.

Chan dug her nails into the strong back and arched up into her. "I can't stop thinking about you," she confessed, breathless from the hot, hungry mouth on her neck. She closed her eyes, feeling the tug on her pants as Sarah's fingers worked them open.

"Me neither," Sarah whispered, dragging her teeth along Chan's sensitive jawline. "When Dave called…" She paused and pulled back. "I was so mad at you. Why do you do that?" Her blue eyes darkened as she took Chan's lips, this time gently, softly.

Chan wrapped her hands in the thick dark brown hair, lost in the kiss. "I…couldn't stop thinking about you," she managed softly between wet, soft pulls of her lips. "When you left the other night…I…the pain in your eyes…"

Sarah stopped her by touching her finger to Chan's lips. "I've been thinking about you too."

"You have?"

"Yes. I've been going insane with jealousy at the thought of you with someone else." Sarah breathed deeply. "I had to find you. Not only because of what Dave said but to see for myself if you were dating. Crazy, huh?"

Chan moved her hands from Sarah's hair and stroked her beautiful face. "Of course not."

"When I think of someone else touching you…" Sarah leaned in as she spoke.

"Don't," Chan pleaded, afraid it would only cause pain.

"I go insane," Sarah repeated. She bent down as Chan raised her chin, offering Sarah her lower lip.

Sarah took it aggressively, biting it, tugging it, igniting both their fires once again. Chan clung to her and kissed her back ravenously. She felt Sarah's thigh thrust between hers, rubbing against her excited flesh. Sarah was here, and she wanted her. Sarah wanted this, wanted to be with her. The thought warmed her, consumed her from her belly out to her fingertips. As the desire flooded her, she felt Sarah's fingers skimming across the satin of her underwear.

"Yes," she cried out softly, wanting, needing the fingers to stroke her swollen need.

Sarah's teeth found her neck as her hand eased down into the panties, gliding over the slick, firm flesh and causing Chan to jerk and groan. Dangerously close to going over, Chan forced her eyes open and her own hand down the front of Sarah's shirt to her crotch. Fingers flying, she tugged open the button only to have Sarah pause in her movements, holding Chan's sex firmly between her fingers.

"What are you doing?" Sarah softly demanded.

"I'm trying to get to you."

"Why?" She raised her mouth, breathing upon Chan's sensitive skin as she made her way to her ear. Sarah lined the ridge slowly with her tongue and moved her magical hand up and down, milking Chan's clit, searing pleasure up into her.

"Because I want to. Want you to feel this too," Chan managed, biting her own lip with determination. She lowered her other hand and eased down Sarah's zipper.

"I don't know if I...can." Sarah took Chan's lobe into her mouth and sucked, causing goose bumps to electrify Chan's skin.

"Yes, yes you can," Chan insisted between gasps of pleasure. Sarah was stroking her harder and faster, trying to get her mind off her new quest. But Chan knew what she wanted, what they both ultimately wanted, and she had to have it. Gritting her teeth, she maneuvered her hand down the front of Sarah's pants, where she felt her excitement through her cotton briefs.

"Argh, God," Sarah whispered weakly.

Chan felt her respond, felt her hot flesh pushing through the cotton, desperate to be touched. "Can I?" she asked, pleading.

Sarah pulled her head back and looked to the ceiling, breathing hard with excitement. "Yes."

Chan tugged the underwear downward, quickly shoving her palm inside, cupping the slick flesh in her hand. Sarah gasped and jerked and then bored her eyes into Chan's with raw excitement.

"Are you okay?" Chan had to be sure.

"Yes," she gasped. "It's good, so good."

Chan felt Sarah's fingers graze the exposed tip of her clitoris. She slammed her head back in pleasure, loving the feel of Sarah on her and the feel of her hand on Sarah. God, yes, it felt so good. Both of them groaning and gasping, kissing furiously as they stroked, tugged and rubbed. She lifted her hand a little, flattening her fingers against Sarah's firm but flexible clit. She assaulted it with her entire hand, up and down, from the tips of her fingers to the heel of her hand. Encasing it in pleasure. There was no way it was going to escape. No way Sarah was going to get away.

"Make me come," Chan begged, floating through heaven itself.

Sarah grunted and lowered to bite her neck.

"Come with me," Chan insisted, knowing Sarah was close. She could feel it. Feel the pressure, hear the sharp intake of breath, the intense focus on her beautiful face.

"Feels so good," Sarah rasped as she shoved her hand down harder and faster, grinding her hips as Chan did the same to her.

The cry of pleasure penetrated through Chan and she rubbed furiously, her entire hand covered in Sarah's warm wetness. "Yes. Fuck yeah." She threw her head back and clenched her eyes. "I'm going to come. I'm coming, I'm co…ming," she cried out to the ceiling above as her body racked and shook with pleasure so intense she thought she would crumble.

Sarah jerked in front of her, a low-sounding moan escaping her throat as she tensed and rocked into Chan. They both stilled and Chan felt Sarah throbbing under her hand. She had come. They had come together. Nothing had ever felt so good.

"You okay?" she asked, feeling her lift up, freeing Chan of her weight.

Sarah pulled her hand free of Chan's pants and then eased Chan's hand up by the wrist. She buttoned her jeans, her eyes avoiding Chan's.

"Hey, are you okay?" Chan reached out and cupped her jaw, worried.

"I don't know." Sarah finally said before glancing away once more.

Chan hadn't noticed before, but her eyes were sunken, her face thin and pale. Again she remembered Dave's concern. "Talk to me," she pleaded, yanking up her own pants.

"I…" Sarah sounded choked up, clearing her throat and clenching her jaw. "I can't. Not right now."

"Why?"

"I just can't."

Chan reached out for her arm as she stepped to walk away. "Then when?" She didn't want her to go. Didn't think she could survive her fleeing once again.

"I don't know. I'm sorry."

Chan watched helplessly as Sarah Monroe walked away from her yet again. Left her standing, sated, head spinning and all alone. The sting was brutal but not surprising. Her body moved somehow, and she returned to the bar in a daze.

"Tequila," she ordered, only dimly aware of her surroundings. The pain she was feeling was unbearable, and she could only hope that the liquor would dull its sharp, stabbing edges.

With a full shot glass in hand, she glanced toward to the door that Sarah had hurriedly breezed out a moment before. Tossing her head back, she downed the powerful alcohol and asked for another.

"Everything okay?" The voice was Leah's and she had her hand on Chan's shoulder.

"Fine," Chan responded with a cold indifference that wasn't there before. She was shutting off all emotion, desperate for the hurt to go away. She eyed the shot glass in front of her, full of golden tequila, promising no more pain. She swallowed it down and cringed at the awful taste.

"You sure?"

Chan turned and forced herself to give the cute blonde a grin. "Yeah, I'm fine. Fucking great." She leaned into her and kissed her young mouth with confidence and carelessness. She was going to forget about Sarah Monroe once and for all.

After swirling her tongue around Leah's for a moment, she pulled away. Even though she had tasted the warm steel of the other woman's tongue piercing, she felt nothing. She was numb.

Leah stepped closer and whispered in her ear. "Wanna get out of here and see where else I'm pierced?"

Chan closed her eyes as the tequila swirled through her brain, seemingly sloshing it around. "Why leave?" she asked, rising to tug the woman along after her.

When they reached the back wall, Chan shoved her aggressively against it and rubbed her through her jeans. At once she felt the hard bud of a piercing nestled in her clit. Leah groaned and drew her closer. Chan felt hot and dizzy as she rubbed the young stranger much like she had done Sarah. As she made her come, she closed her eyes and felt redeemed. This time it would be she who left the woman standing all alone.

She pulled away as Leah shuddered with the aftermath of orgasm. Wiping her hand casually against her jeans, she turned and headed to the door, leaving the young woman calling out after her.

CHAPTER TWENTY

The hallway was brightly lit, reflecting off the polished white floors. Sarah couldn't remember the drive to the hospital, her mind reeling from what had happened with Chandler. The passionate psychologist had somehow gotten to her, making her feel things she had never felt before.

She closed her eyes as her hand remembered the warm, wanting flesh. She could still hear Chandler's voice, tight and insistent. *"Come with me."* The words had reached her, bursting into the dark recesses of her consciousness, exploding with powerful light. Gone were the images of Scottie, drunk and malevolent, his bloodshot eyes full of sinful lust. The images had dissipated, meshing into the blackness of night. No, all she had felt was pleasure, hazy and heavy, overwhelmingly so. Chandler's hand had played her hungry flesh, strumming out the thick pleasure, wave after wave, crashing into her soul.

She opened her eyes, shuddering once again at the thought of her earlier orgasm. The power, the release that tore through her...nothing in the world could've ever prepared her for it. The dreams she'd long had of passion washed away hurriedly, not nearly enough in comparison to the real thing. She thought of the building pressure of insurmountable pleasure, of Chandler working her, filling her up with ecstasy. The pleasure was so great, so conquering, it left her feeling weak and vulnerable.

The rawness it exposed was the reason she had fled. She had trembled as she drove, dangerously close to breaking down into tears. It had felt so good, so amazing, so connected to Chandler. All shook up and emotional in ways she couldn't understand, she had driven here.

Somehow, she had made it.

She slowed in her walk as she noted the number on the nearing wide door. Three eighteen. Feeling a little dizzy with nervousness, she sank down into a chair across the hall from the door.

Sudden and powerful, memories washed over her now that she was so close to her father.

She was sound asleep in her neat little room, which was decorated with anything she could find in red and blue. She loved the American flag and its colors and was determined to someday be the best citizen she could be, a police officer, helping people keep the peace in their lives. And maybe, just maybe, she would even join the FBI. The library book she had tucked under her pillow promised her everything she ever wanted. Structure, excellence, intelligence, and exciting challenges.

A sound stirred her from her sleep and she turned over in a stupor, hoping it would go away. As she tried to return to sleep, the sound took on meaning in her mind. It was constant and blaring, demanding her attention. At once she sat up and threw back her covers. She had to hurry or the neighbors would call the police again. Trotting down the dark hallway, she passed her parent's bedroom. Her mother was dead to the world in an alcohol-induced state of exhaustion, arms spread wide as she lay on her back on top of the comforter. The sight only caused Sarah greater anxiety. She was on her own; it was her responsibility now.

She rushed out the front door, stepping barefoot onto the freezing-cold concrete. Chills shot up through her and she hugged herself in her thin pajamas as she made her way to the source of the loud noise. Her breath showed itself in white clouds as she moved quickly to her father's old Chevy. A screen door slammed shut behind her, causing her to turn. One of her neighbors stood on his porch, staring her down in anger.

"Sorry!" She waved to him nervously and then opened up the car door. Inside, her father lay unconscious, limp and heavy against the steering wheel, against the horn. It was happening more and more often lately, Roy somehow making it home alive and unharmed but dangerously drunk. As soon as he pulled in the drive, or sometimes the yard, his body gave up, passing out in the vehicle, sometimes hitting the horn and alerting her and sometimes not. More than one morning she had found him in his car, nearly frozen with the night air, asleep and

oblivious.

She pushed him back against the seat with all her might. She was only fourteen but she was long and strong, much like him. The angry blare of the horn silenced and he sat slouched, his head hanging. The neighbor banged back inside his house and Sarah breathed a sigh of relief.

Wrapping her father's arm around her shoulders, she pulled him up out of the car. He groaned at her but remained useless as she kicked the car door shut. Walking unsteadily, she dragged him along to the front door, amazed at how she was able to carry his six foot five frame. Once inside, she used all of her remaining strength to maneuver him to the couch, where she released him to plop down like a giant rag doll.

She lifted his legs, made sure his body was entirely on the sofa, and pushed him toward the back of it to lessen his chances of rolling off. He mumbled something unintelligible as she yanked off his heavy work boots and covered him with a blanket.

After returning to lock the front door, she dragged herself back to her bed, where she too collapsed, exhausted. She didn't get a thank you, and never had. She never even got an acknowledgment for caring for her folks the way they should've been caring for her. She figured she never would.

The next morning, she forced herself out of bed and readied her tired body for school. Her father was moving around noisily in the living room, apparently waking up himself. She passed him but did not speak to him as she made her way to the door, book bag in tow. He stood staring out the window, fresh beer in his hand.

"The car's gone." His voice was deep and throaty, still not yet awake.

She froze, alarmed first by the fact that he was speaking to her, and secondly by his words. "What?" Panic rushed through her as she made sense of it.

"I can't find the damn keys." He patted down his pockets with his free hand. "They must've been in the car. Somebody decided to take it." He looked over at her, his eyes bleary, his hair sticking up on one side.

Sarah stood still, fear and shame nearly shaking her. She had forgotten to take the keys. It was her fault the car was gone. She thought about apologizing, about running back to her room in shame. She knew for sure he was going to yell at her. But he merely stood and shook his head.

"I guess I better call the police." He swallowed more of his beer. "You better hurry up or you'll miss your bus."

She hesitated a moment and then moved. He didn't remember the events of the previous night. And she wasn't about to remind him.

That wasn't the last episode with the car. A few weeks later he had wrecked it, running off into a cow pasture and lying there unconscious until the owner found him around noon the next day. Eventually he lost his license and Sarah had to drive him everywhere. That meant picking him up at all hours at Scottie's home, where he spent nearly every night gambling their money away.

Scottie. He not only had taken her innocence, but the majority of their money as well.

She took in a shaky breath and forced her mind back into the now. She willed her nerves to hold out just a little longer. She rose from the chair and brought her hand to rest on the cool door handle and stood for a moment, debating. An orderly broke the quiet, pushing a supply cart slowly by. She glanced at her watch. It was nearing one a.m. Hopefully Roy would be asleep. And alone.

Knowing it was now or never, she opened the large door and stepped inside. A thin blue curtain was pulled even though the bed closest to the door was empty. The room was dim and she moved slowly and carefully, the only source of light being a fluorescent bar that glowed above a sink to her left. Her heart pounded with fright, making her feel fourteen again—vulnerable, afraid and unsure.

She halted just beyond the curtain near the foot of her father's bed. He lay sleeping and she studied him hurriedly, at first thinking she had the wrong room. But as she focused, her breath was stolen from her throat. His face was thin and drawn, his once full cheeks sunken and lined. He was almost completely unrecognizable. He looked worse than Scottie. He looked like a skeleton. A gasp escaped her, and she covered her mouth quickly with a trembling hand. The situation she had been avoiding for so long now slapped her hard in the face, forcing reality on her. She felt herself quiver as raw emotion swept through her.

"Sarah?" a meek voice questioned from the dark corner next to the bed. Her mother rose up out of her chair and approached her. Wrinkles from worry and cigarettes etched her face, aging her beyond her years.

"I'm so glad you finally came."

She raised an unsure hand that eventually settled on Sarah's shoulder. A ragged-sounding cough shook her thin body, punishment for the addictive poison she inhaled on a daily basis. Sarah stepped away, uncomfortable with the contact. She wasn't ready for that yet. There was too much tackling her at the moment, too much to deal with.

She forced hersef to move toward the bed and stood at her father's side. His once thick, dark hair was swept over his head in a soft, thin veil. His mouth was slack and open, taking in irregular, rattling breaths. A strange smell seemed to emanate from him and she noticed some purple splotches on the back of his hands and arms. Panic surged through her as a long pause passed between breaths. She waited, her heart thudding in her ears. She nearly cried with relief when the next breath finally came.

"I was afraid I would be too late," she confessed, her voice cracking.

"They don't think he'll make it through to morning," her mother whispered.

Sarah continued to study him, the man she had resented and blamed her past on. He looked so weak, so helpless, a mere shell of the man she had grown to despise. Every ounce of hate, of blame shook through her, none of it mattering, none of it worth a damn. Another gasp escaped her, one then two. What had she been thinking? Why had she hated for so long? All the while he lay there suffering, his diseased body collapsing upon the man he once was. He was her father and he had wanted to see her, but she couldn't allow it for her own selfish reasons. What had she been thinking? That she would make him pay?

No. She shook her head and hastily wiped away a warm tear. She was the one who had paid. And she was paying now for her harbored anger and spite. She reached out to touch him, desperate for him to know that she was there and she was sorry. Sorry for not calling, for not forgiving. He had only lived his life, never physically harming her, making sure she had a roof over her head. He probably hadn't meant to hurt her. He probably wasn't even aware that he had.

Or maybe he was aware and that was why he had tried to mend their relationship a couple of years ago, calling her, asking her to come around. But she had refused. She had never given him the chance. Her hand trembled, hovering above his. She couldn't remember the last time she had touched him.

Seeming to sense her tight emotions, her mother moved quickly to the other side of the bed. Sarah saw the redness in her eyes, on the tip of her nose. She had been crying.

"Roy? Roy, Sarah's here." Her mother took his limp hand and held it, stroking it. "He's on a lot of morphine. He may not come around."

Sarah pulled her hand back, afraid that if she did touch him, her pain would come spilling out and she would crumble. Suddenly unsure if she could remain strong and still be able to stand, she reached back for the chair her mother had been sitting in. As she settled into it, her father began to mutter through dry lips.

Her mother leaned down, speaking closer to his ear. "Sarah's here." She looked over and nodded at her daughter. "Take his hand, let him know where you are."

Sarah swallowed hard and did as requested, touching her father lightly, feeling his cool, dry skin. She nearly wept at the contact, at his weakness, at her stubbornness.

"Sarah?" His voice was ragged, a mere whisper, his eyes still closed.

Wiping her eyes, she sat forward, grasping his frail hand more tightly. "Yes, it's me." She had to fight to keep from crying. The threatening sobs burned her throat and squeezed her chest.

"Sarah?"

"Yes. I'm here."

His eyelids fluttered but didn't open. His lips moved before the words formed. "I…I'm sorry."

She shook her head, not needing his apology. It didn't matter anymore. None of it. "It's okay," she responded barely able to speak. The emotions she had held buried within for so long surfaced and crashed together like angry waves. "It's okay. I know," she reassured him. "I'm sorry, too."

"Sarah?" Again he called her name and then mumbled words she couldn't make out. His breath rattled as he took in several shallow gasps of air.

He mumbled again and squeezed her hand. Her heart shattered with pain as she listened, wishing she could understand. Hot tears blurred her vision and she wiped at them angrily, determined to see him with clear eyes and clear mind.

"Here." Her mother reached into her purse and pulled out an envelope. She held it out over the bed. "He wanted you to have this."

Sarah took it reluctantly and fingered her name written in neat cursive. She glanced up at her mother, unsure.

"Go ahead, read it. He would want you to."

Tentatively, Sarah opened the flap and reached inside to slide out the letter. She unfolded the notebook paper and read.

To my daughter Sarah,

I hope this letter finds you doing well. I've always hoped that you would find a good life, one that you deserve. I had hoped to see you and make things right by you, but I guess it wasn't meant to be. It's my own fault. All of it. I wasn't a good father and I know that now. I've known it for some time. You were a good girl, Sarah, and you deserved so much better than you had.

I want you to know I never meant to hurt you. Neither did your mom. We were just too caught up in ourselves. But it was never intentional and you must never think it was your fault. The booze. The gambling. They took my attention away from the important things in life. Like our family.

I want you to know how very sorry I am. Sorry for all of it. And I'm especially sorry for not being able to know the wonderful woman I know you've become. I love you. Always have and always will. So does you mother. Please, give her a chance. She's changed, just as I have. I hope you can find comfort in each other.

And I hope more than anything that you find everything you've ever wished for.
Your loving father,
Roy

Sucking in a shaky breath Sarah refolded the letter. Sobs, burning and overpowering, shook her chest. She reached out and touched his hand once again. Swallowing, she said, "I love you too, Dad."

She barely got the words out before the sobbing tore through her. She lowered her head, the sorrow shaking her from head to toe.

Roy lay still, apparently unable to say anything more. His breathing continued on, irregular with lengthy pauses in between. He held her hand, though, and her mother came to stand by her side, resting a hand on her shoulder. They watched him together, and Sarah tried to remember him, the way he'd once looked. She remembered him smiling, tall and handsome, laughing as he chased her around the yard. She remembered the way he danced with her mother, swinging her around the kitchen to one of his favorite songs. Tears welled and fell from her eyes, releasing the terrible pain, one tiny drop at a time.

His breathing slowed, the shallow gasps coming further apart. Her mother reached down and cupped her hand over Sarah's, who held her father's. They remained that way for what felt like an eternity, Sarah quietly battling her tears while her mother did her best to comfort her.

Eventually Roy took in a breath and fell silent for a longer period of time, causing Sarah to look up, waiting for the next breath to come.

But it never did.

She lowered her head and cried as quietly as she could. Her father loved her, he truly did. And she loved him. His life, the choices he made—he didn't make them out of malice. He had made mistakes, but so had she. She couldn't hate him for what he was. He was being who he was meant to be. People weren't always who you wanted them to be. She had to love him for who he was. She could see all of that now. But it took him dying to get her to let go of the pain, of the past.

Rising up, she turned and let her mother embrace her. More sobs came as she felt just how thin her mother was. Her parents were no longer the ones ruining her life, neglecting her for their own fun. They had grown older and weaker and regretful. As she cried into her mother's graying hair, she closed her eyes and held on to her, almost afraid to let her go. Her mother held her too, surprisingly strong for her size.

A nurse entered the room, walking up on them slowly. "I'm sorry," she whispered.

Sarah and her mother lowered their arms and wiped at their eyes.

"He finally went," her mother said, moving to stroke his hair and pajamas. She glanced over at the nurse. "You were right. He was waiting for our daughter."

The nurse gave Sarah a weak smile. "I'm very sorry for your loss. I'll leave you alone with him for a while."

Quietly, she moved away and closed the door behind her. Sarah stared in a daze as her mother continued to straighten and groom her father, folding his hands together and placing them on his chest. She kissed his forehead and whispered to him softly, eventually beginning to hum.

"Mom?" She hadn't stopped to think about just how hard this whole ordeal must've been for her. If anything, she should've come for her. For support.

"Hmm?" She didn't look up.

"Are you okay?"

She stopped straightening the sheets and stood erect, meeting Sarah's eyes. "I'll be all right."

"This has to be hard on you." Sarah knew the pain she was feeling had to be at least double for her mother. They had been married forty years.

"I've known about the cancer for a long time."

"How long?" Sarah had only found out weeks before.

"A little over a year."

"Why didn't you tell me?" Knowing sooner probably wouldn't have changed her behavior. Even so, she wondered why they kept it from her.

"He didn't want you to know. He knew how you felt about him, about us, and he didn't want you coming around out of pity. He wanted you to come around because you wanted to."

Sarah sank down into the chair and buried her head in her hands. There were so many things she wished she could change. Things didn't have to be this way. And she refused to let them continue.

"I'm sorry, Mom. For not returning your calls, for not visiting."

She heard her mother sigh softly. "You don't have to be sorry, Sarah."

"I do." She looked up at her. "I couldn't forgive. I couldn't forget." She glanced at her father's still form and teared up again. "I'm sorry you went through this alone."

Her mother remained by her father's side, looking at her with worried eyes. "Sarah, all I want for you...all we want for you...is happiness." She placed a hand on Roy's shoulder. "We weren't the best parents. We didn't love you like we should've or give you the attention you deserved. We were caught up in us."

"You don't have to explain." Sarah said, not wanting to put her mother through any more pain.

"Yes, I do. You need to hear it. Roy wanted you to hear it."

They both gazed at the pale man who looked so peaceful with his hands folded and his hair brushed to the side.

"So what now?" Sarah asked, needing to be there for her mother from now on, no matter what.

"Now we lay your father to rest."

"What about you? Are you sick?" Sarah took in her appearance and the constant threatening cough, suddenly very much worried for her well-being. Grieving for her husband would be difficult enough, she didn't need to be sick on top of it all. "Have you been checked out?"

Surprisingly, her mother laughed softly. "There's no doubt in my mind that I will follow your father." She smiled warmly at her daughter. "But not anytime soon."

Sarah nodded and lowered her gaze. Her mother moved back to Roy and began humming again, kissing him on the forehead and stroking his hair.

Sarah got to her feet and hugged herself, moved by the love they shared, a love she wished to have someday. As her eyes welled up again, Chandler's face entered her mind. Sarah had left her once again, fleeing into the night with no explanation, fleeing from her own inner fears. Wincing, she turned from her parents.

Chandler moved her, stirred things in her, and yet Sarah kept pushing her away just as she did with anything that caused emotion in her. She glanced back at her mother, awed by her strength. It made her feel a fool, so caught up in her head and the fears it held. If she was going to change, she was going to change everything. Life was too precious to be ruled by her fears, by her demons. It was a lesson hard learned.

"Mom?"

"Yes?"

"I need to go make a phone call. You going to be okay?"

"I'll be fine. Go ahead on home." She smiled first at Sarah and then at her husband. "I'll stay here a while longer."

Sarah took a step toward the door and then hesitated. She suddenly felt overcome with the urge to talk, to share with her mother what happened with Scottie. The anger and resentment she had been feeling had forced her to face it head-on once again, to accept that it happened. And now, Sarah needed her mother to know that as if just by simply talking about it, in time she could mend the hole that had been torn. But not now.

"I'll call you tomorrow, okay?"

Her mother looked over at her, clearly surprised and pleased.

"To check on you. And to help with any arrangements."

"I'd like that."

Sarah returned the smile and gave her father one last look. She thought about touching him again but didn't think she had the strength to withstand the emotions that it would stir up.

Good-bye, Dad. She walked to the door, unable to look back. Outside in the bright corridor, she squinted and took deep breaths. The smell of death seemed to cling to her, like an invisible, heavy mist. She rode the elevator down to the ground floor and walked slowly to the main sliding doors. She needed to call Chandler and talk to her. It was late, but what she had to say couldn't wait.

CHAPTER TWENTY-ONE

S arah drove with the cell phone pressed firmly to her ear.
    "I'm sorry, ma'am, that number is unlisted."
Sarah cringed at the news. "Thank you." She ended the call.
"Damn it!" She slapped her steering wheel and almost slapped herself
for never taking the time to get Chandler's number.

She drove on, determined and swelling with the newfound emotion.
She had to see Chandler and tell her how she felt. She sped, pushing her
truck, needing to confess before she burst from within.

Chandler's house came into view after what felt like an eternity.
Sarah released her tight grip on the steering wheel and slowed to a stop
a ways down from the home. From behind her the headlights of a car
came into view and she held her breath, hoping it was Chandler. But the
car passed by and kept going until it stopped just beyond Chandler's.
The driver killed the engine and the lights but didn't emerge. Sarah
squinted, certain she had seen the car before.

That blue sedan. The car she'd feared was driven by one of
Chandler's lovers. It probably belonged to a neighbor Chandler had
never even spoken to. Feeling foolish, she turned off her engine. It was
late but, still determined, she climbed down from her truck and walked
quickly to the front door. The night felt cool and crisp, sharp against
her warm skin. She rubbed her arms as she stepped up to ring the bell.
Chandler was going to think she was nuts, but she didn't care.

She waited and listened, anxious to take Chandler in her arms once
again. This time she swore she wouldn't ever let go. She rang the bell
a second time and as it echoed through the quiet house, Sarah began

to feel let down. After waiting a few more minutes, she walked away slowly and headed back to her truck. Chandler's absence stabbed her in the pit of her stomach, allowing jealousy to seep in and fill it up.

She wasn't home, and it was probably Sarah's fault. The way she had left her—and for the third time. She had to get to her, but there was no way now. The bar was closed. There was no telling where Chandler was. She would have to look up her number at work or call Dave and get it since he was on duty.

Sarah's throat began to burn as she started her truck. She glanced up to where the sedan had been. It was gone. Exhausted, she drove to her apartment and went inside. All the emotion and trauma from the day weighed her down and she trudged like a zombie to her bed. Chandler, her father, and then Chandler again. She thought about calling Dave, but it was too late. Like it or not, Chandler was going to have to wait.

She closed her eyes and darkness quickly consumed her. She fell right to sleep.

❖

Chan awoke feeling like she had been dragged by her motorcycle. She was weak with fatigue and stiff from the awkward position in which she had slept. She could feel the pulse in her head, which made it ache all the more. Something thumped onto her lap as she pushed herself into an upright position on the couch.

Squinting against the sun, she focused on her cat. Mitote. He rubbed against her hand, purring, saying good morning. She attempted to search her memory banks, but it was just too painful. She groaned and scooted him to the floor. Her legs were bare and it took her a few minutes to locate her jeans, which lay in a heap by the garage door.

How the hell did I get home? She couldn't remember much of anything. She jerked on her pants and stumbled over her boots on her way to the kitchen. Her mind attempted to work as her body tried to catch up. There was one thing she could remember, despite her numerous attempts to forget, and that was Sarah.

Chan rubbed her temple as she realized she had gone out five nights in a row, drinking and dancing and drinking some more. All of it done to fill the void in her life, the hole that Sarah had created by coming into her life and then leaving, over and over again.

She sighed. Suddenly she didn't know if she would be able to move on. Nothing seemed to help the pang, the yearning she felt for her. But it was just too damn much. Chan couldn't handle it. As badly as she wanted Sarah, it seemed that Sarah didn't want her. And Chan wasn't used to being the one who was rejected. It hurt like hell.

She made her way to the kitchen and started some much-needed coffee. The phone rang and she checked the caller ID. It was a number she recognized but didn't know. Someone had been calling her frequently from the same number, but they never left a message so she never answered. She glanced down and noticed that she had on only one sock. As she journeyed through the living room in search of its mate, she heard movement from the hallway.

"*Buenos días.*"

Chan stood very still, mouth agape.

The Latin woman was nude and smiling.

Chan stared, completely stunned. "What are you doing here?"

The woman looked surprised by the question. "I follow you home."

"Last night?"

She nodded.

Fuck. Chan realized she must've run into her at one of the numerous bars she had been frequenting. She stared, trying her best to recall the previous evening, but it was too fuzzy.

As her eyes swept over the woman's body she suddenly felt ashamed and looked away. Seeing a woman in her home brought what she had been trying to forget right in front of her face. She wanted a woman in her home, wanted to wake up to her every day, but not this one.

What had she done? What was she doing to her life? Why couldn't she just go to Sarah and tell her how she felt?

Feeling angry with herself, she asked the question she dreaded. "Did we, uh…have sex?"

"No." The woman moved toward Chan in a seductive manner. "But we could now."

Chan held up her hands before she came too close. She thought carefully. It wasn't fair, how she was behaving. Just because she was hurting for Sarah, it didn't give her the right to lead this woman on.

"Look, whatever I said, whatever I did last night, I'm sorry. I can't sleep with you and I can't continue seeing you." There, it was out.

The woman stopped and stared and Chan felt bad for her.

"I'm sorry for the way I've treated you." Chan meant it.

The woman nodded. "You said all of this last night."

"I did?"

"*Sí*. I thought it was because you drink."

"It's the truth." Chan explained. "I'm sorry."

"Another woman?"

Chan nodded.

"That is all you had to say." Her face softened.

Chan swallowed. "I couldn't say it until now."

"I understand."

"Me too," Chan said. "For the first time in my life, I understand."

CHAPTER TWENTY-TWO

The drive home from work was always slow going. Chan stopped her Durango and relaxed against her seat as the three lines of freeway traffic crawled at a snail's pace. Usually she would fidget in her seat, and switch lanes frequently, convinced the other was moving faster. Patience was a virtue she'd never seemed to have.

Today, however, she was finding the slow ride home a bit soothing, giving her time to think. She'd made several decisions over the past few days and it felt good to go over them, to get things set right in her mind. Waking up to the near stranger in her home and having no memory of the events that led up to it had frightened and concerned her. It had forced her to take a step back and analyze her life. What did she want? What was it that she truly wanted?

The answer was simple. Whereas most people would have reported peace, happiness, health, and love, Chan had bypassed all of them and muttered only one word.

"Sarah."

Sarah encompassed it all. Everything Chan wanted and needed. She no longer wanted to go from lover to lover. The act seemed cold to her now, and she couldn't imagine sharing intimate moments like that with strangers anymore. Sex wasn't just sex. It was deeper, meaningful. The feelings she had were different now.

She wanted to share those intimacies, those sacred feelings with one person only. She wanted to wake up next to her every morning and delicately stroke her skin along with the pale light of the dawning day. To listen to her breathe, watch her eyes as they lightened when they awakened from sleep. She wanted to share her dreams, her thoughts, her fears. She wanted all of it and again she whispered the name of the person who unknowingly held it all.

"Sarah."

Chan eventually drove on, Sarah's face flashing in her mind, making the rush-hour traffic seem to all but disappear. The garage door eased open and she parked her truck and walked into the kitchen, where she tossed her keys on the counter. She felt good, optimistic and calm in a way that surprised her. It was as if the clarity of her realizations had soothed her soul. Her body tingled a bit as she thought about sharing these revelations with Sarah.

A meow slipped into her consciousness and she was startled to see Mitote running over to rub against her legs.

"How did you get in here?" She was pretty sure she had last seen him go out. She crouched down to pet him and noticed something as she did. He had on a collar, one with a little gold-plated tag. She scooped him up into her arms and turned the tag toward the light to read its inscription. *Mitote* was all it said. Puzzled, she cocked her head and watched as he jumped down from her arms and strutted, tail in air.

She moved into the kitchen, confused and baffled, but the phone rang, demanding her attention. The phone was nowhere to be found, so she checked the ID on the base and saw that it was the same number that had been calling so often. She let it go to her machine, expecting to hear the familiar sounds of a dial tone. But when silence came through, she stood and stared. She could hear the faint sounds of someone breathing.

"Hi." Chan nearly crumbled as she recognized the voice at once. "It's Sarah. I've been trying to reach you."

Chan immediately started searching for the phone. This was it. This was her chance.

"I really would like to get together if at all possible."

"Me too!" Chan shouted, tossing pillows off the couch, wishing Sarah could hear her.

"I've been thinking about things, about you and…"

Chan straightened, ears trained.

"I really should tell you in person. Please, give me a call."

Chan dropped the pillow in her hand in defeat as Sarah gave her the number. She collapsed down onto the couch and tried to get her head straight. She felt butterflies inside at the thought of seeing Sarah again. Excited, she stood, hoping against hope that they could meet later that evening.

She was headed toward the hall to her bedroom when the doorbell rang. She hesitated, anxious to call Sarah back, not wanting to be bothered. It rang a second time before she could make up her mind about answering it. Sensing an urgency from whoever it was, she trotted to the door and peeked through the side window. More bells sounded but they were those in her head, alarmed.

Quickly, she unlocked the door and tugged it open. Kim stood in front of her trembling, mascara running down her face.

"Oh my God," Chan whispered as she ushered her inside. "What happened?" She closed the door behind them and locked it and then gently led Kim into the house.

Kim sobbed as she moved, unable to speak. Chan had just seen her at the office and she had been fine.

"Are you hurt?" Chan quickly ran her eyes over her friend and colleague. She breathed a little easier not seeing any signs of injury. But still she felt on edge and glanced around again for the phone. *Where the fuck is it?*

She focused back on Kim, easing her down onto the couch and handing her a Kleenex from the end table. Kim wiped her eyes and took in several shaky breaths, trying to calm down while Chan sat down next to her.

"What, what is it?" Chan probed gently.

"He…he"—she gasped—"he took the dog."

Chan shook her head in confusion. "What do you mean?"

Kim's eyes met hers and they were wide with terror. "I got home the other day and Buster, my dog, he wasn't there. And I panicked and started searching the neighborhood. I thought he just got out, you know?"

Chan nodded.

"When I got back home I checked my voicemail, and there was a message from Michael. He sounded really strange, like he was excited in an evil way, and he said he had taken Buster." She cried some more, unable to stop. Chan waited patiently for her to continue.

"Well, I relaxed a little, at least knowing that he was safe. I was upset, but I knew Michael did it to make me upset. So I just tacked it on to the list of things he's done to report to the police. I figured I would get my dog back."

Chan handed her another tissue, which she took gratefully.

"Michael kept calling after that. Saying that he knows who I'm seeing and that it had better stop."

"Does he know? Did he find out?"

"I don't see how. I make sure I'm not followed. Anyway, he keeps calling and threatening and then…and then this evening, I get home and there's this box by the front door."

Chan swallowed hard, afraid.

"I opened it and there was this collar." She looked up, eyes pooled with tears. "It was a collar I had never seen before, it looked new. It had Buster's name on it and there was blood. Blood on it."

Chan felt the heat of dizziness try to sway her. She reached out and grabbed Kim's shoulder.

"Oh God." Chan stood. "Oh God." Suddenly, her brain began working at lightning speed. She scanned the room for Mitote and found him at his food bowl. She bent down and unlatched the collar.

Kim turned toward the kitchen, watching her.

Chan hurried back to her side, panicked. She held up the collar. "I found this on my cat just now when I got home."

Kim took it slowly and Chan saw the recognition wash over her face.

Chan turned, fear consuming her. She rushed to the back door and turned the knob. It was unlocked. She looked back to Kim as she scurried for her keys.

"We're not safe here."

"What? Why?"

Chan thought of all the times she had found her door unlocked. And how Mitote had mysteriously gotten in.

"He's been here."

Kim stood and Chan grabbed her arm to lead her to the front door. She was afraid to go to her garage, afraid that he would be lurking in the dark hallway. She unlocked the door and pulled it open. A gun came at her face and she heard Kim shriek.

"Get inside!" Michael demanded, shoving his way in.

Chan stared up at him from the floor, where she had landed after tripping over her own feet. Kim shrieked again and began sobbing. Michael kicked the door closed and once again aimed the gun at

Chandler. "You fucked up my marriage! Corrupted my wife! You fucking dyke!"

Chan stopped trying to stand and sat very still. Michael's eyes were wild and crazed, and she didn't want to make any sudden movements.

"No!" Kim shouted, crying. "It's not her, you stupid son of a bitch!"

Michael turned and eyed her with hate. Kim took a step toward him, rage overcoming her fear.

"It's a man. A good man!"

"What!" He lowered the gun a fraction.

Chan stood very carefully, her blood singing loudly throughout her body.

"I don't believe you," he seethed.

"It's true!"

"Then tell me his name."

"No. Not until you give me Buster." She began to cry again. "Please, tell me you didn't hurt him."

Michael grinned and walked up to her. He grabbed her arm and yanked her to him. "I'll tell you about your dog. He's okay now, but unless you tell me where to find this prick you've been seeing, I'm going to cut him up. One piece at a time. Starting with his ears. And I'll deliver every piece to you. Every last one."

"No!" Kim grabbed his shoulders frantically. "Don't hurt him!"

"Who? The dog or the prick?" He grinned suddenly. "Maybe I should make you choose. How's that sound?"

Chan eased closer to him. She didn't know what she planned on doing, she only knew that she had to do something. Kim sobbed loudly and Michael laughed at her. She saw Chandler approaching and suddenly a look of fearlessness overtook her face.

"His name is William, and I won't let you hurt him!"

Chan was a step away when he caught sight of her. In an instant he turned and Kim screamed while reaching for the gun. It fired.

Chan heard the short crack and felt a burning in her belly. Kim screamed and screamed as Chan felt something warm on her hand. The gun fired again. Twice.

Chan pulled her hand away and saw the dark red stain. She was bleeding. She fell back to the floor and heard Kim crying. The room around her hazed. She could smell the gunpowder but couldn't seem to focus. Her ears rang.

Kim ran to her and tossed the gun aside in disgust. She had blood on her hands, but it wasn't hers. Chan couldn't hear what she was saying. She looked past her to where Michael lay on the floor. His chest wasn't moving.

They were safe now. Kim was trembling, dialing on her cell phone. Chan felt dizzy and lay all the way back to stare up at the ceiling.

In the distance she heard sirens. She blinked her heavy eyelids. Sarah. Sarah was coming. With that thought in mind she let her eyes drift closed.

❖

Sarah walked down the steps form her apartment. She had already tried to call Chandler again, with no luck. But this time she had left a message. Hopefully Chandler would call her back. Hopefully Chandler would give her another chance.

Lowering her head to dig out her car keys, she had just reached the bottom of the stairs when someone grabbed her by the shoulders and shook her, jarring her so badly she dropped her keys, frozen with alarm at the brash contact.

"Dave?"

His face was red his eyes terrified. He was in uniform and apparently on duty.

"What are—"

"There's no time, come on!" He tried to tug her along but she stopped to pick up her keys. "Come on!" he cried out as she jogged after him.

"What's going on?" She caught up to him as he opened the door to his cruiser.

"I've been trying to call you for the past half hour," he told her as he climbed inside.

Sarah thought quickly as she eased into the passenger seat. "I've been in the shower." *I was getting ready with the hopes of meeting up with Chandler.* She closed the door and looked to her phone, suddenly worried that she might have missed a call from her.

To her relief, there was only the call from Dave. Nerves awakened, suddenly alarmed, she focused on him as he sped out of the apartment parking lot. "What's going on?"

Her heart fell to her stomach when she saw him clench his jaw. "I'm afraid I have some bad news."

"What? What is it? Is it Nicky?"

Dave shook his head and tightened his grip on the steering wheel. "It's Chandler."

Sarah went weak and her head swam with heat.

Dave reached out and steadied her by bracing her arm. "It's okay, I got ya."

She leaned into him, her breathing suddenly stifled.

"What happened?" *Please, God, don't let it be true. Not now. Not ever. Not Chandler.* She did her best to breathe as images flooded her mind. "That goddamned bike," she whispered.

"No. It's something else."

Sarah felt the strength return to her body. It wasn't the bike. Chandler wasn't lying on some road torn and broken. Thank God.

"She was shot," Dave said, causing her calming heart to jump out of her chest.

"Oh God." The words hit home and she felt sick. *Shot? How the hell?*

Dave continued, reporting the information he had. "I was at the hospital following up on an accident. I saw them wheel her in as I was leaving. Apparently a patient of hers forced his way inside her house with a gun. His ex-wife works with Chandler and she was there too. Sounds like he had been stalking the both of them. The ex is okay. She was able to get the gun from him and shoot him." He paused and looked her way. "But not before he got a shot off that hit Chandler."

"How bad?" she asked, after a long moment of silence.

"It's bad."

Again the sickness, waves upon heavy waves. "No." Sarah wasn't sure if she'd spoken out loud or if her mind was simply screaming the denial.

"She's lost a lot of blood," Dave said. "Last I heard they were taking her into surgery."

Sarah stared out at the road, at the cars zooming by them. Why had she waited? Why had she waited so long to tell her? She would never forgive herself if Chandler died.

"Take me to her," she said simply.

Dave reached out and switched on the lights and siren.

Please don't die, Chandler. Don't you dare go and die.

❖

Soft globes of light stung her sensitive eyes. Chan blinked several times, forcing her heavy lids open. The haze around her slowly came into focus, although she could make no sense of it. Her ears strained to define the steady beeping next to her. She looked down to see her body covered with a light blue blanket. She tried to move but found it difficult. Sharp pain shot through her from her midsection. Groaning, she relaxed against the bed and licked her parched lips.

"Hey, stranger." A familiar voice came out of the darkness that edged the dimly lit room.

She blinked again and focused on her brother's face. "Ha…nk." Her throat felt raw and scratchy.

"Shh. Don't try and talk too much." He reached for her hand, surrounding it with his soft, warm ones. "Do you know where you are?"

Chan stared at him a moment longer, trying to comprehend his words. Meg stepped out of the darkness to come stand by her other side. She bent down and kissed Chan on the forehead. Chan could see that she had been crying.

"You're in the hospital," she said softly.

"I am?" Chan searched the strange room, then trained her eyes on her left arm and the tube running into the vein in her hand.

"Don't worry about that right now. Just concentrate on me," she heard Hank say.

"Am I…?" She licked her lips again. She couldn't make sense of anything. She heard her heart rate kick up on the machine as fear filled her confused mind. *What happened to me? Where am I?*

Hank squeezed her hand. "You were shot." He waited until she found his eyes before he continued. "You were attacked by your friend's ex-husband. He shot you here." His voice quaked with emotion as he rested his hand gently on her belly. "You're lucky to be alive."

Meg began to sob and stepped away, obviously not wanting to do so in front of her.

Chan studied Hank's face and noticed the rough growth of his beard and the shadows under his eyes. She couldn't remember the shooting. At least not at the moment. Her mind still seemed fuzzy. But what she could focus on alarmed her. Her brother and grandmother looked tortured.

"Are you okay?" she asked Hank.

"It's been hard seeing you like this." He swallowed back some rising emotion. "It reminded me of losing Mom and Dad and how lost I felt."

Chan felt the tears slip down her cheeks as she watched her brother cry. Suddenly she was back to that awful time in their life when they only had each other to lean on. Meg had stepped in to care for them, but it wasn't the same. No one could take the place of their loving, affectionate parents.

She knew now that she and Hank had never grieved properly. They had hidden away from the world, clinging to one another. She remembered not wanting to go to the services, and Hank had followed her lead. They had never really said good-bye.

"I'm sorry," she said, hating that she'd made her brother feel that way all over again.

Hank shook his head and Meg came back up to stand beside him. She placed a hand on his shoulder and one on Chan's arm as they all three quietly sobbed.

"We need to do this," Meg said, her knowing eyes comforting Chan. "We've been needing to do this for a long, long time. It's okay to miss them."

"Yes," Chan whispered as Hank continued to cry.

"We have each other and we have a baby on the way." Meg smiled up at Hank. "We've lost a lot but we've gained a lot as well."

She took Hank in her arms and they held each other for a long while. When they drew apart, they both leaned in to hold Chan.

Meg kissed her cheek and wiped away the cooling tears. "Now if we can only get Chandler to stop riding like a maniac, we'll be okay." She cracked a smile and Hank laughed.

Chan grinned. "I'll think about it." She didn't ever want to put her family through the kind of pain they had already been through. She was sorry that it took her nearly dying to see it.

The tears were wiped away and Meg settled back into the chair next to the bed. Chan's eyes had adjusted to the room and she could make out the walls and the chairs even though they were dim. She swallowed and realized how dry her throat was. She looked to Hank, suddenly overcome with thirst.

"Could I have some water?"

Hank moved to the bedside table where he spooned out small pellets of ice. He fed her the ice carefully and she nearly groaned with pleasure as the small pebbles warmed on her tongue. After allowing them to melt, she swallowed them and formed a question.

"How long have I been here?" She waited as her exhausted-looking brother spooned out some more ice for her.

"For a few days," he replied.

Mixed emotions ran through her. Images came, short and fast but dangerously moving. *Michael Gold.* She gasped as she saw his face. *Michael was pointing the gun at her. He was yelling at Kim. Kim was yelling back. Then a sound. A loud bang. And then Chan saw the blood.*

She blinked, remembering nothing more. "Am I?" She voiced her fear again, needing to know. "Going to be okay?"

"I think so." He kissed her hand. "You're too damn stubborn to let the bastard win." He laughed softly through his tears.

Suddenly, with the mention of Michael, she thought of Kim. "Is Kim okay?"

Hank nodded. "She's fine. She wasn't hurt."

"What about Michael?" she whispered.

"He was killed. Kim shot him."

Chan felt a sadness and a strange peace wash over her. Kim was okay; she was going to be okay. Her eyes grew heavy as the peace warmed her.

Meg approached again to whisper to her as she struggled to keep her eyes open. "Get some rest now."

A soft, warm kiss landed on Chan's cheek, and she heard a name in the calm distance. *Sarah.* It floated to her as she drifted off into the soothing darkness.

CHAPTER TWENTY-THREE

Sarah stepped to the side as Chandler's brother walked from the room. He paused in the hallway and pulled his wrists away from his watery eyes. Sarah thought about approaching him but decided against it. She didn't want to intrude and sometimes, she had recently learned, it was just better to let it out. He caught sight of her and, sniffling, he took several steps toward her.

"I didn't know you were here."

Sarah suddenly felt intrusive, having witnessed his private pain. "I'm sorry, I should've gone."

"No, it's okay." He breathed deep. "You're Chan's friend, right?" He studied her and she could see his mind working to place her.

She had been at Chandler's bedside every day, leaving only when her family returned from their brief breaks. Dave too had been there some of the time.

"Yes," she replied.

"I'm Hank." He offered his hand.

"Sarah." They shook and she could feel him assessing her.

"I've met you before, haven't I?"

Sarah sighed inwardly. He was starting to remember. How was she going to tell him that yes, she was the cop who pulled them over? That yes, she had been seeing Chandler intimately. That yes, she was the one who should've told Chandler long ago how she felt. How could she say all that?

"Yes." She offered him no more, the guilt eating away at her.

He was silent for a few moments and then suddenly came to life, snapping his fingers. "You're that cop." He pointed at her. "The one who threatened to arrest her!" He smiled, proud that he had finally placed her. "Have you two been seeing one another?" His voice was light and curious, seemingly surprised by the notion.

She nodded. "Some." *Maybe a lot more if I would've allowed it.*

"She's been awake for a couple of days now. Go on in and see her."

Sarah didn't move. Seeing Chandler asleep and seriously injured had been hard enough; she didn't know what she would say to her now that she was awake. *Hi, remember me? I'm the one who kept running from you.* The courage she had mustered before the shooting vanished. It was nowhere to be found.

"I don't think I can," she confessed softly.

Hank seemed to understand. "I know. It's been tough for me too. For all of us." He started pacing again. "It's so hard to see her like that."

Sarah fought back tears and steadied her weakened body. The past couple of weeks had been devastatingly difficult. She had faced her abuser, buried her father, and lived the waking nightmare of Chandler's fight to live. At one point she thought she would have to bury her too. There were now two people she had neglected because of her pride, because of her fears.

Hank seemed to sense something of her turmoil and startled her by wrapping his arms around her. As he held her, she realized he was a lot like Chandler. Fiery and passionate, a daredevil who was easy with his affection. She had liked him the first day she met him. She had sensed he was a good guy and now she knew it for certain.

He eased away, making sure to hold her eyes. "It's not easy loving a Brogan." His green eyes were similar to Chandler's, and they seemed to read her. "Chan's stubborn. And driven to do what she wants. This won't be the last time she scares you. As my wife says, 'If you love a Brogan, you're in for one hell of a ride.'" He smiled. "You've seen her ride. You know what I'm talking about."

Sarah nodded.

"We may be wild, but we're passionate. And when we love, we love deeply." He paused, then said, as if the words spilled out, "She's worth it, Sarah."

Sarah swallowed. "I know."

CHAPTER TWENTY-FOUR

Sarah strode to the door and pushed it open with a new sense of purpose. She had almost lost Chandler, and she wasn't about to let it happen again. The courage she had lost would have to catch up fast, because this time she wasn't stopping.

Chandler was resting quietly, her eyes closed and peaceful. Sarah rounded the bed and smiled politely at Chandler's grandmother.

"I don't think she's sleeping yet," Meg said. She patted her granddaughter's hand. "Chandler, you have a visitor." She got to her feet and told Sarah, "I'll leave you two alone."

Chandler's eyes fluttered as the door closed behind Meg. Slowly, she opened them and took lengthy blinks before focusing on Sarah's face. A spark flickered in the green depths of her eyes and she smiled.

With her heart fluttering, Sarah smiled in return.

"I would ask how I look, but I'm afraid of the answer." Chandler spoke with a surprisingly strong voice.

Sarah nearly cried at hearing her speak again. She reached out and stroked her face, needing to feel her alive and okay. Chandler looked at her with surprise and sighed at the touch.

Sarah felt the heat rush to her cheeks as she took in her beauty. Some color was back in her face and she felt warm and soft. "You look better than anything I've ever seen."

She meant every word. She had prayed night and day to any and every god she could think of that Chandler would recover. Seeing her, hearing her, feeling her…it was truly a miracle.

"Smooth talker." Chandler's eyes flashed with life and then grew serious. "I'm surprised to see you." She looked off, deep in thought, and grew quiet.

Sarah trembled inwardly, nearly breaking at Chandler's words. "I know. I've run from you a lot. And I'm so sorry. I was just so afraid and…"

"Afraid of what? Of me?"

"Yes."

"Why?"

Oh God, how can I tell you all that you make me feel? Sarah lowered her eyes and forced herself to try. "Because you make me feel, Chandler. Because you reach into me, move me."

"Why is that something to fear?"

Sarah thought and noted just how different they were. She was controlled and reserved, while Chandler was passionate and emotional. It wasn't a surprise that Chandler didn't understand.

"Because I've never felt like that before," Sarah explained. "At first I thought it was just great sex…" She trailed off and Chandler laughed a little.

"The sex was good, wasn't it?"

"Unbelievably so."

A moment of silence passed and then Chandler cocked her head. "You're not falling for me are you, Officer Monroe?" She squeezed Sarah's hand playfully, an obvious attempt to ease the tension. But Sarah didn't respond, her voice overwhelmed by the answer that waited. Chandler watched, her face growing serious. "Are you?"

"Yes," Sarah finally managed to say, her voice thick with emotion. "When I found out you were hurt, I nearly died inside. And I was so mad at myself for not telling you sooner how I felt. For not giving you a chance."

"Tell me how you feel," Chandler said softly.

Full of so many different emotions, Sarah decided to let them out, whether they made sense or not. "Alive. Crazy. Floating. Burning. Elated. And terrified, by all of it. And then with the shooting…I was scared out of my mind at the thought of losing you. Like my heart was being torn bit by bit, my soul ripped out of my chest." She paused and lowered her voice.

Chandler watched and listened, her face coloring with emotion. She tried to smile, but it was obvious she was fighting back tears.

Sarah continued, holding Chandler's hand with both of her own. "But more than any of those feelings," she whispered, "I feel grateful. Grateful at having you here. At getting another shot."

Tears fell from Chandler's bright eyes. "You mean, you actually want to see me again?" she teased.

"If it's something you want." *This is the life I want. The place I want to be. Here. And with you. I don't need to run anymore.*

Chandler looked away, emotion threatening to break. "I'm afraid you'll run again."

The words tore at Sarah's exposed heart. "And I'm afraid you'll stir things in me I've never felt before. I'm afraid you'll grab hold of my heart and force me to feel."

"Then why do this?" Chandler seemed genuinely willing to give her room to be and do only what was comfortable for her.

"Because I can't bear to think of being without you. Because I'm no longer going to let my fears rule my decisions." Sarah waited patiently, having given Chandler all she could at the present moment. But she feared it wasn't going to be enough.

"Promise me something," Chandler finally said.

Sarah nodded. "Anything."

"If you feel like running…instead of taking off, could you try and talk to me about it first?"

Sarah held back some of her own emotion. Chandler was going to give it another shot. It was what she wanted, more than anything.

"Okay," she whispered.

Chandler smiled warmly, obviously content with the promise. "We'll work through things together. It might not be easy, but I happen to think you're cute and worth the fight."

"Well, I think I'll own up to that promise right now, that is, if you don't mind."

Chandler eyed her curiously. "You're not itching to run out on me already, are you?"

Sarah laughed and shook her head. "No. But I do owe you some sort of explanation for doing so before."

Chandler sat up straighter and gripped her hand. "No, you don't. You don't owe me anything."

She didn't want Sarah to feel like she had to do anything. All she wanted was to be with her. "If you want to tell me something, then please do so of your own free will. Don't do it out of obligation."

Sarah patted her hand. "It's okay, Chan. I want to. I want you to know." She inhaled deeply. "My father recently passed away."

Chandler felt her throat burn with emotion. While she was thrilled that Sarah was telling her, she also hurt for her. "I'm so sorry."

"He was sick, and had been for some time." Sarah breathed deep again, obviously searching for strength. "I didn't have a good relationship with my folks. They both drank heavily throughout my childhood. Our home was always one big party. I resented them from very early on and virtually raised myself." She met Chandler's eyes. "I'm sure, with you being a psychologist, you can see what it probably did to me."

"Of course. That alone explains a lot."

Sarah nodded. "It's why I value control so much, why it was important for me to have my life and surroundings absolutely organized."

"It was the only way you felt safe," Chandler interpreted softly.

"Yes." Another sigh. "There's something else."

"Okay."

"When I was thirteen, one of my father's friends began to sexually abuse me."

"That's terrible, Sarah." She held her hand tighter.

"My parents didn't know. They were too drunk to notice it going on right underneath their noses. I resented them for it, blamed them for it."

"I can understand why."

"For years I thought about telling them, of yelling it to them, screaming in their face. But when I walked in that room that night and saw my father lying there so weak, so sick, all of the bad feelings, they vanished. It suddenly didn't matter anymore. Not as far as they were concerned." She fell silent, her voice quivering.

Chandler thought for a long while before speaking. "Have you dealt with your feelings in regard to this abuser?"

Sarah nodded. "I went to see him, soon after I ran from you one night. I confronted him and it helped. I know that he can't hurt anyone else. Not anymore."

"What happened to him?"

"He's in prison." Sarah paused, her voice catching. "He's a prisoner of his mind, trapped in his body."

"I don't understand."

"He was attacked years ago. Beaten nearly to death with a hammer by the boyfriend of one of his victims."

"Oh my God." Chandler covered her mouth, disturbed.

"He's immobile now, unable to speak or even stand."

"Did seeing him like that make you feel better?"

"No."

"What did?"

"Seeing the recognition in his eyes. Knowing that he knew who I was. And that I was no longer afraid. I was no longer his victim."

"I see," Chandler responded. "Are you okay now? Okay with the way things are?" *Have you found your peace, Sarah? Do I make you feel safe, as safe as you make me feel?*

"A month ago, I would've said having my life just the way I wanted was what I wanted. Concentrating on my goals and achieving them, leaving this place and never looking back. Going off to the FBI. I would've said that was what I wanted. That was what made me feel okay."

"What about now? What makes you feel safe now?" Chandler repeated softly, needing to know, dying to know.

"Honestly?"

"Yes."

"You."

"Me?" Chandler felt her bones melt with a warmth she had never felt before.

"Yes. I can't explain it, but I feel like I can tell you anything and that you'll understand, that you'll stand by me. Even if we never had a physical relationship again, I feel like you are the friend I've always longed for, and needed."

Chandler smiled through her pooling tears and reached up to stroke Sarah's face. "We are still going to have a physical relationship, aren't we?" She laughed softly, seeing the desire haze Sarah's eyes as she touched her.

Sarah cleared her throat. "Just as soon as you're ready."

"There's no harm in fooling around a little in the meantime." Chandler leaned in and met Sarah's lips softly, melting into their warmth.

Sarah kissed her back gently and Chandler attempted to shift closer but the pain stopped her. Groaning, she pulled away and was moved by the burning innocence in Sarah's eyes. She was so vulnerable and fresh and alive.

"You sure you're up for all this? With me and my wild ways?" She wasn't just referring to the sex, but to everything. The way she lived her life, with spontaneity and passion.

Sarah sighed playfully. "As much as I hate to admit it, it's what draws me to you."

"Really?"

"Your passion, your emotion. You truly live life, and feel it. So different from me."

"And I love your levelheadedness," Chandler said. "Your ability to live life with a distant, calm assessment. So strong, so wise…"

"So boring."

"What?" Chandler laughed and wiped a tear. "No. Oh no. Hardly boring. Your attitude, your confidence, your quiet, controlled grace. It's sexy. Very sexy. And intriguing."

"It's an illusion," Sarah said.

"No, it's not. Not all of it. I was wrong about you, Sarah. Wrong about a lot of things. You're strong and capable and willing to confront your demons. I'm proud of you for that and honored that you're willing to talk to me about it."

"What about you? What about your demons?"

Chandler thought for a moment, a little surprised at the question. What about her demons? The sense of emptiness, the loneliness, the trying desperately to avoid feeling that void by pushing the limit. She thought about that pain, about the loss she'd never recovered from. Tears tightened her throat. She thought about seeing that pain in Hank's eyes again as she lay in the hospital bed. She saw it in Meg's eyes. And she knew how badly it hurt to feel that pain of loss. Because as she lay there, watching her family cry, she'd allowed that pain to enter her mind. She felt it full force and mourned for her parents in the way she should've done years ago.

"I finally let them go," she said, thinking of her parents and how she'd imagined them surrounded in warm light and smiling down upon her. "I've opened my mind and my heart." She smiled, thinking of her niece, growing inside Kelly, Hank's hand resting on his wife's belly. And then she thought of Sarah, and how whole the woman made her feel.

"I'm ready to live. And I want you in my life. I go home tomorrow," she whispered. "Will you come around to welcome me?"

Sarah smiled, her eyes showing how much the words touched her. "Absolutely."

CHAPTER TWENTY-FIVE

The sun poured in through the windows as Meg opened all the blinds. Chan stood watching, loving the feel of home.

"I don't know," Meg said, eyeing her with concern. "You sure you're going to be okay?"

They had only arrived an hour before, and Meg was obviously worried about leaving her alone. Chan, however, was ready to get her life back.

"I'll be fine." She traced the tops of the cushions of her couch as she walked by, lost in the warm glow of the sun. She stood in front of the back door and gazed out into the yard. Unconsciously, she turned the knob and her heart rate slowed a little when she found it to be locked. She looked down through the pane of glass on the French door, hoping but finding nothing.

"Mitote?" she asked.

Meg busied herself rearranging some of the flowers they had brought home from the hospital. "I haven't seen him."

"It's been such a long time," Chan said, worried about her missing cat.

"Are you sure you're going to be okay?" Meg fussed around her some more.

"I'm going to be fine. Now go." Chan grinned and wandered into the front room.

She expected to find the front door looking overly large and ominous, but it seemed rather plain to her now that she was facing it. Her eyes panned the floor. It was bare, the rug long gone, stained forever with blood. Unlike her life, though, the rug could be replaced.

She continued to look around and relaxed even more as she noted the normalcy of her home.

Meg came to stand beside her, cupping her elbow.

"I guess I'll be shopping for a new rug," Chan said.

It was the only thing that needed to be done, and for that she was eternally grateful. Her body would heal and so would her home.

Meg pulled her in for a hug. "I could stay. For as long as you need me. I could sleep in the spare bedroom."

Chan gave a laugh. She knew her grandmother was worried, but life had to go on. She placed her hands on Meg's shoulder and looked her square in the eye. "Go," she repeated.

"Okay, okay. But if you need me, promise you'll call."

They headed back through the house to the door that led to the garage where they stopped and faced one another again.

"I promise." Chan held Meg close and felt her stifle a sob. She pulled back and took her face in her hands. "I love you," she said.

Meg's eyes widened with surprise. Chan rarely spoke such strong words. Beaming, she said, "I love you too."

❖

Sarah stood at the front door, a nervous wreck. She had hoped to be there earlier but she had spent the afternoon shopping, preparing, and calming her nerves. As the sun set behind her, she took a deep breath and rang the doorbell. She bounced a little on the balls of her feet and tightened her grip on the grocery bags she was holding. She heard the click of the lock before she could muster something suave to say.

Chan opened the door slowly and smiled. An inner glow lit up her form, and Sarah stood in awe, completely turned on by the tomboy in front of her.

"Wow." It was a whisper, but it was heard.

Chan glanced down at her attire, suddenly self-conscious. "I didn't get a chance to change."

She had been busy in her office trying to get caught up on work. Time had simply slipped by as she sat comfortably at her desk doing the work that felt wonderfully familiar. Work she used to put off. She took a step back to allow Sarah to enter.

Sarah stepped inside, her eyes still glued to Chan. "Why would you change? You look incredible."

She was a little thinner than before, her body marked by what had occurred. But she was still strong and athletic looking, proof positive that she would make it through. Sarah swallowed hard, moved by the emotion of what had happened and moved more by the strength of her. She was beautiful.

Chan glanced down and fingered the thin material of her white tank top. "I could've put on something a little more appropriate. This is just more comfortable against my wound."

"No don't," Sarah let out before she could stop herself. "Change, that is." She felt her cheeks flood with heat.

Her eyes swept over the threadbare material stretching taut across Chan's generous breasts. The nipples were soft and the surrounding skin just dark enough to show through the fabric. Sarah nervously looked downward, concentrating instead on the flannel sleep pants, which hugged her hips just right.

Chan watched her and laughed softly. It seemed her innocent choice of pajamas was doing more than most lingerie. "You're blushing, Officer Monroe."

"I know." Sarah was intensely aware of feelings so fresh and powerful she couldn't deny them if she wanted to. "It's just good to see you so…healthy."

"It's good to see you too," Chan said, a little breathless.

Sarah stood very still, trying to get a grip on her swirling insides. The air between them grew heavy and thick, difficult to breathe. Chan was watching her too, her breathing short and shallow. Sarah read her eyes and knew what it was they both wanted. Slowly she bent down and released the bags. Her body tingled, alive with the need to take her in. All of her. Her scent, her breath, her skin. She stepped into her and paused a mere inch away. The lightning between them ricocheted, electrifying her heart, tightening her chest. She could almost see it as it branched upward from Chan's midsection, veining up through her, heating her cheeks, and making her tremble.

Sarah fought to breathe. She reached out, a moment frozen in time, and touched her skin, caressed her jaw. "I want to kiss you," she whispered, somehow finding her voice. She caught her scent as she leaned in, amber and lavender.

"Please do." Chan felt the other woman shudder just before they touched.

Their lips met softly, and Sarah sighed at the feel of her. Warm, plump, and sensuous. Chan's breath caressed her, tentative yet ready, encouraging her further. Sarah pressed in against her and then took the lips into her own, needing to feel as much of Chan as she could. She massaged the warm flesh, holding each lip captive, tasting, feeling, yearning. Her tongue probed gently, slowly lining Chan and then dipping into her parted mouth. It was hot, soft, wet.

Chan moaned as her body swooned. Her tongue touched Sarah's and they teased, lightly caressing as if they were meeting for the first time.

The feel of Chan moving inside shot flames through Sarah. She had to have more, she was desperate for more. She reached out and held her, pulled her closer. But Chan stiffened.

"I have to be careful." She glanced down to her midsection, where Sarah's hands held her.

"Oh, I'm sorry." Sarah moved her hands at once and took a step back, startled and worried she had hurt her.

Chan reacted just as quickly, grabbing Sarah's wrists and tugging her back against her. "Don't be." She brought Sarah's hands up to her breasts and burned a heated gaze into her. "Don't ever be sorry for touching me."

Sarah swallowed against the raging desire rising up through her. Chan seemed to sense it and leaned in to breathe against her neck, voicing her wants and desires. "Touch me, Sarah." Her hands fell away from Sarah's wrists, freeing them.

Sarah held the full breasts in her hands, their weight and warmth electrifying her body. She squeezed and ran her thumbs over the nipples.

Chan shuddered and purred, "Yes."

Sarah watched, noticing everything about her as she stroked the firming nipples. She saw the pulse beat under Chan's skin, saw the twitch of her lip in excitement, saw the fire flame up in her eyes. Unable to resist, she lowered her head and tasted the beautiful skin that beat with the arousal of Chan's racing heart. It was damp, sweet, warm.

"Yes," Chan cried out.

Sarah continued, her own blood heating to dangerous levels. She nibbled behind Chan's ear and held the nipples firm between her fingers. Chan jerked and trembled, completely turned on. She looked into Sarah's eyes with a hazy, heavy look of arousal.

Sarah knew that look, would die for that look. But it was too soon. It was happening too fast. "Wait," she said, stepping back.

"What's wrong?" Chan's heart leapt with fear. She couldn't bear to have Sarah retreat from her again.

"Nothing!" Sarah was quick to respond, seeing the worry in her eyes. She reached down for the bags.

Chan watched her curiously, confused. Sarah headed for the kitchen. She set the goods down on the counter and turned slightly as she dug through the bags so she could see Chan.

"I want everything to be"—Sarah met her eyes before continuing—"perfect."

"It already is," Chan responded coming up to wrap her arms around her. She could tell Sarah was nervous, and she wanted to make her feel as comfortable as possible. Just her being there was enough.

"Not just yet." Sarah retrieved a CD. "Do you have a stereo?"

Chan grinned a little, pleasantly perplexed. "Yes. What are you up to?"

"It's in your bedroom, right?"

"Yes."

Sarah lifted the bags and started into the bedroom. "Give me a few minutes, okay?"

"Okay."

Sarah worked quickly. She opened the CD and placed it in the player that was nestled in the large curio cabinet across from the bed. Next she retrieved the candles and placed them throughout the room, lighting each one. Their glow kissed the room softly, just as she hoped. Then she pulled out all the pale roses save one. She plucked the petals free and let them fall to the bed. Lastly, she pulled out the box of chocolate-covered cherries and debated.

She wanted everything to be perfect. She had never done this for a lover before, and she was a little unsure. But Chan wasn't just another lover. Chan was everything. She decided to open them up.

She placed them one by one on the night table, stacking them into a neat little mound of chocolate. With her hands on her hips, she examined the room and, satisfied, picked up the remaining rose. She pushed the play button on the stereo and adjusted the volume on her way out. With her heart in her hands, she walked into the hallway.

Chan stood waiting, her eyes searching Sarah's for answers. She started to say something but then stopped, the music having reached her. She cocked her head a little, the sound familiar. "Loreena McKennitt." She took a step closer and stood before Sarah, listening. "It's my favorite," she whispered.

The sultry Irish beats of *The Book of Secrets* moved her, spoke to her. It was the most beautiful music she had ever heard. And hearing it with Sarah there, right in front of her, nearly made her dizzy.

Sarah held out the rose. "For you."

Chan took it slowly. "A candlelight rose. Also my favorite." She looked again to Sarah. "How did you know?" She brought the rose to her nose and inhaled deeply. Somehow Sarah was reaching down deep inside her and shining a light into her soul.

"I asked Hank."

Chan grinned at the honesty. She was beyond flattered. "You didn't have to go to all this trouble."

"It's no trouble at all."

Chan saw a new look wash over her incredible face. The halo in her eyes shone like an October moon.

Sarah leaned in and held her face. "I love you, Chandler Brogan."

Chan felt her lip quiver as she responded. "And I love you."

Sarah kissed her, wanting to taste the sweet words she had so longed to hear. Their tongues met and danced, stroked and spoke. Sarah felt Chan tremble and then pull away. She gazed up into her with eyes so full and wild, Sarah nearly gasped.

"Take me to my bed."

It was a demand very similar to the one Sarah had given the night they first made love. Now it was Chan stating her wants and desires. Sarah felt her chest tighten around her maddening heart, ensuring that the desire she felt would never escape. She had never been so turned on in her life.

Chan stood looking at her, all hungry and fiery, busting through her tank top with every ragged breath.

"Say it again," Sarah heard herself say as her flesh pounded with the racing beat of her heart.

Chan spoke again and Sarah watched her eyes spark, her cheeks color, and her lips plead. "Take me to my bed."

Sarah reached out for her, tugging her into her. She claimed Chan's full lips, pulled the words from them again and again. Chan melted against her and Sarah stopped kissing her long enough to bend down and scoop her up into her arms.

"Hurry," Chan whispered in her ear.

Sarah hurried down the hall to the bedroom where she set Chan down as gently as she could.

Chan stood clinging to her as she gazed around the room. "It's beautiful." The candlelight, the rose petals, the music. It was romance she had never experienced firsthand. "You really were listening at that party."

She smiled, teasing, but Sarah's look was serious and Chan felt her quiver.

"This is how I always imagined…" Sarah glanced away, unable to find the words. She had dreamt of this moment from the time she was old enough to understand her feelings. Now it was happening, and it was more overwhelming than she could've ever imagined.

"I understand." Chan touched her cheek, completely moved by Sarah's sensuality. Sarah trembled again as her eyes, full of love, settled back on Chan's.

"Will you show me?" Chan asked. "Show me your dream?"

Sarah nodded, wanting to do nothing else even if it were her last dying moment. Pulling Chan into her arms, she kissed her sweetly, slowly, savoring the way she felt, the way she tasted. Sarah got lost in her and closed her eyes, wishing she could never find her way back. Her fingers traveled lightly down to Chan's sides, easing up the tank top to feel her warm skin. She felt Chan shudder under her touch and pushed the shirt up farther.

Chan drew back and lifted her arms very carefully. Sarah saw the wound and helped Chan remove the shirt.

"I'll be careful," she promised, running her fingers around the white dressing. Her eyes drifted back to Chan's and then up and down her body. She felt a rush of heat as her hands skimmed over the full breasts. Chan sucked in a breath of desire as Sarah caressed them, paying careful attention to the sensitive nipples.

She moved her hands lower again, down Chan's sides to the waistband of the pajama pants. She eased them down slowly, dropping down to one knee as she did so. Chan stepped out of them, breathing heavily as Sarah inhaled the skin of her upper thighs.

"No panties?" Sarah noted, trying to maintain the control she was quickly losing.

"No," Chan managed between ragged breaths.

Sarah kissed the well-muscled thighs and grazed her hands over Chan's hips as she raised to stand before her. "Can you lie down?" she asked.

"Yes. But can we undress you first?"

Sarah nodded, a little hesitantly.

Chan reached out and unbuttoned her shirt, her eyes never leaving Sarah's. She eased the shirt over Sarah's shoulders and let it fall to the floor. She leaned in and felt Sarah's hot skin on her cheek as she unhooked the bra. Sarah pulled it free and Chan couldn't help but reach out to touch the puckering breasts. She stopped, though, just before she touched them, remembering that she needed to go slow—and let Sarah lead the way.

Sarah watched, her breath heavy and thick. Chan lowered her hands to the jeans, which she unbuttoned and attempted to push downward. Sarah helped her and stripped them off. Chan eyed the white satin panties and carefully eased her fingers under the sides to push them down. Sarah took over when Chan couldn't bend any lower. She removed the panties and they both stood nude, the candlelight breathing upon them, just like the music.

Chan sat on the bed. "You want me to lie down?"

"Yes."

She did so, very slowly, settling on the middle of the bed, the cool soft petals against her skin. She watched in wonder as Sarah settled in next to her, lying on her side.

"Close your eyes," Sarah whispered.

Chan did as requested. Sarah took her hands and gathered up as many rose petals as she could. Then, as carefully as she could, she let them fall upon Chan's body. Chan made a sound at the contact and Sarah continued until the last petal fell. She gazed down upon Chan in amazement and then touched her, using her fingertips and the satin of the petals, caressing, awakening, worshipping.

Chan began to move underneath her, writhing, wanting.

"Give me your hand," Sarah softly commanded.

Chan did so and kept her eyes closed. Sarah took it delicately and placed it on her abdomen, just shy of the covered injury. She spread Chan's fingers and leaned in to kiss her. She kissed first the back of her hand and then made her way lower to her fingers. Chan made a soft noise at every touch, at every warm breath that graced her skin.

Sarah continued the soft kissing and then extended her tongue. She used it carefully, licking and lining between Chan's fingers. Chan moaned at the sensation and Sarah continued, tasting her skin exposed between the petals and awakening the skin between her fingers.

"Now give me your other hand," she requested.

Chan did and Sarah led them both up to Chan's chest. She placed them very carefully on top of her breasts. She spread the fingers, just like before, framing the nipples. Chan opened her eyes, anticipating.

Sarah kissed her cheek and whispered, "Eyes closed."

She leaned in and kissed each hand, slowly, lightly. Chan's nipples hardened under her breath. Then she used her tongue, licking in between the fingers and the nipple at the same time. Chan cried out at the sensation and writhed. She began to pant and her eyes flew open as Sarah took each finger in her mouth and sucked, one at a time. Sarah lowered her head and took the nipples inside, sucking them just as she had done her fingers.

Her pleasure mounting, Chan could not resist lifting herself slightly to see.

"Shh," Sarah said, easing her back down. "Don't move too much."

Chan shook her head, the pain the furthest thing from her mind. "I'm not going to be able to lie still," she confessed, trying to sit up. She wanted to touch Sarah. Had to have her.

"No," Sarah said, easing her back down. "You have to be still."

"But I can't." Chan was turned on and nothing was going to stop her, injured or not. The rose petals, the licking, the sucking, it all had started an enormous fire within her. She was about to protest again when she felt Sarah between her legs. "Oh God!" she cried out, feeling the long fingers slide up inside her.

"Shh," Sarah cooed. "Lie back and relax."

Chan did as requested, her heart throbbing between her legs.

Sarah carefully began to stroke, up and down and all around. She worked Chan slowly, as slowly as she could. Chan moaned and writhed but Sarah kept careful control, not letting her get too excited.

"Please, just take me," Chan pleaded, the fire inside her burning out of control. "Please." She couldn't take much more of the sweet, sweet torture.

The words burned Sarah's ears and touched her desire, raising it higher and hotter. She was quickly losing control. Closing her eyes, she concentrated on touch. Chan felt tight and hot and wet. Clinging to her. Bearing down on her.

The music rushed through her, down her arm and into her hand. It poured from her fingers and stroked up inside of Chan in perfect rhythm. Sarah opened her eyes and increased her motion. They fixed on Chan.

"I want to feel you," she said, her voice dark with desire. "I want to feel you inside of me." It was time, and she wanted Chan. Wanted to feel her in every way possible. From inside. She crawled up to her knees and inched closer.

Chan was looking at her with bright, lustful eyes. "You sure?" she breathed.

"Yes." Sarah took her hand and led it slowly to the flesh between her legs. She felt Chan caress her and she jerked at how good it felt. Her own hand continued to pump and she closed her eyes again as Chan slowly and carefully eased her fingers up inside.

Sarah sucked in a quick breath. It felt so good, so full. Heat seemed to spread up from Chan's fingers, igniting every last cell as it journeyed upward into her belly.

"You okay?" Chan asked.

"God, yes." She began to move her own hand again deep inside of Chan. "Don't stop."

Opening her eyes and moving in closer, she kissed Chan then, hard and wet as their hands played the notes of the beautiful music. She felt Chan begin to tense and pulled away and slowed her hand, time and time again, until she herself could take no more and gasped, "I want to come with you, Chandler."

Chan answered with a heated kiss, one full of swirling, hungry tongue.

Sarah pumped her quicker and rocked against Chan's hand. "Oh God," she breathed.

"Yes," Chan said. "You feel so good. I'm going to come."

Sarah stroked her until she felt the walls clench down around her. Then she slowed her thrusting and did it hard and deep and slow. Chan cried out as the orgasm hit and Sarah milked her long and slow, loving the beautiful sight of her face as she came.

Then as she watched and felt her, Sarah came. It hit hard and fast and hot, Chan up inside her, loving her, pleasing her, taking her to new worlds. She closed her eyes and rocked, nothing having ever felt so good. A groan escaped her throat, the pleasure getting better and better and better. She didn't ever think it would stop. She opened her eyes as her body took all it could. Took all of Chan.

"I love you," Chan said.

Sarah crumpled and shuddered, her body trembling, riding out the last little bit. "I love you."

And then it was gone. She stilled, heavenly spent. A few sparks lit and flew up through her. Aftermaths. She jerked as they too seemed to evaporate from her body.

Her heavy eyes focused on Chan.

"I can still feel you." Chan said.

"I can feel you too."

"That was unbelievable."

"Yes it was." Sarah glanced down. "Are you okay?"

"Never better."

"Did it hurt?"

"Are you kidding me?" Chan slowly removed her fingers from deep inside of Sarah. "Come here," she said gently, wanting to hold her, to feel this incredible woman next to her.

Sarah eased up beside her and kissed her neck.

"Are you okay?" Chan asked.

Sarah propped up on her elbow. "I've never been better."

Chan grinned. "Good. Are you gonna kiss me now?"

"Absolutely." Sarah kissed her long and soft and then settled in next to her, relishing in the warm, soft feel of her body.

"Sarah?"

"Yeah?"

"Are you going to stay inside me?"

Sarah laughed a little. "I was thinking about it. Do you mind?"

"Well, no. But it's not a good idea if you were planning on going to sleep."

"Why's that?"

"You know why."

"Well, who said anything about sleep?" Sarah moved her fingers, causing Chan to inhale quickly.

"I'm supposed to take it easy, remember?" Chan teased as Sarah rose back up to kiss her way down her midsection.

"Oh, I'll be careful." She kissed slower and longer as she neared Chan's center. "I'll be very careful."

❖

The sun drifted in and greeted Chan's eyes as they opened to take in the morning. The sheet kissed her bare skin as she carefully stretched. She felt the cool softness of the ivory rose petals that were strewn across the bedsheets. She grinned as memories came, and searched the room for her lover.

As if on cue the gorgeous woman entered, beautifully nude and carrying a gray bundle of fur.

"Good morning," she greeted, leaning in for a soft, lingering kiss. "I'm glad you're up. This guy's been trying to get at you all morning."

Chan sat up and took her cat, who was already purring loudly. She held him up and examined him. "I was so worried about you." She kissed his nose and set him free, thankful he was okay. He plopped down and rolled over, offering his belly.

"He was at the back door bright and early this morning," Sarah said, stroking her face.

Chan nearly swooned from the feel of her. "Did you get any sleep?" They had made love long into the night, and somehow Sarah had made her come two more times without hurting her wound. The woman was an incredible lover in every way imaginable. Chan couldn't have imagined a better lover.

"Enough." Sarah grinned. "You hungry?"

"Starved. I smell pancakes. Did you cook?"

"Yes, I did. No, wait right there. I'll go get it."

"Breakfast in bed?"

"Yes."

"The candles, the music, the roses, and breakfast in bed? Does this fantasy of yours ever end?"

"No." Again the grin. "I'll go get breakfast. And then," Sarah bent down for a kiss, "I'll show you what the chocolates are for."

About the Author

Born in North Carolina, Ronica Black now lives in the desert Southwest, where she spends her time painting, drawing, and writing. A lover of true crime books, she spends any remaining time engrossed in the tales of unsolved crimes and forensic files, where she gets many of her story ideas. Romance, passion, and creativity are her great fortunes, and she shares them all with the woman she loves.

Reading, photography and outdoor sports are a few of her other sources of entertainment. She also relishes being an aunt and she thoroughly enjoys the time spent with family and friends.

In addition to the erotic intrigue novel *In Too Deep* from Bold Strokes Books, she has short story selections in *Erotic Interludes 2: Stolen Moments* and *Erotic Interludes 3: Lessons in Love* from Bold Strokes Books and *Ultimate Lesbian Erotica 2005* from Alyson Books.

For more info on Ronica, visit her Web site at www.ronicablack. com.

Books Available From Bold Strokes Books

Wild Abandon by Ronica Black. From their first tumultuous meeting, Dr. Chandler Brogan and Officer Sarah Monroe are drawn together by their common obsessions—sex, speed, and danger. (1-933110-35-X)

Turn Back Time by Radclyffe. Pearce Rifkin and Wynter Thompson have nothing in common but a shared passion for surgery. They clash at every opportunity, especially when matters of the heart are suddenly at stake. (1-933110-34-1)

Chance by Grace Lennox. At twenty-six, Chance Delaney decides her life isn't working so she swaps it for a different one. What follows is the sexy, funny, touching story of two women who, in finding themselves, also find one another. (1-933110-31-7)

The Exile and the Sorcerer by Jane Fletcher. First in the Lyremouth Chronicles. Tevi, wounded and adrift, arrives in the courtyard of a shy young sorcerer. Together they face monsters, magic, and the challenge of loving despite their differences. (1-933110-32-5)

A Matter of Trust by Radclyffe. JT Sloan is a cybersleuth who doesn't like attachments. Michael Lassiter is leaving her husband, and she needs Sloan's expertise to safeguard her company. It should just be business—but it turns into much more. (1-933110-33-3)

Sweet Creek by Lee Lynch. A celebration of the enduring nature of love, friendship, and community in the quirky, heart-warming lesbian community of Waterfall Falls. (1-933110-29-5)

The Devil Inside by Ali Vali. Derby Cain Casey, head of a New Orleans crime organization, runs the family business with guts and grit, and no one crosses her. No one, that is, until Emma Verde claims her heart and turns her world upside down. (1-933110-30-9)

Grave Silence by Rose Beecham. Detective Jude Devine's investigation of a series of ritual murders is complicated by her torrid affair with the golden girl of Southwestern forensic pathology, Dr. Mercy Westmoreland. (1-933110-25-2)

Honor Reclaimed by Radclyffe. In the aftermath of 9/11, Secret Service Agent Cameron Roberts and Blair Powell close ranks with a trusted few to find the would-be assassins who nearly claimed Blair's life. (1-933110-18-X)

Honor Bound by Radclyffe. Secret Service Agent Cameron Roberts and Blair Powell face political intrigue, a clandestine threat to Blair's safety, and the seemingly irreconcilable personal differences that force them ever farther apart. (1-933110-20-1)

Protector of the Realm: Supreme Constellations Book One by Gun Brooke. A space adventure filled with suspense and a daring intergalactic romance featuring Commodore Rae Jacelon and the stunning, but decidedly lethal, Kellen O'Dal. (1-933110-26-0)

Innocent Hearts by Radclyffe. In a wild and unforgiving land, two women learn about love, passion, and the wonders of the heart. (1-933110-21-X)

The Temple at Landfall by Jane Fletcher. An imprinter, one of Celaeno's most revered servants of the Goddess, is also a prisoner to the faith—until a Ranger frees her by claiming her heart. The Celaeno series. (1-933110-27-9)

Force of Nature by Kim Baldwin. From tornados to forest fires, the forces of nature conspire to bring Gable McCoy and Erin Richards close to danger, and closer to each other. (1-933110-23-6)

In Too Deep by Ronica Black. Undercover homicide cop Erin McKenzie tracks a femme fatale who just might be a real killer…with love and danger hot on her heels. (1-933110-17-1)

Stolen Moments: *Erotic Interludes 2* by Stacia Seaman and Radclyffe, eds. Love on the run, in the office, in the shadows…Fast, furious, and almost too hot to handle. (1-933110-16-3)

Course of Action by Gun Brooke. Actress Carolyn Black desperately wants the starring role in an upcoming film produced by Annelie Peterson. Just how far will she go for the dream part of a lifetime? (1-933110-22-8)

Rangers at Roadsend by Jane Fletcher. Sergeant Chip Coppelli has learned to spot trouble coming, and that is exactly what she sees in her new recruit, Katryn Nagata. The Celaeno series. (1-933110-28-7)

Justice Served by Radclyffe. Lieutenant Rebecca Frye and her lover, Dr. Catherine Rawlings, embark on a deadly game of hide-and-seek with an underworld kingpin who traffics in human souls. (1-933110-15-5)

Distant Shores, Silent Thunder by Radclyffe. Dr. Tory King—along with the women who love her—is forced to examine the boundaries of love, friendship, and the ties that transcend time. (1-933110-08-2)

Hunter's Pursuit by Kim Baldwin. A raging blizzard, a mountain hideaway, and a killer-for-hire set a scene for disaster—or desire—when Katarzyna Demetrious rescues a beautiful stranger. (1-933110-09-0)

The Walls of Westernfort by Jane Fletcher. All Temple Guard Natasha Ionadis wants is to serve the Goddess—until she falls in love with one of the rebels she is sworn to destroy. The Celaeno series. (1-933110-24-4)

Change Of Pace: *Erotic Interludes* by Radclyffe. Twenty-five hot-wired encounters guaranteed to spark more than just your imagination. Erotica as you've always dreamed of it. (1-933110-07-4)

Honor Guards by Radclyffe. In a wild flight for their lives, the president's daughter and those who are sworn to protect her wage a desperate struggle for survival. (1-933110-01-5)

Fated Love by Radclyffe. Amidst the chaos and drama of a busy emergency room, two women must contend not only with the fragile nature of life, but also with the irresistible forces of fate. (1-933110-05-8)

Justice in the Shadows by Radclyffe. In a shadow world of secrets and lies, Detective Sergeant Rebecca Frye and her lover, Dr. Catherine Rawlings, join forces in the elusive search for justice. (1-933110-03-1)

shadowland by Radclyffe. In a world on the far edge of desire, two women are drawn together by power, passion, and dark pleasures. An erotic romance. (1-933110-11-2)

Love's Masquerade by Radclyffe. Plunged into the indistinguishable realms of fiction, fantasy, and hidden desires, Auden Frost is forced to question all she believes about the nature of love. (1-933110-14-7)

Love & Honor by Radclyffe. The president's daughter and her lover are faced with difficult choices as they battle a tangled web of Washington intrigue for...love and honor. (1-933110-10-4)

Beyond the Breakwater by Radclyffe. One Provincetown summer, three women learn the true meaning of love, friendship, and family. (1-933110-06-6)

Tomorrow's Promise by Radclyffe. One timeless summer, two very different women discover the power of passion to heal and the promise of hope that only love can bestow. (1-933110-12-0)

Love's Tender Warriors by Radclyffe. Two women who have accepted loneliness as a way of life learn that love is worth fighting for and a battle they cannot afford to lose. (1-933110-02-3)

Love's Melody Lost by Radclyffe. A secretive artist with a haunted past and a young woman escaping a life that has proved to be a lie find their destinies entwined. (1-933110-00-7)

Safe Harbor by Radclyffe. A mysterious newcomer, a reclusive doctor, and a troubled gay teenager learn about love, friendship, and trust during one tumultuous summer in Provincetown. (1-933110-13-9)

Above All, Honor by Radclyffe. Secret Service Agent Cameron Roberts fights her desire for the one woman she can't have—Blair Powell, the daughter of the president of the United States. (1-933110-04-X)